a benign comedy

a benign comedy

A NOVEL

thomas marshall

WHIPPOORWILL
hill

First printing, 2021

ISBN-13: 978-1-7354947-3-9 (paperback)
ISBN-13: 978-1-7354947-2-2 (ebook)
Library of Congress Control Number: 2021916866

Cover design: Natalie Pryor and Lily Mars
Cover image: Fan Yan, Unsplash
Cover photo: Bridget K. Marshall

For W.v.B.

TUESDAY 12PM

The moving van pulled up just far enough into the dead-end street to have the shamrock on its back door visible. It was the third van this month and all of them had shamrocks painted on them, appropriate symbols for the Bronx families being hauled away.

She closed the curtain and lit the fire under the small, white kettle. He would be home soon. The winter had been especially cold and the month seemed to be in no hurry to move along despite the short number of days. The kettle was just on the boil when the rattle of the latch let her know that he had arrived at the apartment door. He never was allowed a key.

"You're late."

"There was a big crowd."

"Who was it?"

"Some old geezer."

It was inconceivable to her that the sacristan of the church shouldn't know who's being buried, but it was a changing parish and everyone was moving on one way or another.

"Did you get anything to eat at the rectory?"

He was sitting down in the big chair in the living room pulling off his shoes and didn't hear her. She recognized the grunting and went out to get a better assessment. He looked pale.

"The tea is ready. Do you want some boiled eggs with it?"

"I brought home some raisin bread. We'll have that. Did you hear from Tommy?"

AUGUST 1956

"Ma, it's Bennett!"

If there was any danger of the man forgetting his name he was crisply reminded once a month on his visit to the apartment on Naples Terrace. He was also getting quite nimble at catching the door as the young boy would let it close in his face after his announcement. Cautiously holding it half open, he waited for the boy's mother to rush over, offer her customary apology, and lead him to the big chair in the living room. The boy was sitting on the carpet talking to his red rubber motorcycle.

"Tommy, you should always say, 'Mister Bennett is here'."

Behind his blank expression, Tommy secretly considered why such a distinction was important since no one practiced it when the man wasn't present. Rearranging manners for those that live here and them that don't was a tricky process. As soon as his mother went off to the kitchen, he went back to his conversation with the mounted motorcycle policeman. It was a small, inexpensive toy, only six inches long, but it had contrasting white wheels that spun smoothly. So, after a quick trip through the wide, Western valley of the living room floor, he jumped up to explore the mountain range running along the back of the sofa. Bennett nervously watched as the boy leaped wildly about.

"Is that a new toy?"

No answer.

"Be careful with your shoes. You almost knocked over the lamp."

Bennett felt some consideration for the furniture was warranted since he knew firsthand just how tight money was. He was relieved to see the reappearance of the mother and the accompanying highball glass containing two bouncy ice cubes. She toasted with her own glass of 7-Up.

"Good luck to you!"

Tommy looked over to see if anyone was going to ask if he had a mouth. Nothing, they were already onto some sweepstakes ticket business. He swung down from the sofa and stood in front of Bennett.

"Can I have a sip?"

"Careful of the ice cube."

"There's no whiskey!"

"Mr. Bennett doesn't drink."

"Why?"

"I took a pledge not to drink alcohol. That's why I wear this pin on my lapel."

"Never?"

"Never's a long time, Tommy."

Since his mother wasn't offering any more information, the boy bounced off to the bathroom to run his motorcycle around the rim of the tub. He had moved on to the interesting prospect of testing the strength of the ceiling clothesline when he heard his mother's voice asking him to come out and see them.

"Mr. Bennett has some news for you, Tommy."

"How would you like to go home to Ireland with us?"

* * *

"This dial lets us know how high we are in the air, and this one here will tell us how fast we are traveling."

"How fast?"

"Over three hundred miles per hour!"

The captain and co-pilot waved good-bye to the little boy as he was led from the cockpit back to his seat by the stewardess. When he was all buckled in, she handed him his small, blue-and-white Pan Am souvenir travel bag containing brass-colored flight wings. He had to wear them immediately in case he was needed in the cockpit, and the stewardess was only too happy to pin them on his striped polo shirt. When she leaned over, her perfume reminded him of Betty-Ann and he suddenly realized she would not be with him. Kathleen and Eileen wouldn't be, either. He was all alone with the grown-ups.

Since he had been up before daylight, he immediately fell off to sleep even though the plane was still having its baggage loaded on board. No one was happier than Bennett.

"He's certainly high-strung today."

"It's all the excitement."

The old bachelor wasn't at all satisfied with the mother's explanation, expecting the over-tired three-and a half-year-old to be a prayer-book model of behavior. Bridie decided to corral her response with a smile and turned to look out her tiny window.

She was tired herself, with packing earlier in the day for the three-week journey and delivering last minute instructions to the three girls. She made it perfectly clear to Kathleen it was her duty to wrangle Betty Ann and Eileen and they were to listen. As for their father, his promises of good behavior were cautiously considered but Aunt Betty would be on hand for additional reinforcement if needed. Hopefully he'd go to work.

It was a muggy day and the inside of the Douglas DC-6 was too warm for the green wool sweater she had over her shoulders. She laid it across the boy's lap as a little blanket and took his foot off of Bennett's suit jacket. The man himself was busy puffing away on a Chesterfield while paging through a copy of *The Irish Echo*. He was good friends with one of the editors and wanted to see if there was any mention of his trip back home. With the newspaper, his red face, and the two breast pockets bulging with Irish Sweepstakes receipts he looked like a caricature of the returning Yank. At least he didn't drink.

The thump of the cargo door closing made Bridie jump and heightened her awareness of how fragile the whole airplane seemed. The sinking of the *Andrea Doria* a few days earlier had sent a nervous tremor throughout the summer tourism trade, and if a big, sturdy ship like that could go down so quickly this rickety thing wouldn't stand a chance in a catastrophe. She had made sure to stop at Idlewild's chapel beforehand to say a prayer for a safe journey, but when Bennett went to the men's room she took out some extra flight insurance from the lady at the booth.

The weather was clear leaving New York and the view from the plane provided a stunning panorama as it swung past the island of Manhattan. The gleaming spiral of the Chrysler Building looked as grand as it did twenty-five years ago when Bridie first took a job as waitress at Schrafft's Restaurant located in the building's lobby. She was eighteen and it was the most exciting place in the world.

"You never knew who would come in—movie stars, Rockefellers—once, the newspapers even took a picture of Rin

Tin Tin with his handler as they had lunch."

Bennett, sensing that a response was required, looked over the top of his paper.

"Who would that be now, the dog?"

"The most famous actor in America at the time. I remember giving him a biscuit from the bread basket. He was very well behaved."

Bennett stared at young Tommy's two brown shoes, which had landed in his lap as the boy fidgeted about in his sleep. His mother reached over and straightened out his legs so he wouldn't be bothering their escort. It might be best to switch seats.

"I looked in Schrafft's window once. The prices were too dear for me. Who got you the job?"

"My sister, Betty."

"I always considered her the smart one."

Bridie was mentally rehashing the usual raw areas of sibling contention when she felt the playful tap of the newspaper on her shoulder.

"Not as pretty though!"

* * *

They changed seats for supper service and Tommy woke up enough to eat a good bit before going back to sleep with his head on Bridie's lap. She was just about to doze off herself when the sound of grinding metal sent a shiver up her back. Something was wrong. She sat Tommy upright in his seat and put the seat belt around his waist. The grinding noise had gotten worse.

You didn't need any fancy dial in the cockpit to let you know when an engine was on fire because the sight of shooting flames prompted a synchronized scream from the passengers sitting on the far side of the plane. The excitement got Tommy's attention and he was up for it.

"Ma, tell Bennett we're gonna crash."

"Quiet now, don't say that. He's asleep. Get that stewardess's attention."

Tommy started waving frantically at the poor woman who was being besieged by an avalanche of questions as she tried to get down the aisle. She was rescued by the captain's voice squawking over the public address system:

"Ladies and gentlemen, you may have noticed that engine number four has become non-operational. Let me reassure you, there is no need for concern as we have plenty of power with our three remaining engines. The problem will be addressed and remedied when we land at Gander for refueling. We are starting our descent now and will keep you informed as to developments."

A woman in the back row had started to say the rosary and the communal response was quickly picked up by those seated around her. Bridie joined in, barely whispering her response. Looking over, she was happy that Tommy was talking to the policeman on his little red motorcycle. It would keep him busy. When she tried to smooth the cowlick on his head he stopped and looked up at her:

"He says everything will be all right."

True to the man's word, the plane kept on going and made a perfectly smooth landing at the Newfoundland airport, to thunderous applause from the passengers. When the doors were opened, Bridie gave a little squeeze on Bennett's arm to let him know that they could get off and stretch their legs.

"What? Oh, I wasn't sleeping, mind you… was there some sort of announcement?"

"We had had a bit of trouble, but there's nothing to worry about."

* * *

The layover would be a few hours, giving Bridie a chance to settle her nerves with a cup of tea and a scone. Bennett's nerves, which had a good rest during the in-flight emergency, were full on complaining about the boy busy moving chairs about in the waiting area. Why was he always so rambunctious? Fortunately, by sunrise the engine was repaired and Tommy was exhausted as they re-boarded their nine-hour flight to Shannon airport. He awoke just in time for some cereal from the nice-smelling stewardess. She hoped he would enjoy his visit.

"We're going to see Ma's mother."

"That's lovely. Where?"

"Leitrim!"

* * *

Bennett was well organized and the car and driver he had ordered was standing at the curb when they came out from Customs. The driver helped them with the suitcases and off they went, Bennett up in front to avoid the boy's jumping about the seat. Tommy surprised them, however, and settled in, calmly watching with great attention the fluffy sheep and little lambs which he had heard so much about. They were everywhere! Bridie's face, getting more flushed with each passing mile, took her own keen interest in the unusually clear weather and hoped it would hold out until the car made it to the house. She knew the family would be outside waiting.

The hedges along the road hadn't been trimmed all summer,

making it very difficult to see where to turn in from the main road. They went past three times before the driver saw the narrow lane leading up to the old farmhouse. To their surprise, nobody was standing outside and when Bridie pushed open the front door there was nobody home at all. The driver made the mistake of asking the woman if this was the right house.

"Shouldn't I know the place where I was born?"

He was smart enough not to answer and got to unloading the suitcases from the car. Bennett told him to keep his case in the trunk. He would travel on to the Longford Arms. The driver was glad to hear that. They had a good pub there. Bennett could sense Bridie's anxiety and was a little unsure about leaving.

"I better wait until they return."

"No, go and… where's Tommy?"

Bennett, strictly for appearances' sake, made a halfhearted attempt to look around the back of the house. Bridie dashed inside but quickly reappeared, heading straight toward the driver.

"Did you see where he went?"

"I did, madam, but made nothing of it."

"Nothing of what?"

"He was chasing a chicken down the lane."

She looked. There was no sign of him.

"I wouldn't worry, madam; nobody around here would harm—"

She had spotted an old crock of a bicycle up against the side of the house and was doing her best to keep her feet on the pedals. Her shoes, however, wouldn't do at all and she threw them into the front basket. She was just starting off when she heard the laughter. It was her brother, Dan.

"Couldn't you have waited until we had a cup of tea first?"

She jumped off and threw her arms around his waist. Being

so much smaller she couldn't make out the commotion that was going on behind them. When he spun her around, she could see Tommy running up the lane holding the chicken. Behind him was her mother.

"Ma, look who I found!"

* * *

Since they were more than six hours overdue the family had them for dead and went to the church to tell the priest. There were ever so many accidents with the airplanes.

"The mass is being said for you on Sunday."

The old mother told Dan not to make a joke of it and go right back tomorrow and let the man know that, thank God, everyone arrived safe."

"Were you afraid, Bridget?"

"We had a bit of trouble but there was nothing to worry about."

"Ma was praying."

Lena was about to pour another cup for Bridie when she suddenly stopped. "I bet your heart was in your mouth the whole time!"

Bennett, being the experienced traveler, jumped in with his assurances. "Not a bit. They say flying is safer than walking down the street."

Tommy's poker face wasn't quite yet developed so his mother knew an impolite description of Bennett's heedlessness during the emergency was coming. He needed a distraction.

"Here, Tommy, try one of those biscuits that Aunt Lena made for us."

Off he went outside to share his biscuit with his new-found chicken friend. He was distributing the crumbs very neatly along the ground when he noticed a flash of black and white—a kitten!

The little kitten gave the generous boy a wink and said, "Follow me." Down the lane they ran together, traveling for miles and miles until his legs became so tired he was forced to stop and rest beneath the shade of an enormous oak tree. The kitten approved and got all snuggly inside the boy's inviting sweater. Soon they were both fast asleep and would have slept on and on but for the noisy magpie keeping watch above, letting them know that company had arrived. Tommy was still rubbing his eyes as the little girl introduced herself.

"Good afternoon! My name is Deidre. Would you like some tea?"

She had a splendid head of yellow curls, attractively highlighted by the blue and red striped wool jumper that almost touched her knees. A full tea service had been neatly arranged on top of an old orange crate, and the boy was led to the empty, upside-down tin of oatmeal, directly across from a slouching patchwork teddy bear. A scarecrow holding an accordion by one hand stood off to the side and nodded enthusiastically while Deidre explained the protocol to Tommy.

"Please help yourself to the fancy cakes—they are chock-full of either fluffy cream or raspberry jam, I can't remember which. I will pour the tea. We have milk and sugar, so please don't be shy."

Tommy took out his red motorcycle and pointed to the mounted policeman.

"Ooh, we have another guest! How delightful!"

Delightful maybe to the little girl, but the scarecrow was on edge at the sight of the constabulary—the coat he had on was borrowed. His first thought was to quietly slink off, but he decided to stand his ground and play a spirited version of "Dinny O'Brien's Reel." The little girl was ever so pleased.

"Do you know how to dance?"

Tommy shook his head no.

"Then you must watch carefully. I will show you."

She stood up tall and waited for the scarecrow to give her a nod to begin counting off.

"Point, put it in back; point, put it in back; knee two, three, four, five, six, seven."

It seemed simple enough and when she took him by the hand, they were soon a perfect pair, staying in step like two wooden solders. The invigorating music soon attracted a bashful squirrel wearing a gray top hat promptly followed by two adventurous weasels. They were all encouraged to join in and each one displayed great showmanship, the weasel with the white tip on her tail being especially nimble on her high kicks. Even the little black and white kitten swirled around and around gracefully as he accompanied the scarecrow on his tin whistle.

"Switch and switch and point hop back."

Tommy, who never had trouble knowing his left foot from his right, was in mid-air when the magpie let out a screech. As-quick-as-that the music stopped and everyone ran: the little girl to collect her dishes, the weasels into the woods. and the squirrel to the oak tree. Only the kitten remained, stationed at the boy's feet. After she had her picnic hamper filled, the little girl told Tommy:

"We must go. He's coming. I hope to see you again."

She gave a little curtsy and took hold of the teddy bear's hand as she started off down the narrow path. The scarecrow followed quickly, pausing only long enough to accept a Life Saver from the boy by way of a donation. He nodded enthusiastically.

Now with all quiet, Tommy could hear heavy footsteps getting closer and closer and was curious, but his little black and white friend knew better and quickly led him back to the family farmhouse.

* * *

Every day he ate mashed potatoes from his new yellow plastic bowl by the front window of the old house. That was the place where everyone drank tea, talked, and sometimes cried. One time the mother sow came bursting through the front door looking for her young. Tommy was told not to move while Aunt Lena put down the kettle and chased her out with a broom. Then the talking started again as if it never happened.

The afternoons meant putting on the new green sweater and smiling for the Brownie camera; sometimes on top of the old mare with Uncle Dan standing next to him, sometimes in front of the house with Grandma in her long coat, sometimes at church with the priest wearing the funny black hat. Always his face had to be wiped with a tissue mysteriously moistened with something that smelled bad.

One day he was hustled off to Offaly, the place where Da came from and, according to Ma, talked too much about. Da's older brother was beside himself with excitement and would jumble up his words, but it didn't matter because everyone knew what he meant. Another picture was obliged, this time standing next to a thrashing machine—the noisiest thing on earth. While the grown-ups were having their tea, Tommy became acquainted with a cousin named Noel who had the great fortune of owning a red wooden top and, better still, a secret place to spin it—a cave he made in the side of a haystack. Once seated inside their straw cocoon, the initiates of the shadowy club acquired ritualistic tattoos from the fantastic patterns projected on their faces from the filtering sunlight.

"Are you ready?"

"Uh-huh."

Noel wound the string tight and gave a great throw, the top spinning so cleanly in one spot it looked like it was levitating. Tommy took out his motorcycle policeman to show him how fast some things could spin and go nowhere. He too was amazed. After the next throw, Noel doubled the string to gently lift the spinning top and place it into Tommy's open palm. When he spoke, it was like the man in church and didn't sound like Noel anymore.

"It's been said, holding a spinning top makes time stand still. We can stay here forever and never get old."

* * *

Back in Leitrim he ran after chickens, ducks, geese and piglets; petted rabbits, lambs, kids, and donkeys; and watched with his mouth open as the cows were milked. He would describe what he saw each day to the black-and-white kitten as he cuddled in bed. Just when he was getting sleepy the kitten would take him to see the little girl with the yellow curls. Deidre, so excited, would invite him to tea and try to remember what was in her tasty little cakes. Patchwork Teddy got the hang of waving hello and Scarecrow would go on and on about the great improvement in the little boy's step dancing—Life Savers being most appreciated. Squirrel and the weasels were old friends by now and threw themselves into the music with abandon. Only magpie chose not to participate, but instead remained ever watchful, ensuring that they all had time to run away before the heavy footsteps got too close.

One day, while the boy was testing the depth of a hole with a long, thin stick, his mother announced:

"Tomorrow we go home."

The boy scooped the kitten up in his arms.

"No, they won't allow the cat into the country. She has to stay here."

That night when he got into his bed, he had already made up his mind. He would ask the man with the heavy footsteps to let kitty go home with him. He seemed to be in charge.

Everything was in full swing when they arrived, Scarecrow going to town with a lively jig enthusiastically received by all. The dance floor was especially packed because of several new customers the boy had never seen before—four mice, three geese and a polecat everybody knew as Harry. Deidre wasted no time showing the little boy the new dance steps and when Scarecrow took a break everyone found a place around the orange crate to have their tea, the geese monopolizing the conversation with their opinions on modern poetry. Scarecrow had just reached for his squeeze box to begin the next dance session when magpie let out three sharp squawks. Deidre immediately began to pack up her little china plates and, when she was finished, was startled to see the boy still standing there. All the other guests had left.

"I want to see the man."

"You can't. No one can."

"I want to keep kitty."

"Nothing would be the same. You must leave."

By now Patchwork Teddy was in a panic and threw his arms around Deidre's leg. Scarecrow too knew that things were shaping up badly and decided to move off quietly into the woods. He gave the boy a farewell wink for good luck. He would need it. Deidre tried one more time.

"He doesn't remember what it was like and won't understand."

The heavy footsteps were now too close for them to run away. She handed Teddy to the little boy and told the kitten to look cute.

"I will ask him."

She ran a short distance up the path and met the heavy footsteps. The boy was just close enough to see a face both strange and familiar. Confused, he looked to poor little Teddy for an explanation.

"It's you all grown up."

TUESDAY 2PM

Old Tom had gone to bed to take a nap, giving Bridie the chance "to go out and see some well people." Exactly how insulting this was supposed to be taken by the members of the household to whom it was regularly addressed was never broadly considered. Probably just as well, since it was one of those mysterious expressions that allowed a perfect transition from one subject to the next without actually providing any information—all Leitrim women being members of some secret society. On her way down Naples Terrace she stopped to see how they were coming along with the moving. An eager, middle-aged company manager saw an opportunity for business.

"Let me guess, you'll be needing a van yourself soon."

"Wouldn't I be apt?"

"But, begging your pardon, all the Irish are moving away."

"When we moved here, we were one of the first. The neighborhood was mostly Jewish. They all ran off to Riverdale and Co-Op City."

"Ah, today a house is the thing. No more crowded apartment living."

"Where is this one going?"

"Like all the rest, the Irish Alps—Yorktown Heights. Lovely up there."

His warm smile strengthened the genuineness of his opinion. He was rewarded by an unusually candid remark, sometimes more easily given to strangers.

"Too late for us; I don't drive and would be under a compliment to get to the stores."

He tipped his cap to her as a farewell and off she went with her wire shopping cart and her settled memories of the departing O'Neal family. She didn't know them well, but they would always say hello after mass and as far as she could recall never had the cops called. The apartment was a good one with two bedrooms looking out over Broadway. It would have been very hard to get after the war but was considered too crowded now with the three kids. Each had to have their own bedroom. Someone might see an ankle.

At the Grand Union the new Hispanic cashier took special note of the three half-gallon containers of milk that were being loaded up onto the checkout counter by this well-past-child-bearing-years woman. She was eager to honor the march of the maternal mandate.

"Are you minding the grandchildren?"

"He has to have milk with the dinner."

Since no further comment was forthcoming the cashier got back to business and put the groceries into three paper bags and packed them carefully into the wire shopping cart. She then gave it one more try.

"Hope you have a nice day."

"The best part of the day is over; it'll be sleet and rain later… that's a pretty blouse you're wearing, goes nicely with your good head of hair."

She made her way up 231st Street and adjusted her mohair shawl to keep out the wind as she turned the corner onto Kingsbridge Avenue. Old Carty, coming out of his building, spotted her and wanted some news.

"Hello missus, how's himself?"

"He's in bed resting."

"Oh, that's right; he was busy with that powerful big funeral this morning. Caught us all by surprise. I bet he was quite shook up."

"Didn't know one thing about it."

Carty, having spent a lifetime successfully dodging the sacrament of matrimony, was not about to get entangled in some inscrutable domestic peccadillo. Instead, he followed his strong suit of ferreting out a bargain.

"That's a grand-looking loaf of bread you have in your wagon. Would that have been on sale?"

"It was."

"The smaller size, too?"

"No, only the giant loaf."

"You'll need be mighty clever to come up with uses for all that."

"I've had good practice."

AUGUST 1957

The Bond Bread truck had no trouble finding a parking space in front of the playground at 234th Street. It was recently built as part of the neighborhood renewal project with the completion of the Major Deegan Expressway and was too far away from any apartment buildings to be convenient. Anyway, with good local shopping and a reliable subway to get to work, most families didn't own a car. You could always borrow one for an occasion.

"Look who came to see us."

Tommy was running through the sprinklers when he abruptly stopped.

"Who?"

"Your father."

The boy turned his head toward the playground entrance and saw the man in the brown uniform approaching. It was true. He excitedly waved his arms and ran toward the deeper end of the sprinkler area where about a foot of water had collected.

"I can swim!"

Bridie walked up and led Tom to a bench facing the sprinkler pool. After inspecting his general appearance, she asked:

"Are you finished for the day?"

"All done, just have to bring the truck back."

"I can swim!"

Tom stood up and took a couple of steps forward.

"Let me see that now."

Tommy had lain face-down in the water and started moving his arms and legs in a circular motion—like the swimming he had seen on television. Around and around he swirled, all the time keeping his belly firmly planted on the pebbly bottom as his arms and legs made a great splash with the water. Of course, he actually didn't go anywhere, but it didn't matter because it looked like he was swimming and that was what was important to him. The father smiled and gave a big salute bringing his hand up to touch his driver's cap. As he turned to go back to the bench, Bridie yelled out for the boy to come out and dry off. It was starting to turn cool.

"Here, get this towel around you. What happened to your stomach? It's all red."

Tommy wasn't paying any attention to his mother as she swirled the thin cotton towel about his body. He saw a rare opportunity for adventure.

"Can I ride in the truck?"

"Get dressed and we'll go around the block."

As soon as he got his polo shirt pulled over his damp head, he was off to stand in the front of the truck. There was only one seat, so his father told him to hold on tight as they eased out onto the street and made their way around Broadway. Bridie waited for them at the entrance of the playground and was glad to see the truck return.

"You made it back safe. We don't want him getting hurt before school starts next month."

"What school is that?"

"The public kindergarten over near the Concourse; our parish school wouldn't take him. Said he was too young, but they'll take him afterwards for the first-grade next year."

"I'm going to be five in December."

The father lifted Tommy down from the truck and rubbed him on the head.

"Soon you'll be big enough to drive the truck yourself."

* * *

By late September the corner of 230th Street and Kingsbridge Avenue had become an unavoidable Scylla and Charybdis for the young boy. Behind him lay the ominous windows of Dr. Clyne in whose office vaccinations for far-fetched diseases were being injected with vicious delight to accommodate the opening of another school year. To even turn in the direction of those windows brought terror. But there was no escape. Gaping open like a seductive flytrap was the swallowing door of the yellow school bus, the sinister vehicle which would force him to appear before this teacher person—a most humorless woman! She didn't look, speak, or act like anybody he knew. Why did he have to go there?

His first visit to the schoolroom taken on the public bus with Bridie held out the promise of an interesting visit, but then suddenly it happened: she left! He was to spend the rest of the afternoon alone with this questionable collection of riffraff. The only thing he was sure of was the predicted about-face of the teacher woman. He was convinced that the smiling, pleasant face was a front and sure enough, as soon as all the mothers were gone her true grim nature revealed itself. He had had good experience picking out phonies.

As the weeks went by Tommy got the hang of what was

expected and would make halfhearted attempts to participate when he was in the mood. His innate ability to feign interest was sharpened here, as was his talent to flatter strangers with smiles, winks, and double talk, his teacher being particularly susceptible. The group games were generally boring and the individual tasks valueless. The only assignment he found beneficial was the nap, his contrived snoring always a popular lark.

Slowly, individual dealings with the other children were tentatively explored, barter being the primary reason for establishing contact. Chewing gum was a particularly valuable exchange medium and Tommy always had a couple of sticks of yellow Juicy Fruit happily provided by his sister Eileen. A stick of gum was often traded for a cupcake, a marble, or a book of matches. These deals would be made in strict secrecy as Tommy was sure the woman would find some reason to void the transaction. The concealment also added a stimulating air of intrigue which was sorely lacking from the mundane games selected for their amusement.

At his age Tommy took no notice of the well-mixed ethnic makeup of his 1957 kindergarten class which would have been a poster child for future sociologists. To him they were just fellow travelers having to endure the antiquated ritual of public education. Like all children, he was naturally aware of differences but his interest would only be aroused when novel implications presented themselves. One day a boy named Guillermo caught his attention by throwing the ball with his left hand. Why? On questioning, he showed Tommy how he tied his shoes—the other way around! Tommy tried it and his laces ended up in a big knot. The woman had to help him untangle them and then had the gall to insinuate that his relations were somehow behind this preference for favoring one hand over another. She was obviously deranged!

After a few months of endless humdrum, a keen bit of excitement presented itself on the bus ride home—the new driver got lost. Tommy immediately recognized the sauce of the problem as a whiskey bottle was rattling about quite noisily between the brake and clutch pedals. This improvised route, careening erratically through new neighborhoods, was welcomed as it provided a great opportunity to yell asinine insults out the window. What was the chance you would ever see these people again? Tommy had just told a startled passer-by that his mother wore army boots when the incessant crying of Louise two seats in front made him stick his head back in and gallantly consider her predicament.

"You have chalk on your dress."

"What?"

"It's pink, see right here."

"I don't care! We're lost!"

Although being lost and screaming out the window was like a dream come true, the sight of her tear-stained face had a sobering effect on him. He went to discuss the situation with the driver. On the way to the front he noticed most of the other children were crying too. What was the problem? Fortunately, the Irish twins who lived in his parish had no fear of the unknown and were involved in their customary wrestling match, which had spilled out into the aisle. Tommy stopped long enough to give a good kick to the one he disliked more. It wasn't often you get a chance like that. He had just realized he kicked the wrong one when the bus driver yelled out to him.

"Do you know where we are?"

"No."

"What good are you then?"

Tommy walked up near the front window and held on to the metal bar as the bus made a sharp turn out from Jerome Avenue.

"The other driver goes down this street."

"Kingsbridge Road?"

"I don't know the name."

The driver, although not satisfied with this answer, restrained himself from any further disparagement and drove straight on. Tommy meanwhile recognized the huge brown building they were passing as the Kingsbridge Armory and knew that this was the right way home, but he wasn't saying any more. Let the guy sweat.

Down the big hill they went and after another bit of advice from the boy they turned onto 230th Street. He could see the mothers waiting on the corner and as soon as the bus opened its doors all the distraught children ran into waiting arms—all except the Irish twins who had fought to a draw and bounced happily down the stairs together, heedless that they were ever lost in the first place. Tommy was left alone with the driver.

"Ya did all right, thanks."

The driver ran two fingers across his lips indicating how one could keep his mouth shut. Tommy, already knowing there was nothing worse than being a snitch, nodded his head. He turned and was met with the reddened face of Bridie waiting at the bottom of the stairs.

"What kept you?"

As the other mothers hovered to hear his answer, he stood still just long enough for the bus to leave and then made a mad dash toward the small grocery store down the block.

"Ice cream cone!"

* * *

"It was very dangerous times."

"Why?"

"Because if you ever got caught, you'd be killed for sure."

They had been waiting for the TV to warm up so Tom could watch the Saturday afternoon races from Aqueduct. Their talk started off on the difference between a mule and a jennet when the boy's interest turned to bicycles. Did his father ever have one?

"I had a lovely Raleigh bicycle and it was very handy—we used it to transport the dispatches."

"What's that?"

"They were orders given out during the Rebellion. I would pedal up to Birr and leave the bicycle in the alley beside the woolen shop. While I was inside someone would put the rolled-up orders in the handlebars. When I got the piece of butterscotch from the old lady in the shop, I knew it was time to pedal off down to Tullamore. Again, I'd leave the bicycle, this time outside the Phoenix Arms Hotel. When I came out from using the toilet they would be gone."

"Who put them there?"

"I never knew—but it wouldn't have mattered—I never would have told."

Even over the sizzle of a leg of lamb Bridie heard enough to come out into the living room to put an end to any dubious exploits.

"The dinner will be ready in a half hour. Which horse do you have?"

"Da was a hero."

Ignoring the boy's remark, she turned her attention to a gray horse entering the starting gate.

"Number two has a pretty coat."

"That's the winner... quiet now, they're off!"

Being attractive was no hindrance to her running ability as the gray got off to an early lead and was still going strong right up to the 16th pole…

"… come on girl…"

At odds of eighteen to one you couldn't realistically expect her to outlast the big, black mare that was the favorite coming up fast along the rail. But for a high-hopes horse player…

"… hang on, just a little more…"

There was no doubt about it; the pretty gray was beaten by a half-length. Tom got up to pace the room. Bridie started back to the kitchen, but took a moment to harbor her opinion.

"You would have been better off putting the two dollars in a glass in the cupboard. The result would have been the same and you'd have your two dollars saved."

In the ensuing sullenness brought about by another losing Saturday afternoon, the boy was given the chance to assess the joys of a short-lived fantasy versus the dreariness of persistent practicality. The apple never fell far from the tree.

"She almost won."

"She did that—next time we'll get 'em."

* * *

The following June finally brought an end to the disastrous experiment of kindergarten, and with this forfeiture of educational accountability a new level of devilment was instilled in the boy. The summer looked promising.

One of the first rituals to be observed was the yearly pilgrimage to Rockaway Beach where Bridie's cousin Bea resided in a bungalow with her husband Jack. This congenial visit, simple enough on the face of it, required elaborate and well-prescribed preparations from which there could be no deviation. First off was the jamming to the bursting point of a gleaming, black patent leather travel bag brought out just for the occasion. The most threadbare towels in the house were immediately packed because they were sure to be lost at the beach and you didn't want to lose good ones. That may have made good economic sense, but unfortunately due to their flimsy nature they were utterly useless for drying the shivering, skinny bodies of Tommy and Eileen coming out of the freezing ocean water. With quivering blue lips, they would stand on the corner of the beach blanket endlessly wiping and re-wiping their arms and legs with towels that had the absorbency of ceramic tiles. Last summer Eileen took the initiative to "accidentally" leave them rolled up and buried in the sand only to have some well-meaning beachcomber run up and return them to Bridie. Now they were back in the bag!

Next on the packing list were the venerable bathing costumes from the mysterious recesses of the hall closet, sufficiently reeking of mothballs as to make one instantly nauseous. What had she expected, a swarm of locusts? The boy was ordered to put his swim trunks on under his cotton summer shorts where they would itch terribly for the next four hours until they arrived at the beach. Why was this necessary? Couldn't he use Aunt Bee's bathroom to change like everyone else? Don't ask. Better to go off into the bedroom to play under the bed while Bridie continued with her predetermined inclusion: a box of tea, a tin of powdered mustard, two cans of Spam, toothpicks, iodine, Band-Aids, a jar of healing ointment, a bottle of Pepto-Bismol, a wool blanket, two extra pairs of white socks, suntan lotion, saltines, bobby pins, tissues, a new deck of cards, and a carton of Chesterfield cigarettes. Lawrence of Arabia went to the beach with less, and he had a camel.

It was Eileen's job to go to Peter Reeves for specialty items such as the cookies to be savored on the two-hour subway ride. The boy, peeking out from underneath the bed, was only too happy to over-exert himself, thereby ensuring an early state of exasperating exhaustion.

"Can I come?"

Eileen's smile said it was okay but he better hurry before anyone notices. She handed him one of the two cartons of empty 7-UP bottles which had a return ransom of two cents per bottle and off they went. She was very happy to have one hand now free to wave to some of her girlfriends standing across the street and also to give Kevin McCormick a slap as he ran by and tried to grab her hair. Tommy, being in watchdog mode, had given her an advance warning that a red-headed boy was approaching. He now really had to be on his toes since they would have to maneuver through the alley on the way to the low stairs. The alley was a place anything could happen.

Teeming with dozens of kids of all sizes, this extended sidewalk between two buildings was always awash with several overlapping games involving a pink Spaldeen. The unstated rules of the alley made it very clear that no passerby was to interfere in the play action and no responsibility was assumed for bodily injury. Anyone of advanced age or physical limitation would avoid the alley completely because it was not uncommon to get run into, hit in the face with a ball, or be bushwhacked by a kid in a hurry on a bicycle. But no one really complained. Having been ordered out of their all-too-small apartments and told to not come back until supper time, where else did you expect them to go?

As hazardous as these competitions were there was no comparison as to the danger of having to walk by the leering, squatting figures involved in the moronic game of pitching pennies. Always situated at the end of the alley, these participants were not the familiar, freckle-faced, exuberant youths challenging each other to throw a ball onto the building roof. No, these were smoking, swearing slackers with the unofficial title of juvenile delinquents. Tommy thought they were great.

"Ssss... ssss..."

Eileen ignored the snake-like greeting from the one with the worst complexion and grabbed Tommy's hand to keep him from wandering any further to see who had the closest penny to the wall.

"Hey kid, wanna play?"

"We're going to Rockaway."

For some inscrutable reason this remark was immensely amusing to their stunted intelligence and precipitated a grotesque group pantomime complete with pathetic drownings, silent screams, and contrived cries for help. Eileen quickly saw her chance and hustled the boy down the low stairs to the relative safety of 231st Street.

"You shouldn't talk to them."

"Why?"

She was concentrating on holding his hand and trying to get across the busy street. It was not really a pedestrian crossing, but a time-honored place where everyone took their chances of dashing across. Only when they got to the safety of the opposite sidewalk did she turn to answer.

"They're not nice."

They did, however, know how to wear their dungarees in the most roguish manner and Tommy was still considering their five-inch turned-up cuffs when the man in Peter Reeves asked him to put his return bottles up on the counter next to Eileen's.

"Six and six is it? Twenty-four cents. Do you have a penny?"

Tommy's hand disappeared into his pocket and re-emerged with an overflowing palm to the man at the counter.

"Good lad, a whole handful of them! Well, first we'll take

one to make your sister's deposit a quarter even. Thank you, young lady. And I can be using those pennies of yours, so we'll count off…"

When finished he gave a dime and a nickel to the boy in exchange. Eileen led Tommy to the cookie aisle where she could investigate in private.

"You didn't have any money… you picked them up from their game, didn't you? Did you?"

"Look, Marshmallow Sandwiches!"

* * *

Only Eileen and Tommy raced up the stairs to the token booth and pushed through the subway turnstile together ahead of Bridie and Tom on this journey to Rockaway; the big sisters were too busy now. Kathleen recently graduated from high school with honors and had an important job as a secretary downtown where you had to dress up every day and be ladylike. You wouldn't want to be the one not showing up for work when you're just starting off. Betty Ann, too, never letting any grass grow under her feet, quickly emulated Kathleen's high school career trajectory and took up her sister's former position of shop assistant at Horn & Hardart on the corner of 231st and Broadway. She knew how lucky she was to get a good job in the neighborhood while going to school and wouldn't dare ask for a day to go to the beach. So, they were both out of the picture and cunningly embellished their presumed disappointment with exaggerated regrets while taking secret delight that they were free from the tedious obligation and the accompanying blistering sunburn. Perhaps even more cleverly concealed was the new cycle of separation now starting for this first generation in America.

APRIL 1929

His brother was the one to go, him being the eldest. Young Tom was supposed to stay home with his mother on the farm and the way of life he loved to talk about too much. But it turned out the brother had a bad ear, or at least bad enough that the certifying doctor said he couldn't be accepted for emigration. Young Tom would be eighteen in the spring—the spring of 1929—and would take the brother's place. It sounded like a grand adventure, and wouldn't he be back soon enough?

He made a few farewells before he left. He rode over to Philipstown to visit his favorite uncle who raised yellow canaries and had a draper's shop in town. It was his delight to show young Tom all sorts of ingenious practices, like how you can make a man's suit new again by turning the cloth inside out or why you should always put a double lining in a pair of trousers because the seat gets worn out first—all that riding on the bicycle. It was a cheerful, lively place with fabrics slung about and birds singing and customers laughing. When the old uncle heard the of the lad's journey, he took out a special ten-pound note hidden in a safety pin packet under the counter, and gave it to him for luck and safe passage. Then they had tea and scones in the little room in the back and it was there the nephew promised to post one of those famed picture cards showing all the tall buildings of the great city. By the time young Tom was back on his bicycle to return home, the whole town had heard the news and many came out from their shops and houses to give a great hurrah for the boy, who responded by standing up on the pedals and waving triumphantly. But as the gray dust from his wheels settled and they turned back into their houses any momentary elation was shattered by the sorrow of the old ones sitting by the windows knowing full well what it meant.

"Another one we'll never see again."

Closer to home he stopped by to call on his childhood sweetheart Fanny Doyle, who was very mad that he should go to America and she was to stay in Offaly. As a way of making amends for his thoughtlessness he gave his cherished Raleigh bicycle to Fanny for her pleasure. He pedaled and she rode on the handlebars up to the small roadside workshop where he unbolted the main crossbar to make it easier for her to ride. He then went to her house to say goodbye to her mother, who cried, and to her father. who was glad to see the last of him. Fanny wouldn't go to the train station to see him off because she considered it bad luck, but instead made an enormous bread pudding for the journey. It always remained his favorite dessert.

His brother, disappointed at first that he wasn't the one to get to travel, came to realize how fortunate he was when they took a last walk together around the farm and young Tom said goodbye to the childhood donkey they used to ride in the local races. Where would you find a better friend? No, the farm was his life and he was grateful to stay. He vowed to keep things as they were until the brother got back and asked him not to change. Young Tom, always on the threshold of exaggeration, promised to leave all his bad habits behind and come back a better man. When the donkey heard this, he turned and gave out a great kick as if to say, "Even I don't believe that." They laughed and lit up a couple of Woodbines as a parting gesture and headed back to the house. The old mother was busy all day making a fancy dinner for his last meal. She wouldn't say what she was planning, but young Tom's favorite was turkey and mashed parsnips and it would be no surprise if she outdid herself making quite a feed.

The next day he boarded the train in Tullamore and waved from the greasy window in the third-class compartment to the small send-off party. It was a six-hour journey to Queenstown, and it was lucky his mother sent along a jug of buttermilk because he had half the bread pudding eaten by Heuston Station in Dublin where he had to switch trains. Several times he took out his bank notes and counted them: eighteen pounds and several half crowns and shillings in silver. He never had so much money and would be well set in America with such a tidy bankroll. At Limerick Junction he was suddenly wedged in between a buster of a man who smoked a terrible smelling pipe and a small woman wearing a big overcoat and floppy hat. You could barely see her face. It was funny they had to pick his seat since the train wasn't that crowded and there were plenty of available spaces. So squeezed was he that it was impossible to even open the small book of ghost stories Major Sherlock gave him as a farewell gift. All he was able to do was gawk about the compartment and that's when he noticed the old woman two seats over waving to him. Like pulling cotton out of an aspirin bottle, he finally was able to extricate himself from his human bondage. He had no sooner tipped his cap to his petitioner when he got his instructions.

"Sit across from me. I hear the tea trolley on its way down

the aisle and I would like you to order two teas for us, milk and a lump of sugar each."

Young Tom did as he was told and graciously offered to pay the sixpence to the serving steward. By the time he had pulled his hand out of his pocket he was in a full panic and on his knees looking under the seats. The old woman asked if anything was wrong.

"My bank notes! I've lost them!"

"Do you have any coins or did they take them also?"

He came up from under his seat and gave the steward a shilling. After he received his change he sat down and waited until they were alone.

"What do you mean?"

"I mean rattling coins make ever so much noise. They'd have to be really good for you not to hear them being scooped from your pocket."

Young Tom looked over at the couple who had sandwiched him in his seat. He was halfway standing up when the old woman pushed him back down.

"Finish your tea. You rushing over there will just result in a big ruckus. We'll handle things in an orderly fashion. The train conductor should be coming by shortly to check for tickets. Read us a story from your book in the meantime."

Was she mad? How could anyone be just sitting and smiling with grand theft running rampant throughout the place?

"Nice and clear; it'll keep you from worrying."

He took the book from his jacket pocket and started with the legend of a banshee who could turn herself into a cat. He was just up to the part where a crock of goat's cheese goes missing when he felt a tap on his shoulder.

"That's a great tale, one of my favorites. Tickets please, lad."

The conductor! He fumbled through his jacket, showed the

ticket and received another punch on the stub. He looked anxiously at the old woman but she had a finger on her lips to not speak out. The conductor gave her a tip of his cap.

"Lady Bernard, always a pleasure to have you on board. I see you're on your way to Cork. I wish you a pleasant stay."

"May I have a private word?"

Being quite a large man, he tilted his head sideways and leaned down low so she could whisper next to his ear. When he had straightened up his face was beet red.

"We'll just see about that... you two over there, up and out of that seat!"

They at first put up all sorts of protestations, but when the eighteen pounds were spread out across the seat and young Tom guaranteed that his Uncle's ten-pound note could be traced back to the bank in Philipstown the jig was up. The money was returned to the young man and the thieving couple were hustled up to the front compartment where they would be met by the police at the next station.

Young Tom sat back down across from Lady Bernard.

"How did they know I had that kind of money?"

"Well, you were counting it often enough, but if the smaller member of the team didn't see that when she made her first pass, they surely noticed your traveling case and your fresh face."

As he looked at his reflection in the window she commented:

"The expression is 'never having left the ashes.' Nothing to be ashamed of, but it appears you're on a big journey. Canada?"

"No, New York... I'm sorry, your ladyship, I had no idea who you were or I wouldn't have been a bother."

"Nonsense, it was my duty to help you and besides I've enjoyed your recitation. There's a touch of the dramatist in you. In case you're wondering, I always travel third class. I think first class is overindulgent and completely boring. You meet the real people of Ireland here."

"I'm terribly grateful. There must be some way of thanking you."

"You know, I can't remember the last time I had a piece of homemade bread pudding. It's one of my favorites!"

TUESDAY 4:30PM

"I was dreaming of buttermilk."

Old Tom was on his way to the bathroom, having gotten up from his two-hour nap. Bridie had been in the living room carefully removing the candle grease from his good Sunday pants with some brown paper and a hot iron. She ignored the remark but took notice by way of the wall clock that it was time to put the light under the potatoes to boil. After taking her lamb chops from the ice box, she looked through the kitchen curtains to see that the sleet was coming down heavy and worried that it would turn to snow. Then he would have to go back out to see that the church steps were cleared off. She waited until he came out of the bathroom and finished coughing to ask if he would have to go back out again. No answer. When she went back into the living room to investigate, she found him standing barefoot in the twilight, pajama tops tucked carelessly inside his old brown pants. He never looked at her but spoke as from a performance.

"Candlemas, a candle less."

"Almost three weeks gone by already; you can tell now the

days are starting to get a bit longer."

She turned on the table lamp nearest the door and looked to see if he was all right. The sudden illumination seemed to break his trance and started him off towards the easy chair where he grunted his way through socks and slippers. When he was finished, he rewarded himself with a Chesterfield and asked:

"What's it doing out there?"

"Sleet, the sidewalk is looking slippery already."

JUNE 1935

"They call it an Irish banjo."

Young Tom remembered the first time he heard the expression and he nodded thoughtfully at the line of men furiously flinging shovelfuls of dirt in front of Kilbeggan's Bar and Grill. All the remaining lines on the telephone poles were going underground and strong backs were needed to dig out and fill in the accommodating trenches, vigorous work indeed and sure to bring on a terrific thirst. The foreman, showing insightful sensibility, made arrangements for growlers of beer to be brought out from the bar when the men took their breaks—with his portion of course being free of charge. The smart ones knew how to grab opportunities when they presented themselves.

He tugged on the big brass door handle and tipped his cap to the late-arriving young waitress running in ahead of him. Being just half nine the place was empty except for two black supply porters at the end of the bar accepting a small glass of ale as an expression of the establishment's appreciation for their services. Their big smiles clearly confirmed the service sector's preference for deliverance to an Irish saloon. Young Tom waved to his cousin behind the bar and weaved his way through the scurrying waiters setting tables for the lunch trade. After hanging up his jacket, he was still adjusting the cords of his immense white apron around his waist when his cousin called him over.

"It's going to be a hot one today."

"Good for business. I'll bring the empties down to the cellar. Do you need any refills?"

He shook his head no and young Tom noticed how old he looked. A completely different person from the one he met when he arrived over five years ago. He also knew the man had something more to say so he quietly waited. Finally:

"Are you happy?"

"I'm doing all right. The job at the A&P has turned out to be permanent. They moved me up to the dairy section the other day."

"With your mother having been a dairy maid I shouldn't wonder you'd be an expert. That's grand, but you'll still be able to help me out behind the bar?"

"I don't go in until noon and then there's my day off—Sunday."

An elderly gent with a bad case of the jitters had planted himself at the bar and the barman understood the call to duty.

"He's in tough shape today. I'd better not keep him waiting. Come back up later and have a sandwich at the bar."

Young Tom acknowledged the wink with a smile and lugged the crate of empty bottles down to a cellar reeking of stale beer. He knew the small open window at street level would be no help. There wasn't a wisp of a breeze and the day was already a scorcher. He took off his apron and hung his white shirt up on the nail near the St Ignatius Loyola Church calendar. He needed to have it fresh-looking for his dairy counter customers. The manager at the A&P insisted his boys look and act like gentlemen.

"It's best to keep him buttered up."

He was pleased with his little pun until it brought back memories of his mother and the farm. Was she feeling any better? How was the brother managing? It was sad to hear about the old donkey dying. That was at Christmas time when he received their card. He of course sent a card, too, but couldn't give out many details. With them having such great expectations on his occasion in America there was no way he could turn the cousin's hard luck into a day at the races.

Sweeping up the soggy sawdust from the floor he thought back to when he first arrived and how his cousin greeted him at the pier. He looked like the Lord Mayor of Dublin, dressed in a long-tailed coat, striped pants, and top hat. He gave him a great big hug and instructed the chauffeur to put his battered suitcase into the trunk of an enormous limousine. Then off they went.

"Where to?"

"Atlantic City."

The toot of their horn at the main entrance of the Traymore Hotel had more people jumping to attention than reveille at a barracks. Directing their limousine to the red carpet, a white-gloved hand opened the door where they were transported from the familiar to the sublime, starting with a lobby more befitting a pontiff's palace than a hotel. Young Tom was just starting to enjoy the taste of the salt water taffy offered to him by a small boy on holiday when he noticed the chauffeur handing his bag to an eager-looking lad in a pillbox hat who immediately disappeared into some small room with sliding doors. He became suspicious and questioned the cousin.

"Ho rong can huh reath in dar."

"Pardon?"

His cousin waited patiently until young Tom had freed the

candy from his front teeth.

"How long can he breathe in that closet?"

"That's not a closet, that's the elevator. He took your bag up to our suite."

"How would he know where that is? We haven't talked to anyone yet."

"It practically has my name on it."

Putting claustrophobic trepidation aside, Young Tom took the assurances of the elevator operator that the confining contraption was indeed safe. The proud general manager ran up ahead to hold the penthouse door open for the gawking greenhorn, unveiling a suite twice the size of the old farmhouse! The young man had died and gone to heaven.

Young Tom was still recalling the four faucets in the bathtub—two for hot and cold fresh water, two for hot and cold salt water—when he heard the demand from upstairs.

"We need ice up here, quick."

Young Tom knew it wasn't his cousin calling down from the bar; not by the sound of the voice, since everything was partly muffled underneath the floorboards. No, it was because there was no familiar "please" or "thank you"—hallmarks that a gentleman never loses, regardless of how his particular circumstances may have been altered. He didn't bother to reply.

With a freshly lit cigarette in his mouth, he hoisted a big block of ice from the storage box and violently chopped it into cordial chunks, filling up two large ice pails. He then put on his shirt and apron and humped the buckets upstairs.

"What kept you?"

The manager pushed him aside and grabbed a handful of ice to wrap in a dishtowel as a means of revival. When young Tom peered around the manager's shoulder, he could see the old cousin in a twisted heap on the floor behind the bar.

SEPTEMBER 1958

"Sputnik?"

"That's right, the first artificial satellite launched into space."

Tommy went over to the window to investigate but came back looking suspicious.

"I don't see it."

"What? Oh, it's not up there any more. It fell back to earth."

"Then why did they do it?"

Betty Ann missed matching the other red queen that was in the corner of the Concentration card game. Bob jumped on the chance and made the connection. With a big smile he gave Tommy an atta-boy pat on the shoulder. The younger brother interpreted his sister's frown to mean he should share his distracting chattering with her competitor.

"Why is your hair so short now?"

"Regulation from boot camp; proper hair length is part of my uniform."

"Can I touch it?"

Bob bent his head down low and Tommy gave it a long, vigorous rub, taking enough time for him to miss seeing the ten of hearts Betty Ann had uncovered and left on the board. When her turn came around again, she collected it with the ten of diamonds. She then went on a tear and matched up the remaining eight cards on the board to win the game. Bob was stunned.

"I was waiting the whole time for that ten of hearts to turn up! That was a lucky guess."

"No luck, skill. 7-Up time!"

With Betty Ann gone Tommy stood enchanted watching Bob shuffle the playing cards.

"My father mixes them up the other way—one hand into another."

"That's old-fashioned. This is the way they'll do it aboard ship."

"How long will you be gone?"

"Six months, maybe longer if there is action."

"What kind of action?"

Bob looked around to add to the suspense then quietly whispered in the boy's ear.

"Russians."

Betty Ann returned with two large and one small glass of 7-Up. Tommy barely gave her time to sit down.

"Bob's going away a long time."

"Let's hope not. Did you tell him you're going into first grade in St John's next week?"

Tommy ran into the bedroom and quickly returned with a pair of navy pants, a white shirt, and a sky-blue tie with a school emblem. Instant enthusiasm was always Bob's strong suit.

"That's a cool uniform!"

"Maybe someday I'll get to fight Russians too."

Betty Ann, sensing a topic she had no interest in, moved on from the conversation and over to the red and black Magnavox record player. Fast dancing was on her mind and it didn't take her long to decide that Bobby Day should lead the way. Once he got spinning, it only took a wink and a wave to get her Bobby on his feet. Tommy jumped up on the sofa to keep clear of collisions and to carefully observe how things would shake out.

He rocks in the treetops all day long
Hoppin' and a-boppin' and singing his song
All the little birds on Jaybird Street
Love to hear the robin go tweet tweet tweet

Bridie, hearing the music, came out from the kitchen and smiled when Bob reached over and grabbed her hand for a spinning Lindy hop move. With her red hair flying, he quickly spun her back to her original starting point and scooped up Betty Ann again, right on refrain.

Rockin' robin, (tweet tweet tweet)
Rock-rock-rockin' robin' (tweet tweedly dee)
Go rockin' robin 'cause we're
Really gonna rock tonight (tweet tweedly dee)

Since it was a hot September day the block of wood that was used to keep the front door open for a possible breeze was in full force, giving unlimited access to the apartment to anyone who just happened to be passing by. So it was no surprise to Tommy when Deidre came scooting in and sat next to him on the sofa. Being a gentleman, he knew it was his duty to play host.

"Would you like some 7-Up?"

"Yes please. Where does the music come from?"

"It comes out of that music box."

"The dancing is very lively. I would like to learn."

"Watch, they're great at it."

But that takes practice and Betty Ann knew it could be better, so she didn't hesitate to restart the record to tighten that slingshot move. Over and over Bob wound her up and flung her out at arm's length until she was satisfied, they finally out-bopped the buzzard. Laughing, they flew the coop to get some city air and have a cigarette. The dance floor was available for newcomers.

Tommy was just putting the needle down on the record when his mother's public announcement message echoed out from the kitchen.

"Be careful you don't scratch it; she just bought that one yesterday."

As Tommy spun his partner around and around on the living room carpet, he could hear Deidre laughing.

"Music from a magical box—Scarecrow would be ever so jealous!"

* * *

The transition to Catholic grammar school was not as traumatic for Tommy as stand-up comedy routines would have foretold. It was quite seamless, actually, since by now Tommy's hodgepodge of humbuggery was sufficiently conniving to cajole the gaggle of nuns assigned to St John's Parish. For the ones who looked like they held a hammer when the place was first built, he would steer their recollections to the accomplishments of his much-cherished eldest sister whom he hoped to emulate in exemplary good behavior and high standards.

"Oh, so you are Kathleen's little brother? She was a good student."

"She said I was lucky to have you as a teacher."

With Kathleen as the focus of the old woman's well-worn

cerebral cortex, the conversation could now be skillfully turned to this beloved sister's present situation, giving Tommy the opportunity to enthusiastically expand upon her impressive business career downtown where she had to be up early every morning and take a lot of time in the bathroom—all of this success being the result of her solid parochial school foundation.

And much better to keep the small talk right there because in social comportment Kathleen was always a sure bet whereas Betty Ann was somewhat of a crap shoot as far as school behavior was concerned. Being able to charm the birds out of the trees when she felt like it, she also possessed a deep-seated urge to garner attention by occasionally attempting some ill-conceived stunt. Now, although this was one of her more impressive qualities as far as Tommy was concerned, he had to tread carefully because at this introductory stage of his eight-year sentence he wanted to remain the innocent—easier to deflect blame onto those with confirmed reputations. Any mention of Betty Ann therefore would be handled gingerly, mostly relying on confusing the old nuns' memory of circumstances.

Eileen would be his ace-in-the-hole because she was still in the system, just entering the sixth grade. Her quiet and unassuming nature could be effectively utilized in spying on any inevitable enemies he would obtain in disturbing this reserve of religiously-induced conformity as well as providing excuses and planting misinformation to his present handlers. He in turn would be more than happy to play the cute little brother if it would in any way advance her social standing among friends. No need to mention the misfortune befalling the ill-mannered lout causing her any trouble. There were plenty of half-deranged miscreants malingering outside the nurse's office who could be easily bribed for this type of dirty work. They seemed born for it.

For the younger members of the religious order a special brew of adorability and precociousness would be whipped up to gain extraordinary exemptions from the mundane assignments obediently obeyed by the rabble under her questionable authority. Along with this personal manipulation, cultural camouflage techniques would also be employed, taking advantage of the large number of Irish numbskulls in the class—"it wasn't me; it was him you told" being a standard misdirection. Not quite sure, she would suppose a mistake in identity could have been made and would quickly withdraw from her oppressive requests. And once the seed of doubt was sown, she was easily intimidated into believing that even the most egregious and flagrant abuses may not have actually taken place. The teaching profession is not for everyone.

No, the great leap forward for the young Irish prince would not be within the confined walls of parochialism but in venturing out alone for the first time onto the streets and alleys of Naples Terrace. Here was uncertainty, chaos, cruelty. Like Dante, it was best to have a seasoned guide for this inferno and in Tommy's case that would have been be an older brother. Almost indispensable in his ability to provide air cover from both physical harm and mental intimidation, an older brother would also offer feedback in the development of effective antisocial behavior, sneering and posturing being highly regarded. These, and other manly practices, were not as simple as they appeared, but had an idiosyncratic nature that took careful coaching to master and were secretly guarded by hardened warriors who had no intention to share with the unrelated. Faced with this formidable handicap of no fraternal sponsorship, the boy had to rely on his own fertile imagination to mold this bloated mass of illogical behavior into a serviceable sphere of survival. He had to develop street smarts.

When first out on the street geometry plays an important role, starting with a half-circle mentally drawn from the front steps of the apartment building. The radius is your escape route back to relative safety when menacing circumstances present themselves. The actual time it takes would be tested under non-suspicious circumstances and cloaked under the usual excessive energy of a hyperactive five-year-old. Here was the beginning of judgment—just how far should this green fuse be extended today? Was an investigation of that Kool-Aid stand across the street worth the risk? What about the moron sitting atop the fire alarm box? Was his motive worth an investigation? The general temperament of any migrating mobs would also have to be carefully assessed. Could this be the day when casual assimilation might be attempted? A foreign presence was an invading virus and would be immediately detected. Waiting until some inevitable calamity to occur might the best approach—to be a nonchalant bystander. All would have to be given careful consideration. One thing was certain: life required an ever-increasing expansion of this half circle of existence.

Sitting alone on the cold cement steps like Rodin's *Thinker*, he was forced to consider the relative merits of obtaining a friend. Companionship presented appealing aspects, both in terms of obtaining secret street information as well as providing possible protection from bodily harm, since Tommy was running a bit on the thin side compared to some of the uncaged busters he'd seen roaming recklessly. A friend could also be a useful trading partner for items where a certain level of indifference had set in; hardened portions of Play-Doh or bent Erector Set beams. Yes, there were advantages in making welcoming contacts, but something would undoubtedly be required of *him*. Was the burden of friendship worth it? He decided to consult with his red motorcycle policeman and was busy racing him around the top step when he realized he had company.

"Whaddya you got?"

"Him."

"Let me see it… I said give it to me!"

"No."

Tommy, having the advantage of being three steps above the brute, was able to slide from under his rapacious grab for the policeman. Once on his feet he ran to the glass front door of the building and turned to gauge the gap. He was surprised to see he wasn't being chased. Instead he was given a piece of the code.

"Sissy!"

And then he left. Tommy snuck down to see which way he went and was shocked to watch him knuckle-walk into the building across the street. A regular delight to look forward to.

Back in the apartment he was told to wash his hands for dinner where he did his best to show appreciation for cold leg of lamb by pushing it around the plate hoping it would disappear. Eileen was much more direct and used her gagging technique to have Bridie reluctantly reach over and remove her portion, leaving her quite happy with just the mint jelly. As was often the case, something in the boiled potatoes released a nostalgic fervor in Tommy's father resulting this time in a rousing recollection of sitting around the turf fire in Ireland eating stirabout.

Given a chance to look away from the intimidating gray meat still occupying his plate, the boy challenged the significance of such a seemingly dismal activity.

"Wasn't that boring?"

Bridie chuckled at the boy catching on to the obvious so quickly but the father was not to be put off by any lack of appreciation and sallied forth confidently.

"Not a bit boring. That's where I learned almost everything I know."

An uncomfortable silence resulted which held the possibility of a severe mood swing. Tommy picked up on Eileen's frozen facial expression and offered a follow-up question.

"Like what?"

The father's voice became very soft as he leaned across the table to be closer to the boy's ear.

"Things like being careful when you go following the Wil-o'-the-Wisp; he'll have you enchanted and the next thing, you'll end up being led straight into the bog."

Eileen, now trying to appear interested, wanted to know why this atmospheric apparition takes such delight in luring people to their death. Bridie was ready with the answer.

"There's no why to it."

Fortunately, the anguish involved in trying to unravel another of his mother's mysterious aphorisms was cut short by the sound of the front door opening. Tommy slid out from his chair to see who it was.

"Ma! It's Betty Ann!"

Betty Ann's return meant freedom from the gray meat. He would go out into the living room to make room for the working sister to eat.

Snuggled in the sofa's soothing seclusion, Tommy realized that neither the evocative folk tales of his father nor the gnostic sayings of his mother would ever help him in dealing with the demons he was now forced to confront in this new concrete jungle. No, the ancient ashes of Ireland's turf fires could not be rekindled. What was needed was an up-to-date guide based on a realistic portrayal of 1950s America. Fortunately, centered triumphantly in the living room was the perfect instrument for extrapolating practical solutions from comparable situations:

television.

It took a bit of time for the boy to consider all the models available to fit his particular circumstances. At first the free enterprise system of hiring someone to solve your problems was very appealing and westerns provided plenty of material to choose from. The bounty hunter in *Wanted: Dead or Alive* was certainly cool enough and he seemed to like his horse, but for sheer ruthlessness you couldn't top Paladin in *Have Gun—Will Travel.* In style points, Tommy particularly liked how Gilman in *Trackdown* rolled and smoked his cigarettes while staring danger in the face, but the guy was a Texas Ranger and probably couldn't be bribed. Likewise, Matt Dillon in *Gunsmoke* was too square to kill someone for just bothering you, but the show was worth watching just to see the way Miss Kitty could hold her liquor. In the end, the world of the western was undoubtedly a good venue for cultivating acceptance of violent outbursts, but did not offer the subtlety that the boy craved.

Shows featuring farm life presented all social conflicts in clear black and white terms—someone was right, and someone was wrong and they must pay. The boy liked that aspect but was skeptical of their overly complicated schemes, especially when they featured an animal smarter than any of the characters. On the plus side, either *Lassie* or *Fury* would certainly have solved his companion problem but he had repeatedly heard, "There is no dog being let in this apartment." He never bothered to ask about a horse. *The Real McCoys* was completely eliminated from his consideration set. Their response to problems was simply not aggressive enough.

Alfred Hitchcock Presents and *The Twilight Zone* provided unique insight into psychological warfare; Tommy keenly observed the effect both shows had on family members. For instance, the incessant suspense kept Eileen in a very fluid state, tossing her cruelly between muffled screams and fits of hysterical laughter. Kathleen, on the other hand, maintained her characteristic cool when viewing but then would nonchalantly saunter off to bed to silently suffer nightmares. Only Betty Ann serenely incorporated the episodes into a worldview that rationalized crazy things happening because crazy things *can* happen. For the boy's part, the story line went above his head most of the time but he was perceptive enough to appreciate the value of fear—whether real or imagined—in reducing one's enemies to a harmless state.

Conveniently, as is often the case with self-absorbed boys of Irish parents, it was during this period of pathetic anguish that he experienced a euphoric episode. He brilliantly realized that at his command was the one weapon omnipotent in all situations—a dry sense of humor. Newly inspired, he set off to eagerly devour the formulaic comedy shows offered—*Ozzie and Harriet*, *Abbott and Costello*, *Love That Bob*—all in search of a personal technique that would flaunt this deterrent to its best advantage. But even with these exalted expectations, the power of hurtful wisecracks and callous comebacks in crippling the most fearful opponent would astonish him, delight him. Here was higher authority! Here was vocation! The life of the amusing, unloved jokester lay before him.

OCTOBER 1930

"Whoever took this picture should be ashamed."

Young Bridget looked up from her letter writing to notice the young man standing above her holding her passport book.

"And why is that?"

"Doesn't do you justice—much prettier in person."

"I don't think the immigration authorities in New York will be much concerned about how I look. May I have my passport, please?"

"Well now, that's just the thing. They should care very much. You see, you'll be a great danger to all those other girls in that wonderful city who can't hold a candle to you. Quite unfair, actually."

She stood up from the table in the third-class lounge and held out her hand. The young man shook it vigorously and occupied the chair across from her.

"Very pleased to meet you, I'm sure. Since I have you at a disadvantage, let me introduce myself. Johnny McCabe is my name. Sit down, sit down, Miss Bridget Kiernan. We have another important matter to discuss here."

She took her time moving her chair a little farther away from the table before sitting. When satisfied:

"Do you work for the steamship line?"

"Me? Oh, no, no, no. They would never have me. Actually, that's why I'm on this ship in the first place. I'm running away from work. Terrible I am at it."

"I didn't know there was any work in Ireland to run away from."

"Nor in Scotland, me being one of the first to board in Glasgow. No, you see I'm afraid my father has the funny idea I would follow him in his profession."

"That sounds very important. What kind of profession?"

"Men's fancy goods. Dreadfully boring. Always scurrying after gents with a measuring tape. Not for me at all."

"What *is* for you?"

"Greasepaint. I have acting blood on my mother's side and I'm hoping those magnificent brains that put together Broadway shows will recognize talent when they see it."

Young Bridget couldn't hide the thin smile forcing its way out. She tried to reclaim a bit of authority.

"You mentioned another important matter. What that might be?"

"Bee! What a perfect name for you. Not this stuffy Bridget business."

"Some people call me that, but it's Miss Kiernan for you."

"My humble apologies. How rude, how presumptuous on my part. But I get carried away. You asked about the other detail I must bring to your attention—a most shameful one."

"What?"

"It says right here, in black and white, with only the smallest traces of a butter stain, that yesterday was your birthday. You can't deny it."

"I don't."

"Eighteen years old and I wasn't invited to the celebration!"

"There wasn't any. I was awfully sick to my stomach and stayed in bed most of the day."

"Seasick!"

"It's a little better right now; I'm not so shaky."

"But you're out here writing a letter home telling them about the wonderful voyage."

"Yes."

"You know, you do a terrible job of hiding that little bow smile of yours. Let it out, the Irish have good teeth. Not my strong suit at all. Hopefully there will be a bit of distance between me and those in the front row of the theater. But we mustn't let this momentous occasion pass unheralded. Join me in the dining room for some tea and a scone—that's right, it rhymes with gone. I'm sure it will do your stomach wonders."

It became a ritual for the next seven days. Young Bridget would be seasick in the morning and would recover just enough to have tea and scones with Johnny McCabe in the afternoons. She was ever so glad to see the Statue of Liberty and know that she would be getting off soon. They docked at 44th Street and went through the new auxiliary immigration office. Johnny was through his inspection line a little ahead of her and waited. He noticed the small cardboard suitcase she was carrying and was impressed by the courage of this red-haired lass to make it on her own in America. He walked alongside out the front entrance.

"It's quite a big place, isn't it?"

"I never saw the like."

"I've been to London, of course, but this is the tops for sure. I hope to see you again. I'll be staying at the Hotel Astor—at least until my funds give out. Why don't you leave me a message and we'll resume our mutual admiration of strong tea and warm flaky things? Will you?"

"I might."

He shook her hand solemnly and walked off in the direction of Tenth Avenue. He was just out of sight when young Bridget's sister ran up and gave her a big hug and kiss.

"You made it!"

They walked up to St. Malachy's Church in the Theater District and lit a candle in gratitude of safe passage, afterwards stopping at Bickford's to have a small sandwich. Having solid ground under her for the first time in eight days inspired a great appetite in young Bridget. During her piece of apple pie, she related the details of her trip. Her older sister was not too impressed.

"Was that him I saw prowling across the street before I met you?"

"Johnny? Yes, he had just said goodbye."

"And that's just how it'll be—goodbye. Don't need the likes of him coming around."

SEPTEMBER 1935

The shock of the poor old cousin dying on the floor of the saloon was compounded by the hardened insistence of the landlord for Tom to vacate the apartment they had shared; the ability to pay the rent trumping any lingering nostalgia for the old man. So, with urgency being thrust upon him and funds being quite limited, he was forced to consider the favorite locale of the funny papers—a rooming house. After visiting a few lodgings and getting a glimpse of the customers being accommodated, the idea of sleeping in Central Park seemed not such a bad idea. There were still plenty of shanties around that would probably take him in. Luckily he took the advice of a co-worker and went up to Mrs. LaTrey's place on West 74th Street. She took one look at him with his well-worn traveling bag and got down to business:

"Have you got a job?"

"I have."

"Who recommended you?"

"Mike Slovak."

"The butcher at the A&P?"

"That's the fellow."

"And you also work at the supermarket?"

"In the dairy section."

Satisfied by the young man's employment record, Mrs. LaTrey adjusted her glasses for the touchier part of the interview. "Not in any kind of distress, are you?"

"Pardon?"

"You know—trouble. Not trying to hide from anyone?"

"No ma'am."

"All right then, there's a trial period of one month. Any violation of the rules and you'll be asked to vacate the premises."

"May I ask, how much would you be charging?"

"Eight dollars a week—with two weeks in advance."

"Including meals?"

"Half board. Our main meal is supper. Right now, we have only two boarders but we always wait 'till everyone's home from work, Come in."

Tom followed her through the vestibule into the dining room which was expertly laid out for the evening's meal. From there they went into the sitting room where she approached the occupant of a pair of gray trousers whose identity was concealed behind the late edition of the *New York Daily Mirror*.

"Mr. Bennett, may we have a word?"

A pink face with a pair of spectacles perched atop his nose peered around the newspaper.

"It's a wicked world we're living in, Mrs. LaTrey."

"You know, Mr. Bennett, how I strongly advise against reading such stimulating accounts before mealtime. It is not beneficial for your digestion. We have a new boarder who I would like to introduce. His name is… is… I don't know his name!"

Bennett had just seen a *Movietone News* featuring Clarence

Darrow and wasn't going to waste a good opportunity. He put his hand up to Mrs. LaTrey indicating he would take charge. Slowly rising from his chair, he made a scrutinizing turn around the man standing before him. When he got back to where he started, he took off his glasses, furrowed his forehead and spoke in a consoling, reassuring tone, insinuating sympathy for any sinister secrets.

"*Why* won't you tell us your name?"

"I was never asked."

* * *

Over the next few weeks they became friends. Undoubtedly both being Irish was a foundation, but there was an understanding between them that went beyond the obvious. Professionally settled himself, Mr. Bennett saw in the younger man a certain potential and encouraged him to take advantage of the unique opportunities America afforded him—hard times or not. The first thing was to figure out what he was good at.

"I see you like to play cards," Bennett observed.

"You can learn a lot in a place like this."

"You know, being an insurance man, I can tell you there is a great association between games of chance and what we do."

Even with an unlit cigarette stuck to his lips, Tom's accusation was unmistakable. "The Scotsman cheats."

"What?"

"He's good at it, too."

"You're not playing for money, I hope. Mrs. LaTrey strictly forbids gambling on the premises."

"No money is shown. We use matchsticks to keep track."

"How do you know he cheats?"

"I watch him. Sometimes he deals from the bottom of the

deck, other times he'll palm a card or float a card to the top and shuffle the rest. I even think he has the cards marked.

"That's a very serious charge to make of someone. You have to have irrefutable proof."

"Oh, I'm not going to accuse him. I want to learn."

The next day when Tom got home from work, he washed up quickly so he could be the first one in the sitting room. It didn't take long for his tutor to show up.

"Fancy a game, Tom?"

"How about a little blackjack?"

The Scotsman put on his thick, black spectacles and pulled a deck of cards out of his jacket pocket. He was just about to shuffle when Tom reached over and took up the deck.

"Do you mind? I splurged and bought a fresh pack of cards today. I figured we could retire this old batch."

Tom put the old deck in his shirt pocket and snatched up the heavy eyeglasses his opponent had discarded.

"You know, I always wondered if I need specs myself. Let me have a look."

He started by examining one of the old cards taken from his pocket. It was like wearing binoculars.

"I'm seeing all sorts of things but I don't know what they mean."

"If you would be so kind as to return my goggles and spread the old deck of cards face down on the table, I will give you a demonstration of how it works."

Tom did better than that and neatly placed all fifty-two cards face down covering the whole table. He started by pointing to a card smack in the middle and asking:

"Would you want to guess what that card could be?"

"The five of clubs."

Tom flipped the card face up. "Amazing. How about this

one in the corner?"

"Ace of spades. I suggest we save some time."

The Scotsman started from the top row and quickly identified the first card, the next one and then the next—moving on as fast as Tom could turn them over. When he was finished, he took his glasses off and rubbed his eyes so he wouldn't have to look at Tom as he spoke.

"Well, I guess you hold all the cards now."

Tom had the figure in his head of how many matchsticks he had lost and was immediately reimbursed the four dollars and twenty-five cents. When that was settled, he asked:

"How do you do it? I don't see any marks."

"You're not supposed to. Wearing these magnifying lenses allows you to observe a series of dots placed in certain positions—like a semaphore code. Once you get the hang of it you can read them very quickly. By the way, what happens next?"

"What do you mean?"

"Do you run about the house shouting we have a card sharp in our midst?"

"Why would I do that? You made good with me, but I want to learn, especially the other tricks."

"What tricks? Sorry, I think you dropped something."

He handed Tom a card.

"The ace of spades. I don't remember missing any cards.... Wait! There's already an ace of spades in the deck!"

"But here's another one you must have dropped... and another... and one more."

He put three aces of spades face up on the table. Tom checked the back of the cards and they looked like they came from identical decks.

"No way you could ever lose with a talent like that."

"Oh, you could lose a lot more than you realize, that's why I'm not going to show you anything more until I get to know you a little better."

"How about coming to the dance with me and Bennett tonight up at the Roscommon House?"

"Whiskey, women, and song: temptations I cannot resist."

"We'll eat, then head out. I'm a bit ashamed to admit it, but I never got your name."

"Johnny McCabe—at your service."

* * *

After supper Tom shaved and put on his best black suit jacket with his almost-matching pants and was greeted by the overwhelming smell of Kreml Hair Tonic when Bennett entered his room. The man's hair was so well lacquered it would have withstood a hurricane without flinching. Pulling his prized gold watch out of his waistcoat pocket he reminded the younger man of the streetcar schedule.

"Better hurry, we have only five minutes to make it to the corner."

"With the three of us, makes more sense to take a taxi cab."

"Three? Who else?"

"The Scotsman. He's even offered to pay."

"Why is he coming with us? I thought you said he cheats."

"Nah, he's just a good player, that's all."

They went downstairs to the sitting room and no Johnny. Tom was just about to go upstairs and knock on his door when the man himself dramatically appeared at the top of the stairs.

"My, my, my!"

If there was a parapraxis in Mrs. LaTrey's possessive you couldn't blame her. As was her habit to be reasonably nosy, she wandered by just in time to see McCabe's descent from above. First, there was the flawlessly-fitting three-button Glen check blazer with fashionable narrow lapels, all properly accented with a clean, white handkerchief. The man knew a good tailor. Underneath was an open-collared, white shirt redeemed from any blandness by a jaunty blue and white ascot made up just a bit too rakishly. The light gray gabardine trousers were triple-pleated with quarter-inch turn-ups and they offset the charcoal-colored blazer brilliantly. Black loafers, distinguished by a tight basket weave, assured a lightness of foot guaranteed to reassure any dancing partner that this was a gentleman who would leave their toes unharmed. Hair was combed straight back without any oily creams or preparations, the wavy texture projecting a hint of romantic boldness. Like a jaguar, he noiselessly descended two steps at a time, all the while maintaining perfect posture.

"Bonsoir, messieurs-dame. Are we all set for an exciting evening?"

Mrs. LaTrey, looking for something to do besides blushing, got busy flicking cigarette ash from Tom's jacket and clumsily excused herself as the men headed out to the street. Tom went up to Central Park West to hail a taxi, allowing Bennett to get better acquainted in his usual humorless style.

"I'm an insurance man. My motto is you can never be too well covered."

"Afraid I'm totally naked in that department. You see, acting's my game and I'm between parts right now."

Bennett eyed the expensive ensemble and couldn't restrain his disapproval.

"It's all about priorities, you know. Always wise to plan ahead."

"My dear Mr. Bennett, fortune brings in some boats that aren't steered. For me a planned life is simply unlivable… ah, the luck of the Irish! Tom found a taxi. Allow me, my good fellow."

* * *

Roscommon House was a dance hall located on the second floor of a rundown building in the Highbridge section of the Bronx. Situated directly above a saloon, its reputation stipulated both an early arrival and timely exit; this based on the inclination of the inebriates downstairs fancying some dancing once they finished off a fifth of whiskey. The phrase "the jig is up" was never more befitting than when these stumbling sots had hit the dance floor—fighting being more of their specialty. Since the dances were held on Saturday nights this caveat of knowing when to leave was reinforced by the whingeing of unwanted chaperones worried about being able to get up for mass the next day.

The depended-upon clientele were high-spirited young Irish immigrants looking for some fun and companionship and a break from the weekday drudgery most of them faced. Besides being reliable customers for the club owners, this pool of naïve greenhorns was also ideal fodder for local gangsters looking for new recruits. With good paying jobs hard to come by, exaggerated offers of easy money were very hard to refuse and once ensnared the dance hall was no longer good enough for them. They had moved up—or so it was said. It was only through some unflattering picture in the crime section of the newspaper or, worse still, a terse obituary notice that you learned the job didn't turn out as well as expected.

A rotating schedule of local bands provided the entertainment, which was quite good considering their amateur status and their inability to practice during the week. Most of their talent was developed back home in Ireland as simple pub entertainment, but that ability to match lively melodies with witty lyrics was fully exploited when given the opportunity to perform to a much larger audience. This new venue, however, did bring additional responsibilities. As the night wore on, they had to constantly assess the mood of their listeners, tempering their musical selections with just enough sentimentality to elicit good-natured nostalgia all the while being mindful of the Irish proclivity for melancholy—themselves sometimes being the most affected!

Tom, Bennett, and Johnny were halfway up the stairs to the dance hall when they had to jump aside to avoid the tumbling body of a former patron. When he reached the bottom, Johnny ran down to help him up and put him straight on his feet. The assistance was not appreciated:

"Get your hands off me, I don't need any help… say, aren't you Tyrone Power?"

"Shhhh! Not so loud. Don't want anyone else to know."

"Wow, yeah, I get ya. But… but who are those two you're with?"

"My good man, you must have banged you head more than you realized. Why, that's none other than Pat O'Brien. And surely you must recognize Spencer Tracy? Pat, the gentleman's hat, if you please."

Tom picked up the crumpled fedora, slapped it onto the guy's head, and spun him in the direction of the bar.

"Remember, not a word to anyone."

"Oh no, not me, you can count on it."

He was off happily mumbling to himself when the trio again attempted the stairs. This time they made it to the top unimpeded and were graciously greeted by a giant of a man guarding the entrance.

"Evening, Mr. Bennett. Tom, I see we have ourselves a new customer. Who might he be?"

"This is Johnny McCabe, a fellow boarder at LaTrey's and a great guy to know."

"Well, any fella who's a pal of yours is okay with us. Go right on in. Oh, and don't mind the rubbish I had to give the heave-ho to. We don't allow the likes of them in here."

As they entered the big hall, the band had just finished their first set and the over-heated dancers were scurrying around and lighting up cigarettes to catch their breath. Johnny spotted the service bar at the far end and offered to go for the initial round, but first wanted Tom to set him straight on the ground rules.

"It took a fearsome force to propel a full-grown man so violently down the stairs. Does such a creature have a name?"

"We call him Finn McCool." "Ah, the fabled Irish protector. And would you know the particular indiscretion our airborne acquaintance committed to earn membership into 'the likes of them'?"

Bennett immediately looked away so Tom knew that it was up to him to deliver the disagreeable description.

"The man was a masher."

"Tsk, tsk, tsk, naughty, naughty. Mustn't have any of that. Anything else I should know?"

"Mr. Bennett takes only ginger ale."

McCabe threw his hands up in feigned horror and ran toward the bar. Bennett took this quiet moment to consider the image reflected in the large glass mirror displayed behind the bandstand. For him, there indeed was a strong resemblance.

"I'm a bit taller, of course."

"Who's that?"

"Spencer Tracy."

"He seems to go easier on the hair tonic."

"That may be, but that unkempt look is out of date. Today's ladies prefer a gentleman who is well groomed."

"You may be on to something; every time I see him in a movie he's playing second banana to that peacock with the moustache."

Bennett couldn't quite remember if Clark Gable had a moustache or not. Sometimes he does, sometimes he doesn't. He would check the current copy of *Life* magazine in the sitting room, but for now he had another concern.

"Speaking of being on to something, I don't understand this new-found admiration for Johnny McCabe. 'A great guy to know.' Can you really verify the verisimilitude of such a statement?"

"We had our little talk in the sitting room and I was all wrong about the man. I think he could be very handy to have around."

"Well, he's certainly stylish, I'll give you that. But he has a recklessness about him that I would give a wide berth to. Like I told you many times, Tom: it's the slow and steady tortoise that wins the race."

"He's slow enough getting those drinks over here. I'd better extract him from that host of sparrows he's charming."

Tom went over to the bar and pushed his way through to give Johnny a tap on the shoulder.

"We're gathering a mighty thirst standing over there. Did you forget us?"

"Oh Tom, just the man. Let me introduce you. This is Elizabeth and Margaret and Connie and—who was it again?"

"Bridget."

"Ah yes, Bridget. Who would have thought that good old Schrafft's Restaurant employed such beauties? Outstanding really! I must visit it sometime. Ladies, let us venture over to poor, lonely Mr. Bennett and share some of your radiance with him."

Tom grabbed his drink out of Johnny's hand and watched them descend upon the venerable Bennett. They had him surrounded. It was only after he had taken a sip from his own glass and had put it down on the bar that he noticed not all of them left. One was staring at him.

"Isn't anybody going to ask if I have a mouth?"

"Pardon? Oh, I see, forgive me. What would you like to drink?"

"Rye and ginger, please."

Tom jumped to it and ordered from the young bartender. He held things up fiddling for change from his pocket, and further when he couldn't find the nickel that dropped to the floor. Finally, he turned back to the patient woman in the cheerful, summery dress.

"Here you go. Good luck now!"

"Thanks, you too."

He nodded toward the open window and the pair of folding chairs that were available. The fresh air felt good. He shook a cigarette toward her from his pack of Chesterfields but she declined.

"I'm sorry, but I don't smoke."

"Probably better for you that you don't. I myself find them relaxing. Yours is a lovely name but I bet you take a bit of ribbing for it. Every Irish service girl is Bridget."

"Smart enough of you to remember it."

"Why wouldn't I?"

"He didn't—me or the name."

"Who. Johnny? Do you know him?"

"We were temporarily acquainted on the passage over from Ireland. I thought after eight days he would have remembered something."

"When was that?"

"It'll be five years this October."

"And you haven't seen him since?"

"He gave me the address of his accommodations, the Hotel Astor. I was to stop by for tea. When I did they never heard of him."

"Well, we're both at the same establishment now."

"Oh, I see. May I ask where?"

"Mrs. LaTrey's place."

"A *rooming* house?"

Tom quickly picked up on the disparagement.

"I used to stay with my old cousin at his grand apartment on Riverside Drive. He had been quite the man at one time: the proprietor of five saloons, chauffeured limousine. It was the time of my life when we would go down to Atlantic City. You never have seen such luxury."

"What happened?"

"He lost all his money gambling in the stock market. Ended up being the barman in one of the saloons he used to own. He passed away this June and I had to find my own place. Old Mrs. LaTrey isn't half bad."

They both sat silently and sipped at their drinks. When Tom was finished, he put a cigarette in his mouth and shook one out for Bridget.

"I still don't smoke."

"Oh, sorry, that's right. Would you like another rye and ginger?"

"I didn't mean to belittle your accommodations. I'm just living with my sister in a small little apartment on Tenth Avenue. You're not doing half bad considering the shock of your cousin dying and all that's happened. Only I was surprised to hear *him* living there. He was supposed to be the big shot actor. I guess the roles were too small for him."

"That's a lovely tune their playing now. Do you think there could be any chance of our getting the hang of a foxtrot?"

"They say everything's easy when you know how."

Encouraged by the expressive melody of *Down By the Salley Gardens* they traveled once around the dance floor, ending up at the exact spot they started off—always a good indicator of efficiency. On landing, Bridget had to adjust the toe of her stocking, giving Tom a chance to wipe his heavily-perspiring face while expressing his pleasure at their artistic display.

"Well, we made it back in one piece."

"Excuse us!"

Tom came out from behind his white handkerchief just in time to see Johnny grabbing hold of Bridget's arm and whisking her back onto the dance floor. Whizzing around the other dancers like they were wooden Indians suddenly made Tom's wigwagging dance steps the equivalent of a dog looking for the head of its bed. If that wasn't enough, the man could talk and dance at the same time!

"Why didn't you tell me you were the girl from the *Caledonia*?"

"If I have to tell you, it's not worth the mentioning."

"Come on now, that's not fair. How was I supposed to imagine that shy, young lass turning into a stunning Irish beauty? It was only when I saw you holding onto Tom's arm for dear life that I recognized the same startled expression you had when first seeing New York. So, let me have it, what have you been up to?"

She told him about being an au pair for a well-off Jewish family and taking care of their two little boys. It was her first job and she was very nervous but they were kind to her and the work of course was not too hard, considering her coming off the farm.

She also got to see how people with breeding did things correctly and with a sense of style. It was very good training and the boys were lovely—spoilt maybe, but still no problem at all.

"And after that?"

"Waitressing."

"At Schrafft's? Like the other girls?"

"That's right."

The band had finished their version of *Molly Malone* and without so much as lifting a chin from a fiddle they moved on from poor dying Molly to the romantic rhapsody of *The Galway Shawl*. Bridget was a bit unsure.

"I'm afraid I don't know how."

"Don't even think about it. Just follow my lead… three steps and turn… three steps and turn… that's it."

Since most of the regulars had cleared off the floor due to the formal nature of the dancing all eyes fell on the dashing dandy and the reluctant redhead taking command at center stage. Johnny was in his glory.

"Don't look down at your feet; they will take care of themselves. Keep your chin up and look over my shoulder; there, that's it. Oh, by the way, I'm very pleased that things have turned out so well for you."

"One, two three; one, two three… Now that you know all about me, what about your acting?"

"*Conversation Piece*."

"I thought it might be."

"No, no, the name of the last show I auditioned for. Big stuff, too, Noël Coward and all that. Had a good run in London before it landed here. I considered myself most appropriate for the role of a Regency Rake."

"I can see why… one, two, and three… what happened?"

"Well, after being looked up and down by the great bard

himself, they gave me one of his musical numbers as an audition."

"Ooh, which one?"

"*There's Always Something Fishy About the French.* A sentiment with which I quite agree, but alas, the musical director said I was out of tune. Can you imagine? A clear case of professional jealousy if there ever was one."

"When was that?"

"Last September."

"And nothing since?"

The music had stopped and the impressed female onlookers offered appreciative applause for the stylish dancers, them being the only ones on the floor. Johnny ceremoniously bowed and gave Bridget a little spin by way of an acknowledgment. Since the band was going on a break Johnny suggested a respite at the beverage bar.

"Have you had no auditions since last September?"

"Not in the legitimate theater. I've been trying my hand at a new venture."

* * *

Tom was back at the A&P during the week and only got to see Johnny rushing out of the house a couple of times early in the morning. He finally caught up to the man on Friday evening just as he was coming in the doorway. Mrs. LaTrey normally didn't make exceptions if you missed supper, but…

"Mr. McCabe, you are late and you know we have our rules."

"It's perfectly all right, missus. I've been so busy on the new job time just slips by. I'll just nip out to the beanery and procure a poached egg on toast."

"An egg? For your supper? Ridiculous! Although I encourage

moderation, I also applaud appropriate industriousness. Tonight's meat loaf can be served at room temperature and there are plenty of mashed potatoes that are still warm. If you seat yourself at the dining room table, I will prepare you a proper plate."

"You're just like a mother to me. What would I do without you?"

Tom walked behind as Johnny threw his arm around Momma LaTrey and wondered if he was always like this or did it take practice to be so shameless.

"If it's permissible, I'll keep the gentleman company while he eats."

"Certainly, Tom. I'll make a pot of tea so you help yourself."

Tom took the chair on the other side of the table and passed the butter dish so Johnny could start on the sliced bread. He spread the butter thickly on two slices and slapped them together for a sandwich. Tom waited until his mouth was full to remark:

"There's no Blarney Stone in Scotland, as far as I heard."

"Hmmm… no, not that I know of."

"But you do have the fair folks living amongst you?"

"Oh, you mean Billy Blind and the like. Yes, quite popular."

"I bet your mother showed them a kindness and was granted a wish."

"What the deuce are you talking about?"

"Your secret. Why anyone would believe half of what you tell them?"

"So that's what's on your mind. Well, I'll have you know the scintillating topic of conversation in my village for years revolved around how I was conceived during one of the biggest thunderstorms in memory... you get the picture?"

Mrs. LaTrey was standing frozen with a platter of meat loaf

in one hand and a giant bowl of mashed potatoes in the other. Tom jumped up to help her.

"Please, madam, allow me."

Once relieved of her plates she disappeared back into the kitchen.

"She probably thinks you're the devil now so she won't mind me sneaking a little meat loaf sandwich for myself."

"Ah, a man with a hearty appetite. Eat mightily, my good friend, you will need your energy. Fortune awaits us."

"I hope she recognizes me."

"You will be given a most well-deserved introduction. Last Saturday, at your superbly entertaining dance pavilion, you may have noticed my conversation with a particular gentleman who arrived late in the evening."

"The fella with the fancy chin whiskers."

"Yes, Nicholas is well known for his classic Van Dyke, very befitting for someone working for Jake the Barber."

"I could have taken him for the tsar of Russia. Are you going into the haircutting business?"

"In a way. Close shaves will be my specialty. He'll be back tomorrow night at the dance. I already briefed him of our acquaintanceship and he wants to give you a try."

"At what?"

"I don't know, but remember; it was a bold man that first ate an oyster."

"Sounds a bit fishy."

"It doesn't matter. After I get set up I'll bring you in. You said you wanted to learn some of my tricks. As luck would have it, we're being given the biggest stage in town."

* * *

Devil or not, the next night had Mrs. LaTrey waiting at the bottom of the stairs to catch his descent and he didn't disappoint. A tuxedo! She had never seen one on a real person, only in pictures in the magazines, it being ever so new and exciting. But as soon as he stepped down into the foyer, she told him to wait right there and returned with a small white rose which she gently put through his buttonhole.

"Why, Mrs. LaTrey! That's lovely. However did you manage?"

"I must confess, when I answered the door this afternoon and saw this big parcel being delivered for you, I had to ask the delivery boy what it was—you know, in case they made a mistake."

"Yes, of course, Quite sensible."

"Well, when I found out it was a *tuxedo* and that you were probably going to wear it tonight, I just thought a white rose would be the perfect accessory and ran around to the florist to pick one out. It does look dashing on you."

"My wonderful Mrs. LaTrey, I don't deserve you."

"No, you don't, and we'd better get a move on since you took up half the night getting yourself into that thing."

Tom and Bennett had heard about the tuxedo business from her nibs earlier in the evening and had decided to pay it no mind at all. He didn't need any encouragement being a glamor boy. Tom ran off to find a taxi cab, and when it arrived, they all waved to Mrs. LaTrey who had come out onto the brownstone steps. She was so proud of her gentlemen boarders.

With no flying philanderers to avoid, their ascent up the stairs to Roscommon House was uneventful. Finn McCool was especially impressed with Johnny's monkey suit and was very enthusiastic in his praise:

"That really makes the place look classy."

"Most appreciated. By the way, I understand you take an interest in those poor unfortunates who during these hard times don't have much going for them. The Sisters of Charity, I believe. If you could kindly make an anonymous donation on my behalf?"

Johnny palmed a roll of bills into the Giant's hand so no one could tell how much. McCool grabbed him by the arm before he could turn away.

"This means a lot to me. Thanks a million."

As they entered the dance hall Bennett offered to go first for the drinks because he saw a potential life insurance policy swaying at the bar. Tom and Johnny said they would wait by the open window hoping to get a breeze. While lighting a Chesterfield, Tom took a reappraising look at Johnny's evening suit.

"What's that black sash you have wrapped around your waist?"

"It's called a cummerbund. Originated by the British military in India, its purpose was to provide a cooler alternative to the waistcoat. As you may notice, it is very important for the pleats to be facing upwards and should cover both the shirt and the waistband of the trousers. Any other manner would be ungentlemanly."

"It's good for covering up a big belly."

"Judging by the protruding protuberances of the males in my family I would say that is an unequivocal eventuality."

"Speaking of a big bulge, that was quite a bundle of cabbage you handed the Giant back there. What's the idea?"

"Just what I said, a lot of people aren't as lucky as us."

"No, they aren't. Then I have to say you're a good fella to give a damn."

"All right, don't overdo the accolades. Bennett isn't the only one in the insurance game, you know. I did a few inquiries and found out McCool has a soft spot for the kiddos stuck in the shantytowns. So, a few dollars is a good investment. A big fellow like that could come in very handy some time. Might even be able to use him at the new joint."

"This new joint, that's why you're wearing the get-up?"

"Exactly. Nicholas will by stopping by and then we're off to a fancy party of big rollers. It will be a kind of test balloon for my blackjack racket. If it works smoothly there, we can move ahead with the casino they're planning up in Harlem. Tonight is a sort of dress rehearsal for me."

"Well, break a leg."

Johnny smiled at Tom's correct use of the expression for good luck. There was something inherently guileless about the man and, as an actor who had to continually struggle to connect with an audience, he felt a surge of jealousy for someone who could so easily engender endearment. To beguile must surely be an Irish privilege.

"The same for you, too. Nicholas will fill you in on that job tonight. When I see you at the rooming house tomorrow let me know what it is and we'll compare notes."

Bennett arrived with their two whiskey and sodas and his large ginger ale. He cheerfully clinked glasses. Tom could see the man was bursting to tell but too polite to boast so he winked at Johnny to get him on board then set the stage for Bennett to relish his triumph.

"Well now, how did you make out with that fellow at the bar? Any luck for the business?"

"Best of health, gentlemen. Ah, yes, the prospect standing at the bar. Yes indeed, you can rely on good ol' Bennett to close a deal. He was doing a touch of celebrating tonight; got a promotion at the collar and shirt factory—been moved up from the shrinking room. Feeling buoyant about life and his prospects for advancement."

"A good time to bring up dying."

Bennett looked sharply at Johnny's face to detect any facetiousness behind this comment. He was satisfied there was none and chalked it up to his naïveté with the business.

"Actually, McCabe you're onto a keen insight. When a man is on top of his game is the time to clearly think of the future. It's my job to open his eyes to the opportunity."

"Looks like his eyes are outside of his head right now the way he's dancing on rubber legs."

At Tom's comment Bennett quickly turned around to the dance floor and saw his newest client swaying a buxom brunette recklessly hither and thither. The other dancers were trying to stay out of the way and yelling for him to watch out.

"Oh dear, perhaps a bit too much celebration. There goes the Giant to usher him off the floor."

"Who's the beneficiary? Is the ink dry?"

Bennett's head swung fiercely back to the face of Johnny McCabe.

"What are you insinuating?"

"I used to be pretty good at changing letters around so no one could notice—making an 'F' into a 'B' and what have you. You know, schoolboy stuff when the bad marks got to be sent home."

"No, I don't know."

"Well, suppose our shrinking violet out there suddenly cracks his head open. You got to pay out right away but he hasn't had time to tell anyone that they are the beneficiary."

"You would change the beneficiary to your own name!"

"No, not me. I'm not the greedy sort. Maybe somebody like Mrs. LaTrey. Somebody always looking to do good."

"I see and I did *see* tonight how generous you were with our greeter. But such a course of action—however honorable in its intention—would be blatantly illegal. By the way, the situation you described, an accident, would in this particular case result in a payment of double the face amount of the policy. It is sometimes called a double indemnity clause."

Johnny seemed lost in thought, until: "It's a great script."

"How's that?"

"An insurance scam, but you need a fiery accomplice—a redhead—someone like that Schrafft's waitress standing over there."

"Bridget."

"Thanks, Tom. For some reason I can never remember her name. Yeah, that's it. Bridget charms some simpleton to cook up a scheme fraudulently collecting a double indemnity policy on a schlemiel she can't stand. Pretty good, eh?"

Bennett was clearly shocked by this scenario but at the same time fascinated.

"What you're proposing is utterly despicable."

"That's just why it would make such a great stage play, or better yet a movie. You know, the more I think about this—"

"Why are you staring at me?"

"*You*! You would make a great insurance inspector. The guy who figures out the scheme!"

"Well, I have the professional background to play such a part."

"You have acting ability also! Trust me, coming from the theater I know talent and you have what it takes to light up the big screen."

"Do you really think so? I always had a fancy to try the stage, but of course obligations being what they are, I chose the more conservative approach."

"Prudential in every aspect. We all make our sacrifices, but it's never too late, old man. Give it some thought."

"Oh, I do. Just the other day I was reading a few lines from *King Lear* to Mrs. LaTrey, and—"

"Excuse me; have you seen where Tom got off to?"

It didn't take them long to spot Tom and Bridget awkwardly shilly-shallying in a corner of the dance floor. Tom was enamored enough to try a waltz but he was stuck in the box step. She tried to get them moving forward.

"That's it, one, two, three; you've got the timing down. Let's see if you can step out on your right foot and I'll follow along. Go ahead, be bold!"

"One, two, three… how we doing?"

"We're progressing—off we go!"

Like a ship with a fresh breeze in its sails, Tom and Bridget were soon moving briskly along the line of dance. However, with keeping time and remembering to switch leads and keeping his arm straight and his head up, looking where he was going was too much. He wisely passed.

"You'll have to do the navigating."

"We'll stay along the perimeter to avoid collisions with the more experienced dancers."

When Bridget made mention of the better dancers, she had her eye on Johnny and his bubbly partner now taking over the dance floor. She was quite impressed. "He's quite the showman. I think he called that a weave step."

"Who's the lamb he's leading about?"

"She works with us at Schrafft's."

"What part of Ireland?"

"Not one bit Irish. She's from Dumfries."

"Scottish, the same as Johnny."

"Yes, I guess, but you'd hardly know it. He doesn't have any accent. Hard to understand her sometimes. She sure can dance though. Much better than me."

"Not in my book."

Tom was enjoying Bridget's little bow smile when he felt the tap on his shoulder.

"Changing partners, please."

Just like that Bridget was whisked out of his arms and the gal from Dumfries was spun over in her place. Tom came to a complete standstill and when he tried to start up again he was off time to the music.

"Sorry, you'll have to excuse me. I'm a beginner."

"Oooh, nothing to it! I'll back lead until you get the rhythm again."

And like a little tow truck she pulled him steadily along, but once his own motor kicked in she unhooked the hitch.

"There, you have it now, your lead. My name is Gavina, by the way."

"I'm Tom."

"Oooh, we all know that. Hold your arm out straight and I'll be under it."

Tom did as he was told and watched in amazement as she twirled underneath his arm and came right back to him on his next lead step.

"Weel dane! You didn't lead with the right foot until you gathered me back in."

"How does everyone know my name?"

"Nae everyone, but all the girls at Schrafft's do."

The music ended and Tom thanked Gavina for the pleasure of her company. He was flattered by her little curtsy and wink before she ran off to meet up with her workmates. Standing alone now on the dance floor he made his made way to the service bar where he expertly shouldered his way through the crush to emerge with two rye and gingers—an extra just in case. Turning to go back to the chairs by the open window he was met by an outreached hand taking hold of one of the glasses. It was Nicholas.

"Thanks very much. I admired the way you made it up to the barman so adroitly. Johnny McCabe tells me you're Irish—slàinte! After we finish our beverages, shall we go someplace affording a little more discretion?"

Knowing when a question isn't a question, Tom drank silently and then followed him past the Giant into a small office at the front of the hall. After Nicholas had accommodated himself behind the desk, Tom took the only other chair in the windowless room. Like a child playing patty-cake, he started to rhythmically clap at each pocket in search of his cigarettes only to remember he forgot to buy a pack while at the bar. Nicholas picked up on his absent-mindedness.

"Perhaps you would like to try one of mine."

As he opened his suit jacket to bring out his gold cigarette holder the sturdy shoulder holster was impossible to miss, but Tom wasn't letting on. He wasn't sure if it was a calculated display or not. Likewise, after accepting a light for the tar-colored cigarette, he withheld the urge to cough and was stone-faced as to the dreadfulness of the taste. He acted as if he smoked them by the carload. Nicholas rocked back on his chair confidently as he made clear just how important he was.

"I'm on very friendly terms with the manager of the establishment and he lets me use his office. Tell me, Tom, how long have you been in the country?"

"It was six years in April."

"And how are you doing?"

"Reasonably well. I'm the head dairy man at the A&P."

"Johnny says you're a sharp fellow."

" 'Twas kind of him."

"Oh, Johnny's a shrewd one all right. How would a little extra pocket money sound to you?"

"It would sound very pleasant, very pleasant indeed."

"Good. You see, there's this particular truck in Hunts Point. Do you know where that is?"

"Up in the Bronx?"

"That's right."

"Is it you want me to stand watch on the truck for protection?"

"Ha! Yeah, you're going to protect it all right—by moving it to a warehouse."

"I'm to drive it?"

"What else? Are you familiar with Myrtle Avenue?"

"That I wouldn't know."

"It's in Brooklyn. How good is your memory?"

"I could memorize my poems and prayers with no bother at all."

Nicholas took out a small piece of copy paper and handed it to Tom.

"Those are the addresses: the pickup place in the Bronx and the delivery point in Brooklyn. Commit them to your memory now."

Tom read the addresses twice silently, closed his eyes for a moment, and handed the paper back to Nicholas.

"Okay, what are they?"

"The Bronx is 540 Coster Street between Randall and Oak Street."

"Okay, and the other?"

"It's 394 Myrtle Avenue, between Vanderbilt and Clermont."

Nicholas propped the paper in the desk ashtray and used his matching lighter to set it on fire.

"You are never to repeat those addresses to anyone. Understand?"

"Absolutely."

"Here are your instructions: You are to arrive at the Bronx address tomorrow at exactly 10PM. The truck will be parked outside the building on the street. You are not to look into the back of the truck. You will be watched. The keys will be on the floor of the driver's cab. Got it so far?"

"Yes."

"You will drive the truck to the Brooklyn address. Since you don't know Brooklyn, take the Brooklyn Bridge. It's not too far once you get off."

"Right."

"No, stay straight on Myrtle—get it? When you arrive at the address, the main door to the warehouse will be raised and you are to drive straight in. You are to shut off the engine and leave the keys on the floor of the cab the way you found them. Talk to no one and leave the warehouse. Your job is done. With traffic not being heavy on a Sunday night it should take you no more than an hour. Any questions?"

Tom sat quietly, considering, and Nicholas offered him another filthy cigarette. He was impressed the Irishman had such good taste in tobacco. Finally:

"It's all very clear, no questions."

"Good. The job pays two hundred. You get a hundred now."

Nicholas arranged ten sawbucks into a neat pile on the desk.

"I like to pay out in smaller bills; draws less attention. Go ahead, they're yours."

Tom picked up the stack and folded it towards him for luck.

"And the rest, how will you deliver?"

"Ah, I like a man who speaks up for himself. I'll drop by here next Saturday. With the dance crowd it's less conspicuous, us meeting."

"Very well."

"You leave first. I'll stay back awhile."

Tom was fingering the one hundred dollars in his pants pocket when the Giant gave him a nod to step over his way.

"You're a nice fellow, so I'll tell you."

"Yes?"

"He's a good one to stay away from."

"Why would that be?"

But the Giant was finished saying any more and looked away. Tom could hear the office door opening again and he quickly moved into the dance hall where he saw Bennett talking to a young couple near the bandstand. They looked like they wouldn't mind the interruption.

"Pardon me. I was wondering if you saw Johnny?"

"Oh, Tom, let me introduce you to Danny Bellingham and his fiancée, Mary. We were just having a little chat about their future. McCabe is at the bar."

"Pleased to meet you and very best wishes on the upcoming marriage."

Tom ran over and grabbed Johnny by the shoulder.

"He wants me to drive a truck."

"What? That's great! *This* lovely lady is about to go to night school for bookkeeping. I was just telling her the road to learning is always under construction, and to be successful—"

"Very enterprising. Please excuse us."

Reapplying his hold on Johnny's shoulder, Tom steered him over to a quiet spot by the windows.

"I don't think you heard me."

"I say! Lifting cases of milk all day gives you quite a grip. I heard you, and that's great. Did he pay you any money?"

"One hundred samolians."

"Then you made a good impression. That puts us both in solid… but why the February Face?"

"I don't know how to drive."

"Not even a little bit?"

"Never sat behind the wheel. If it was a horse and cart now, I'd be in good shape."

"A horse and cart? This is the age of mechanization! When do you take off?"

"Tomorrow night."

"Hmmm… then we must act with haste. Tomorrow we'll meet at our midday repast and afterwards practice a few motoring runs. You will do magnificently. So tonight you must cast aside all cares and doubts and enjoy the pleasures offered… oops, there's Nicholas letting me know my curtain is about to go up. I bid you adieu, my rustic traveler."

Tom watched from the open window as Johnny and Nicholas got into a limousine and drove off. It didn't look that difficult. The chauffeur looked no smarter than him. The more he thought about it, he knew plenty of ignoramuses who were driving all sorts of lorries. One fellow hadn't drawn a sober breath in years and he had no trouble. An afternoon of moving back and forth should be plenty of practice. He was picturing his uncle in Ireland zipping along with his motorcycle and sidecar when a well-sculpted hand suddenly appeared, presenting a pack of Chesterfields. It was Bridget.

"The barman said you paid for them but got distracted and left them on the counter."

"Did you ever drive a horse and cart?"

"The cart having just the two wheels? No, my brother Dan would be the one to take that into town. We didn't have a wagon and would use the neighbor's, the nephew not letting anyone else be in charge but himself."

"Where was that?"

"Leitrim."

He finally took notice of the cigarettes being held out for him.

"How did you get them, now?"

"I think you can be a bit heedless."

"Oh right, I left them at the bar. Thank you very much. I did notice you have very lovely hands. You must have a special beauty treatment."

"Digging potatoes when I was young."

"In Leitrim?"

"Didn't need to go any further than that to find them. One of the few things that grew there."

"Not in Offaly. We could grow oats and barley, root and green vegetables, and of course the best pasture for grazing you could find anywhere."

"Sounds like full and plenty. I thought Offaly was just an old bog and not much else."

"What? That old bog gave us all the peat you could ever want, but the best part was the droves of wild asses roaming free. There was real fun going out to catch one. Once tame enough, I would take the ass out with the little cart, more times than not rather than the horse."

Bridget noticed the change on Tom's face.

"You didn't want to leave."

"Well, it was my brother who was supposed to come, but with his bad ear, I took his place and at the time was eager enough for the adventure, being young and foolish you see, but it's taking me a little longer to get established than I had figured when first starting out but that's the price of experience so they say."

"We'll be heading out soon."

"Who?"

"Me and my sister. That's her standing over there next to your Mr. Bennett. She's always very interested in business and he seems to be a wizard."

"Will you be here again next Saturday?"

"I hope to be. I enjoy the music."

"Well, Bridget, I'll look forward to seeing you."

"Bridie."

"Bridie it is. Will you have a cigarette before you leave?"

He opened his new pack and shook one out toward her.

"Heedless."

* * *

The Sunday mid-day meal was always the most memorable of the week, and Mrs. LaTrey kept to her impressive standards by delighting her rooming house guests with her famous fried chicken. Where she learned the tricky technique of crispy yet tender was a calculated mystery, encouraged by her hinting at a LaTrey pedigree dating back to sailing-ship days of New Orleans. The warm weather had her omit the traditional potato logs and instead a substantial salad comprised of fresh lettuce, carrots, purple cabbage, hard-boiled eggs, and quartered tomatoes was provided, all topped off with shredded cheddar cheese. The menu, loaded with enough salt to melt a block of ice, would bring welcome relief to anyone suffering nerve cell damage from the previous night's overindulgence. After saying a quick grace, Mrs. LaTrey was bursting with exciting news.

"I'm very pleased to welcome two new guests to our little family! Firstly, Miss Katharina Holten. Nina, as she likes to be called, is from Sweden."

"Norway."

"Pardon?"

"Trondheim. It's in Norway."

"Oh, I see. Well, anyway, you are very much welcome. Also, we want to extend a warm reception to Mr. Clyde Bowman who is recently arrived from Kansas City."

"Chicago."

"Why did I think Kansas City?"

"I don't know. Perhaps because they're both in the Midwest?"

"I'm sure you're quite right, but more importantly welcome to New York."

"Thank you."

After allowing the newcomers to be seated, Bennett smoothly introduced himself and explained how delighted he would be to give them any help needed in acclimating themselves to their new surroundings. Tom and Johnny, their mouths already full of chicken, mumbled greetings in a moist, cheerful manner, but that was it as far as courtesies. The objective, for Tom at least, was to get going with the driving practice as quickly as possible and if that meant only three pieces of fried chicken and just one piece of the peach shortcake that Mrs. LaTrey made for dessert, he would suffer. However, as much as Tom was full of anxious energy, Johnny was devoid of any initiative. The debilitating effects of being out the entire night were catching up to him. As his appetite petered out and his eyelids became heavier and heavier, he tried to convince Tom that a short nap really wouldn't take up that much time. But Tom wouldn't have it. Johnny's compromise was to bring along a flask for a stimulant.

On Johnny's advice, they changed into some rough work clothes and headed over to the West Side train yards. Being a Sunday, the tracks were full with idle freight and passenger cars, but it was the large truck facility next to the yards that Johnny was interested in. Looking up dejectedly at the imposing chain-link fence, he accommodated his weary head by resting his chin on the wire mesh.

"Are you a good climber, Tom?"

"There's barbed wire on the top, too."

"I see that. Therefore, I think we should enter like gentlemen."

Johnny conjured a set of thin metal gadgets from his back pocket and started to fit each one into the new Yale lock that secured the heavy chain around the gate. On the third try the lock sprang opened. Tom was impressed.

"Picklocks!"

"Very handy to have, and we'll lock it behind us to avoid detection. As you can observe, we have a very nice selection of motors to choose from. I suggest we start with that medium-sized lorry over there."

The door to the cab was unlocked, but after looking around on the floor there was no ignition key to be found. Johnny went to the front of the truck, unhooked the hood, and disappeared. It was only a minute later the engine started and Johnny reappeared to slam the hood back down. Tom was again impressed.

"How did you do that now?"

"A little trick with spinning a few wires together."

"Could you have used a picklock to start it up?"

Johnny took out his flask and threw his head straight back as he took a generous gulp. Wiping the mouth of the flask with his handkerchief he made an offer to Tom but was declined. He took out the ring of picklocks and handed it to Tom.

"Go ahead and try it on that truck there."

Johnny took another slug of the flask as he watched Tom

mount the cab. He soon heard the sound of the engine starting up and Tom yelling out the opened window.

"It works just fine."

* * *

They practiced for three hours, forward, backward, changing gears, using hand signals, tooting horns, turning on headlights, even parking in tight spaces. Johnny was right. Tom did magnificently. He would be ready for his 10PM appointment.

Once back at the rooming house Johnny went straight off to bed while Tom went in to check on Bennett sitting alone in the parlor reading *The Brooklyn Daily Eagle*.

"It's a shame, you sitting in here on a beautiful sunny afternoon. Did you not get out for a walk?"

"No, but I had a lovely time talking to our new house guest."

"She's not bad looking at that, but you better watch it. She'll be saying one thing in her language and you'll be thinking she said something else."

Bennett took the paper from his lap and folded it neatly before placing it on the reading table. It was his way of setting things straight.

"Miss Holten seems like a very charming young woman; however, I was speaking of Mr. Bowman, or Clyde, as he likes to be addressed."

"Oh, him, is it? And what puts a smile on his face?"

"He seemingly has many hobbies: shooting, canoeing, horseback riding."

"That's good if he likes the horses. Maybe he'll come to the track with us. Does he have a car?"

"Yes, as a matter of fact, I believe he does."

"That's handy, too."

Tom sat down on the chair across from Bennett and started to look at the race results from the day before. Bennett was annoyed.

"I see you have no interest in his line of work."

"I assume he has some sort of job or the madam wouldn't let him in the door."

Tom put the paper back on the table as a courtesy and waited for Bennett to refold it to his satisfaction before asking:

"Well, what does he do?"

"I don't know exactly. He seems to be self-employed and travels quite a bit."

"Sounds a bit mysterious that, but if he's his own boss then he can take off and do what he likes. Not a bad way to make a living."

* * *

Tom set his alarm clock for 7PM and took a nap. His plan was to take a bath and put on his best suit jacket and black trousers for his first job behind the wheel. He also would give himself plenty of time to get up to the Bronx since he wasn't exactly sure which trolley or elevated train went to Hunts Point. The last thing he wanted was to be late. He wasn't sure how long the truck would wait for him before they found another driver. It was just a little after eight when Bennett stuck his head into Tom's room.

"You look very well-presented. Going out for the evening?"

"I was able to pick up a bit of extra work. Shouldn't take me too long."

"Glad to hear it. Remember to pay yourself first and put a portion away for savings."

"What's the best way for saving today?"

"Well, I'm not actually impartial you know, but I feel a good life insurance policy which pays a reliable dividend provides exceptional value in these uncertain times."

"Could you open an account for me with one hundred dollars?"

"One hundred dollars! Of course, that would be an excellent start."

Bennett watched as Tom rummaged through his sock drawer and magically pulled out a roll of bills.

"Should be a hundred smackers right there. I'll give you another hundred next week. Set up a policy for me, will you?"

"Of course, I'd be delighted to. I must say, I am very pleased by the way you have prudently put money aside for a wise investment. Tomorrow we will formally fill out the required documents for your coverage. Who would you like to have as your beneficiary?"

"Can't tell you yet. I have to find out her last name."

* * *

Tom rode the elevated subway line up to 149th Street in the Bronx and then took the streetcar that ran along Southern Boulevard to Randall Avenue. He walked the rest of the way to Coster Street. The area was deserted except for a few scattered shanties, and although he couldn't see anyone because of the darkness he had the feeling of being watched. He was glad to be able to keep the gold pocket watch from his late cousin out of sight because the clock on the Morgan & Bros. warehouse told him the time: ten minutes to ten. He was in good shape. As he looked down Coster Street, he saw the number 540 and sure enough there was a black, canvas-covered truck sitting in front of it. Just enough time for a cigarette before climbing aboard.

"Any chance of a fellow getting a smoke?"

It took Tom a few seconds to make out the figure of the man standing in the shadow of the building. It was a hobo.

"Sure enough, I have plenty to spare. Help yourself."

Tom shook out a few cigarettes toward the stranger. He took three from the pack and asked for a light, putting Tom on alert. There's no way you live in a hobo camp and don't have a match. It was an attempt to see what else he had in his pocket. Tom carefully rooted for a book of matches and tossed it high in the air for him to catch. He was surprised to see the man had a third arm. It turned out to be a fellow traveler stepping out from behind him.

"Mighty generous of you. Maybe you wouldn't mind making me a gift of those shoes of yours. As you can observe, mine have seen better days."

He pointed to a shabby pair of work boots. As he lifted his foot to pull the right one off, the sole started flapping about like a fish yanked out of water. Tom had taken a few steps backward when he felt a tap on his shoulder. It was another tramp.

"And I think your fine jacket is just about my size, too."

Before Tom had a chance to answer, two more customers popped out from the darkness and something told him his pants were going to fit one of them for sure. He turned to make a dash for the truck when suddenly the one who was bent over taking off his boots went flying across the pavement. Someone had kicked him in the behind. The next one to hit the ground was the chap standing right next to Tom. Out cold on the ground. The other three quickly ran off down the street leaving Tom face-to-face with two escaped strongmen from the circus. They were clearly annoyed.

"Are you the driver?"

"For 540 Coster? Yes."

"Get going."

Tom ran to the cab and jumped in. He was about to start the ignition when he realized he hadn't found the key yet, forcing him to search the cab floor. Nothing—and no matches to see! He was still groping about when suddenly a beam from a flashlight showed that it was right next to the gas pedal. He never turned to see who was holding the light but just grabbed the key, started the engine, and put the truck into gear. It was only after he was at the end of the street that he was bold enough to look into the side view mirror. Nobody.

* * *

"Pull that truck to the side."

It was the first words Tom heard since he left the Bronx and he was none too pleased. He thought he was home safe. After leaving Coster Street he made his way across Southern Boulevard to the Third Avenue Bridge and down Second Avenue without a hitch. At Houston Street he crossed over to go down Bowery then across Worth and finally down Center Street. He had just turned onto the Brooklyn Bridge approach when a cop stepped out of his traffic booth and ordered him to pull over. He was already thumbing through his violations book looking for a fresh summons page when he walked up to Tom's window.

"I guess you didn't see the sign indicating no left-hand turns."

"Good evening, officer. I saw no notice of a sign."

"It was right in front of you."

Tom twisted his head out of the cab window. There was a small sign that looked like an upside- down arrow standing near the sidewalk.

"Missed it completely."

"Probably in too big a hurry. What have you got in the truck?"

"Oh, a bit of this and that."

For the first time the traffic cop looked in the cab at Tom.

"Where are you from?"

"Ireland."

"That much I figured. What part?"

"Offaly, right outside of Tullamore."

"Are you now? Well, you better not be telling me any lies. I'm from Westmeath myself and used to go into Tullamore all the time. It's not a bad little town. How long have you've been out?"

"Just over five years."

"And how long have you been driving?"

"It's my first time behind the wheel. Trying to pick up a little extra cash."

"Nothing wrong with that, but I bet you have no license."

"None at all."

"Then I'm going to tell you what to do. The first thing tomorrow you go down to the motor vehicle office and get an application. You'll be asked to take a written test on the rules and regulations. What school did you go to?"

"The Christian Brothers."

"Then with that good learning you'll have no trouble understanding the little rule book they give you to study from. After that comes the road test and before you know it the license will be in the mail."

"I appreciate the assistance."

"That's as may be, but don't let me catch you turning onto the bridge again without that license. Good luck and off you go."

The cop blew his whistle to stop traffic, letting Tom turn out onto the road safely. He felt like the eyes of the policeman were burning through the back of his head as he went up the ramp to the bridge, but looking out the side view mirror he could see all was clear. Once off the bridge he went straight ahead and had no trouble reading the street addresses. Before he knew it, he was at 394 Myrtle. As he was told, he turned to enter through the main warehouse door and proceeded a good piece before shutting off the engine. It was pitch black. He felt his way along the truck aiming for the dim street lamp coming through the open door. It was a great relief to be out on the street and he would celebrate with a cigarette, something he had put off so as not to distract himself when driving. Walking down Myrtle Avenue he intended to ask a passerby for a light when he remembered: he didn't leave the key in the truck!

He ran back to the warehouse and found the big doorway pulled down and locked. All he could think off was not getting his other hundred dollars and no more jobs after this. Walking back and forth in front of the building he had just decided to go back to LaTrey's and get a hold of Johnny when he felt the tap on his shoulder. It was an elderly gent using his cane for attention.

"They don't open 'till the morning."

"I got a bit of a problem. I was supposed to leave this key in the cab of the truck but forgot. Now it seems I'm locked out."

The stranger looked at Tom's unlit cigarette still sticking out of the corner of his mouth.

"Are you trying to cut down?"

"Don't have any matches."

He rummaged through the pockets of his cheerful, blue-plaid Mackinaw jacket and found a small box of matches.

"Keep them. You know, from what I'm told something funny goes on in there."

"Sounds like you're none too fond of the proprietors."

"I mind my business."

Tom noticed his wink and threw away the soggy cigarette from his mouth.

"But when a thing may be profitable?"

"How profitable?"

Tom's own pocket search resulted in two dollars and a nickel. The old man took the two single dollar bills and left the nickel.

"You may need it for car fare. Follow me."

He led Tom down the side alley and pointed up to a dirty window on the next floor—officially making him the second-story man. Tom carefully fitted his feet into the niches of the red bricks and climbed until he was eye-level with the window. Getting his thumbs underneath the sash was no problem and once he gave it a good shove it opened easily and he was able to pull himself up and in. When he looked out to say thanks all he saw was a shadow disappearing down the alley.

Tom turned into the office and walked straight into the desk. After rubbing his knee, he could see a light coming from underneath the door and slowly opened it a crack. The garage area was flooded with light but no one to be seen. This was his chance. Opening the door just enough to slip out, he tiptoed down the metal staircase which led to the garage floor. Once down, he used the coverage of a stack of barrels to assess the situation. So far, so good. He was close enough to sneak up to the truck. Luckily, he left the window down so he was able to gently toss the key onto the floor without having to risk the racket of opening the door. He was about to turn and slither back when he noticed the canvas covering to the back of the truck was up, making it very tempting to see what was in it.

Fortunately, he hadn't skipped school the day the priest told the story of Lot and the missus because just as he decided it was best to mind one's business a sudden noise coming from the other end of the warehouse forced him to peek under the truck—two heavy boots pushing a wooden dolly! Someone was coming back to unload. Crouching low, he made his way back to the safety of the barrels, but here he would have to wait. It was too risky to try to dash back up to the office. He might be seen, especially when there were more heavy boots on the way to help with the unloading. From all the laughter it seemed like a jolly enough place to work.

"Talk about the Midas touch! Imagine the amount of dough you could get for just one of these crates."

"Maybe they wouldn't mind me taking one for my old age."

"You'll never see old age if caught."

"If I was the driver, I would have taken the lot."

Peeking out from behind the barrels Tom saw the last load being rolled out of sight. This was his chance! Taking two steps at a time up the staircase, he was back in the office and looking down at the alley from the window ledge. It suddenly was much higher than before and there was nothing to grab hold of to climb back down. The only way was to jump for it. The thin-soled shoes didn't take much of the shock out of the landing and he was pitched forward onto his knees. Looking up at the window and seeing he was undetected, Tom tucked in his shirt and assumed a nonchalant gait, trying not to attract attention leaving the alley. He walked straight into the tail end of a gray horse.

"Say hello, he's friendly."

It was the milkman with his horse and wagon parked on the sidewalk. Tom rubbed his nose and gave the horse a pat on the head. Seeing a metal pail hanging from the wagon he took it down and approached the driver.

"Seems like he could use a drink."

"That's why we stopped, to catch our breath. There's a hydrant across the street. Here, give it a turn with this."

He threw Tom a small wrench which he grabbed in midstep on the way to the hydrant. Filling it to the top, he held the pail up high while the horse drank enthusiastically and then placed it on the curb for him to get at when he was ready again. The milkman had disappeared into the truck in the meantime and came out to ask Tom:

"Would you be partial to a drop of buttermilk?"

"I would, sure. It's my favorite."

Tom hopped up on the bench next to him and accepted the half pint bottle of buttermilk. He noticed he was drinking alone.

"Not going to join me?"

"Oh, I have something a little stronger."

He slipped a flask from his back pocket and took a healthy swig, wiping the spout with his sleeve. On the offer, Tom declined, but shook out a Chesterfield in appreciation of the consideration.

"Thanks very much, don't mind if I do. The name is Willy, Willy McNiff. Oh, and that's Dandy. He's been hauling me and this old wagon around for eleven years without missing a day. Sunday being his day off, naturally. And while he's not winning the Jockey Club Gold Cup any time soon, he's still pretty grand as far as I'm concerned."

Tom introduced himself and nostalgically told the saga of him selling a horse's tail to a traveling rag man and the resulting commotion when his father found out. Willy nodded politely.

"Well, anyone from Offaly loves horses, that's for certain. I know a lot of good gamblers from there. By the way, I hope you don't mind me asking…"

"What's that?"

"Was it worth it?"

"Coming to America?"

"No, jumping out of that window. I see the knees of your trousers are torn open. Must have been a fair height."

"I'm surprised you could see me."

"I didn't. I heard the landing and I know there's no business back there this time of night."

Tom remained on the driver's bench while Willy went down to get the bucket and adjust the bridle on Dandy. He was still considering how much to reveal when Willy got back on board and decided to keep it simple.

"It was worth it."

"Good, and I'll tip my hat to you for having the guts to go sneaking about. From what I've heard something funny goes on in there."

"It seems to be a regular comic strip. But it has nothing to do with me. I just forgot to leave a key to the truck that I was dropping off. I slipped in and threw it on the floor of the cab like I was told. Nothing more."

"What was in the truck you were delivering?"

In an instant, Tom was the kid who just had the blindfold removed and saw everyone in the game for the first time. He certainly *was* part of the funny business, whether he wanted to admit it or not. He started to get down from the driver's bench when Willy asked, "How far you going?"

"Manhattan."

"Stay on board. We're heading that way and Dandy likes company."

OCTOBER 1958

"Go outside and play."

Tommy had just finished his bacon and tomato sandwich on toast and was all set to watch *The Three Stooges* on afternoon TV when he heard the command from the kitchen. His mother wanted to tidy up the living room and didn't want him underfoot. Or something. Anyway, he had to go, so he placed his plate on top of an ashtray where it was sure to fall at the slightest vibration, and slid down onto the floor to find his blue and white sneakers. While down there he gave his motorcycle policeman a quick run under the lamp table and up to the arm of the sofa where he could look for any trouble in the wide valley below. All safe. He then placed him safely in the toy box and went into the kitchen to receive a kiss on the forehead and instructions.

"Be a good boy and be back in time for supper."

"Okay."

He stopped at the top of the courtyard to survey the extent of the engulfing chaos and was pleased to see no immediate threat. He was still deciding whether to dodge left or right once at the bottom of the steps when he suddenly heard someone singing.

"Higgledy-piggeldy my black hen,
She lays eggs for gentlemen.
Sometimes nine and sometimes ten,
Higgledy-piggeldy my black hen."

It was Deidre.

"Where are we going?"

"I don't know?"

"Why not ask your motorcycle policeman?"

"I can't bring him outside."

"Why?"

"They make fun of me."

"So?"

Deidre began singing about the black hen again and performed a little dance in the courtyard with both hands clasped behind her back. Finally, after she had completed a big circle, she stopped in front of Tommy and held out her hand. There was the red motorcycle! Tommy laughed and spun him around the stoop a few times, all the while chattering away. After he finished, Deidre came over and asked, "Which way?"

"He said to the right."

"Then we shall follow his advice."

Once around the corner the volume of noise became almost deafening— a stickball game! But it wasn't, it was a contest.

"Fifty dollars if you can do it!"

"And if I can't?"

"You pay me five."

Tommy made his way up to the corner by the fire alarm box and stuck his head between two teenage girls just in time to see the money placed in the hands of some guy dressed in navy whites. He was the trusted third party.

"What are they doing?"

The girls simultaneously looked down at the boy they didn't know was there. It was Eileen's little brother!

"It's a bet. The super from across the street has bet Billy O'Shay he can't hit the ball onto the roof."

"If he does, he'll be the Shay-Hey Kid! Come on up here and have a better look."

It was the fat guy from the back of Sweeney's that always gave Tommy a dime when he and Betty Ann visited their father bartending. He swept Tommy up onto his shoulders, leaving a skinny leg dangling on each side of his massive ears. Up there he even smelt more of beer.

"Which roof?"

"The big building down the block, at the end of Godwin Terrace."

Tommy looked down the rows of small kids, teenagers, young guys, and tradesmen just off work lining the hill from Naples Terrace almost all the way down to the big building. The word had gotten out about the challenge and interest was high. Looking further up, Tommy saw his mother's head sticking out from the kitchen window. Tommy waved and the vibration got the fat guy to look up also.

"Hello missus!"

She waved back and went to resting her elbows on the window pad to comfortably take in all the excitement and hear the encouragement from Billy's supporters.

"Limber up, Billy. You can do it!"

Tommy watched Billy take a few practice swings with the sawed-off mop handle. The sound of the swish was impressive. He also seemed to have a lively entourage: a semi-circle of older teenagers like himself standing right behind.

"Who are they?"

"They're on deck. After Billy wins his money they'll give it a try."

Billy put the mop handle behind his back at waist level and twisted this way and that. Next came a few toe-touches holding the mop out straight. He was ready to go. The super handed him a brand new Spaldeen.

"Good luck."

The crowd cheered as Billy strode up to the designated starting spot at the top of the hill. He tipped his NY baseball cap and bounced the ball a few times to get the feel of the return, the smell of the new rubber enhancing his confidence. Tommy took out his policeman so he could watch.

Billy gently tossed the ball an arm's length above his head and let it bounce once, having it precisely at chest level for his fierce swing. He made good contact and the crowd was impressed.

"Oooh!"

It was hit so high and so far, everyone strained to see where it went. The fat man started twisting this way and that, forcing Tommy to hold onto the little hair that remained on his head. Finally, it landed with a violent bounce in the garden of the big building at the end of Godwin Terrace. A tremendous shot indeed, but far from landing on top of the six-story building. The crowd was gracious.

"Good try, Billy."

"He lost his money."

The fat man was trying to gently untangle Tommy's fingers from hair, stiff with old-fashioned Brilliantine that he, but just about nobody else, continued to use. When freed, he explained to the boy, "He has two more chances."

The Spaldeen was retrieved and relayed up the hill and into

the hand of Billy O'Shay. Shouldering the stickball bat like a parade cadet, he marched with his back to the crowd, all the while squeezing the ball forcefully as if trying to release its full physical potential. Once done, he determinedly returned to the designated home plate. Another cheer arose from the crowd.

"Beers all around, Billy! We're counting on you!"

A toss in the air and a true bounce gave Billy a target he could muscle.

"That's it now!"

Unfortunately, the spectator's reaction was a rush to judgment, for although the ball was crushed it traveled in a low trajectory and only hit up against the building at the first-floor level, still a great distance down from the intimidating height of the roof. The exuberance of the ball being relayed up the hill was now more subdued, kind of like staying to see an exciting movie a second time. Nonetheless, on its arrival the ball was respectfully handed to Billy. But this time, as he walked silently alone trying to muster the resources needed to achieve this Herculean task, Tommy realized everything was wrong.

"He should do it the other way."

The fat man put Tommy down from his shoulders for a rest and to hear him better.

"He should stand the other way to hit the ball."

Tommy demonstrated swinging his imaginary stickball bat and making a whoosh sound when he hit the ball. The fat man was amused.

"That may be the way for you, but Billy's a lefty. He has to hit it from the other side. Okay, he's getting ready to try again. Up we go!"

It was soon after being replanted between the Brobdingnagian ears that he suddenly had company.

"Move over."

It was Deidre.

"Where?"

"Put both legs on one side of his head and I'll sit on the other shoulder."

Tommy recklessly swung his legs over the lacquered hair while Deidre sat gracefully and flattened her dress about her knees. She was keenly interested.

"What are they doing?"

"Trying to hit a ball up on that roof."

"What did the ball do that they want to get rid of it?"

"It's a bet."

Billy took a few practice swings when he arrived at home plate prompting Deidre to ask Tommy the meaning of such a ritual.

"His does things the other way."

"Oh, he's left-handed, like Kathleen's Billy."

"He had to be."

"Why?"

"After a baby is born and you see him grabbing things with his left hand you name him Billy."

"Who told you that?"

"Nobody, I made it up."

Meanwhile, Billy O'Shay was having his problems. On throwing the ball up in the air the bounce returned unevenly making him miss completely. The super was quick to state the rule:

"You're allowed two swings. Another miss and I win."

You had to hand it to Billy at this point. Almost anyone else would have been defeated by this disheartening descent, but somehow, he reached deep within, bringing forth a resurgence of purpose to hit his best shot yet. The crowd's roar of delight sent the super running to home plate to get a better look. He was worried.

"Remember, it has to *land* on the roof!"

Like a pink Sputnik still ascending, still sending back hope, the gallant Spaldeen climbed and climbed where no ball had gone before in order to complete its mission. And in this timeless moment, as all heads tipped further and further back to marvel at its flight, there stood Billy O'Shay pointing toward the roof with his mop handle. To Tommy, looking through the scattered hairs of the fat man's head, here was a legend in the making—no matter how fleeting.

"It won't make it."

It could have been exceptional eyesight or just wishful thinking, but the super was right. Within seconds of his prophecy, the sound of the ball thumping off a fourth-floor window of the big building produced a head-snapping response from the crowd, releasing more neck tension than a convention of chiropractors. No one moved as the ball bounced wildly around Godwin Terrace. It had let them down and was angrily abandoned to gravity's heartless web where its frolicking leaps were soon reduced to a listless roll, relentlessly being dragged to the sewer at the bottom of the hill.

The super was particularly giddy as the winnings were handed over by the summertime sailor, prompting him to deliver a warning to those who would dare take up the challenge.

"Not as easy as you thought, is it? Well, that's enough for today. Your champion has been defeated. I'll give you some time to go home and think about those fifty dollars. See you tomorrow."

The show was officially over. Tommy was again dethroned from the fat man's shoulders and given a pat on his head. He stood very still as the crowd passed silently this way and that, his head again presenting an agreeable landing point for an occasional friendly hand that wished to acknowledge the little boy but not bother with a conversation. Deidre, who had been practicing a new hornpipe step while waiting, looked over just in time to see Tommy dodge the slap of some pre-teenage ruffian, leading a pack of dimwits. Missing his target's head seemed to enrage the prowling menace.

"Jerk!"

"Jerry Lewis."

"What?"

"He's the biggest jerk around."

The cinematic reference slowed his aggressor down long enough for Tommy to follow up.

"But doesn't have root beer spilt all over his shirt!"

Like a wounded hyena, the hooligan was immediately set upon by his pals who made fun of his dirty tee-shirt and being squashed by a young squirt. They punched and pulled him toward the low stairs in a circle of mocking contempt. Tommy watched in satisfaction as he spun the wheels of his motorcycle policeman with his thumb. He was slightly startled when he realized someone was talking to him.

"I hate those guys."

Tommy recognized him as the boy who occasionally stuck his head out the window across the street from his own kitchen window. Being properly identified justified a response.

"Why?"

"They took my ball from me."

"Where?"

"In the alley."

"I don't know how to play those games."

"I could show you."

"But you don't have a ball."

"Do you?"

There was an old rubber ball in the toy box which was hard, discolored, and didn't bounce. Tommy thought it was best not to mention it.

"No."

"I know where to get one."

"Where?"

"Meet me tomorrow after school at the fire alarm box. Bye."

* * *

"Time to go to bed."

Tommy was comfortably situated on the living room floor enjoying the closing musical number of *The Gary Moore Show* when he heard the announcement. Contorting to a standing position, he made a surprisingly humble and unharried exit.

"Good night."

He gave his mother a kiss on the cheek and Betty Ann a hug. Eileen took his hand and walked with him into the bedroom where she made sure the covers were in place.

"See you tomorrow."

"See ya."

Eileen left the bedroom door slightly open, so the light from the living room would provide a reassuring beacon. Normally, it was Tommy's listening post, a place where he could hear what was really going on as opposed to the unimaginative blather he was constantly being fed. But not tonight. The boy was still excited from the day's activities and wanted to complete the adventure. This was the real reason behind his uncharacteristic acceptance of going to bed devoid of the usual convoluted confrontation whereby he would attempt to justify more late-night television as being critical to his cultural development. He would save that challenging face-off for another night.

"Here's your thingamabob."

It was Deidre.

"It's not a thingamablob. It's a stickball bat."

"Oh."

"And you didn't cut the mop part off."

"Is that important?"

"Of course."

Tommy took out a butcher's saw from his underwear drawer and made a nice smooth cut. He put the mop part on Betty Ann's pillow and pulled the covers up to make it look like a head was waiting for her when she went to bed. She'd find it funny. He then proudly presented his handiwork to Deidre.

"See, that's how it supposed to look."

"Excellent. Let's go!"

The crowds watching Billy O'Shay were puny compared to the throng awaiting Tommy as he left the building and headed for his place of honor at the top of the hill. And were they ever exuberant!

"Here's the lad now who can do it!"

"Hip, hip hooray! Tommy will show the way!"

Tommy had on his *Rebel Without a Cause* dungarees with the big turned-up cuffs and a red and blue striped polo shirt so all the people pressed tightly together could catch a glimpse of him—he was only five feet tall, after all. The photographer from *The Daily News* was kneeling in position for his first shot and Tommy obliged with a tip of his Bronx Zoo ball cap. There was genuine affection in the applause as he stepped up to home plate.

"We're all counting on you, son."

"We know you won't let us down."

His first practice swing was so powerful that it blew the hat off Dennis O'Leary and uplifted the ears of a dachshund being held in the arms of a cute girl with curly hair. The crowd immediately sensed that this was no ordinary stickball bat, but a powerful magic wand. Only someone truly special would have been chosen to use it. Thingamablob indeed!

The building's superintendent, however, was not impressed; just another quixotic Irish kid—and a puny one at that. There will be easy money to be made today.

"Well, I see we have a new *challenger*. A bit on the small side I give you but mighty energetic and we don't want to discourage the lad now, do we? In the spirit of good fun and sportsmanship, I will make this an open wager. I will *triple* the amount collected from the audience if he is able to hit a ball onto the roof of the building at the foot of Godwin Terrace. Do we have any takers?"

A large laundry basket was eagerly passed around both sides of the street and returned into the hands of Mike the Cop who plopped it down at home plate. He would stand watch as the money was counted by Edith Williams, the smartest girl in the fourth grade. Despite rude remarks from the repugnant boys in her class, little Edith kept to the task and whispered her final tally into the policeman's ear, and he immediately announced:

"Fifty thousand dollars—oh, and 25 cents."

The super gawked in astonishment at the bulging money basket. He didn't realize many people had waited all their lives for an investment opportunity like this, and, when they were told that young Tommy was about to undertake the challenge, immediately went to the savings bank and emptied their entire account. There was no way to save face by backing out now, so the super changed his tactic from compliment to reproach.

"Remember, little boy, you have to hit the ball all the way up to the roof of that building, way down the street. And let me remind you, your big shot hero couldn't do it..."

The crowd suddenly spotted Billy O'Shay standing with his

head bowed, defeated.

"...so, let's see you try."

That humiliation had to be erased and Tommy was up for it.

"Okay."

Another new Spaldeen was handed to Tommy by Mike Hosty, the man whose athletic reputation rested on having successfully lasted ten rounds with Jack Dempsey. The significance of the torch being passed to the next generation wasn't lost and the crowd became ecstatic as the boy symbolically bounced the ball ten times to signify the coming together of the two events. You could feel history-making in the air.

Before beginning his quest, Tommy of course took the time to wave to his mother watching comfortably from the kitchen window and also didn't miss the chance to shoot a mischievous wink toward his sisters sitting atop the front seat of Billy's brown and white Ford convertible. He especially appreciated all three sporting a stylish, mop-top hairdo for luck. His final acknowledgment was another tip of his cap to the television cameras, which was not only bringing the anticipated contest to a worldwide audience but, more importantly, to the exuberant crowd at Sweeney's, where his working father was proudly reminding everyone his son was right up there on the TV.

Tommy's intensive scientific analysis led him to the conclusion that hitting the ball from a bounce resulted in a loss of angular momentum equal to the square of the circumference of the ball. According to his calculations, this significantly hindered the projectile from gaining the most advantageous height and distance and was subsequently verified on a ground-breaking episode of *Mr. Wizard.* What he would cleverly do instead is gently lob the ball into the air and hit it on the fly, thus approximating the force of three fig newtons. To those who didn't understand the dynamics, Tommy explained it as a kind of skinny hurling stick.

The crowd became very quiet as Tommy took his position at the top of the hill and proudly placed his red motorcycle next to him on the street. Deidre, too, was in place, racing back and forth on the roof of the target building holding her sign: *Up Here!* She wanted to protect her twenty-five-cent investment, and—

"Why are you up?"

"I have to go to the bathroom."

"Well, don't dilly-dally. You have school tomorrow."

"Okay."

The next morning Eileen gently gave Tommy a nudge, letting him know that it was time to get up. Since there was an unexpected lull in the morning rush for the bathroom, Tommy was able to dash in and make a halfhearted attempt to brush his teeth. Any water that missed his mouth while rinsing was enough to claim he had washed his face. Once freshened, it was off to the kitchen to see what type of breakfast he could avoid. Front and center today was a bowl of cold cereal that his mother enjoyed but he found dreadful, only the addition of three spoonfuls of sugar making it somewhat palatable. The mandatory One-a-Day vitamin tablet was also on the table for his consumption. Tommy was never able to swallow the thing and would make believe he took it, instead sneaking it into his pocket and then offering it to one of his classmates as a piece of candy. He was never sure what he found most amazing: that they fell for the line in the first place, or that they could actually enjoy chewing the bitter pill. Maybe he was more convincing than he realized.

The school day was mostly uneventful with the sole entertainment being the afternoon fire drill. Their first-grade teacher, Mrs. McGowan, had never practiced the drill before and sent her class off in the wrong direction, down the hallway instead of up and out the main entrance. Now, the smallest boy who was at the head of the class line should have seen the whole school assembly charging toward them and, needless to say, turn the class around to go with the flow. Unfortunately, Nature bestowed this position on Michael Muldoon who, besides being a shrimp, was also was the devil himself when given the chance, and here it was, served up as neatly as a banana split from Woolworths. He wasn't going to let it pass.

"Look out!"

Muldoon forged ahead, creating a deep crevice in the phalanx of the oncoming seventh grade girls' class. The resulting mixture of screaming and laughter alerted the accompanying nun that something was amiss. However, she was too small to see over her charges.

"Stop right there! Turn around!"

Muldoon's particular brand of devilment seemingly infected the girls as well because, knowing clearly that they shouldn't, they turned and immersed themselves into the eighth-grade boys class following closely behind and only too willing to let them snuggle in. Brother Michael, who always wore a whistle attached to a leather cord, started blowing furiously and shouting madly at the boys who were on the fringes of the melee. Now fully satisfied, Muldoon adroitly redirected his class down the unoccupied part of the corridor and out onto the street where the whistling and shouting within could be clearly heard. With the principal and all the other teachers staring, Mrs. McGowan came marching toward the boy for an explanation of the ensuing chaos, but was met in mid-step by Muldoon's screeching, unassailable defense.

"It was *you* who told us which way to go!"

Since there was no way to get back into the building past the commotion, the class was dismissed for the day. On his way home Tommy was thinking of Twinkies as an excellent candidate for an afternoon treat when he saw some sort of black object flopping around in the corner of the low stairs. This of course required immediate investigation, but he was not alone in his curiosity.

"Must have fell out of his nest."

He was a tall, lanky teenager. Although the street was busy during this time of day, his superior height and age dictated caution in determining his intentions.

"What is it?"

Stooping down, the teenager brought his cupped hands over for Tommy to examine.

"A pigeon!"

"That's right, even at this age they look like the adults."

"What will you do with him?"

"I'll keep him until he can fly. He may even want to stay with us."

"In your house?"

The teenager laughed and walked with Tommy through the alley holding the bird gently in his hands. When they got to Naples Terrace he nodded toward the roof of the building on the corner.

"Not in the apartment, dopey. Up there. I have a coop."

"We have a canary named Charlie."

"You like birds?"

"Uh-huh."

"Come on, follow me."

But Tommy turned to look up to his kitchen window.

"I have to go."

The teenager noticed the boy's mother waving.

"That's okay. Next time I see you I'll show you the coop.

What's your name?"

"Tommy."

"I'm Elgin. See ya!"

Once inside the apartment, Tommy started to remove his school clothes as he walked: black, ripple-soled shoes kicked off in the vestibule, jacket flung across the arm of the big chair, school tie hung on a door knob. His mother trailed after to gather up the rejected jetsam as well as any relevant information about school. It was harder for him to tell lies when he was occupied with something else.

"You're home early."

"Uh-huh."

"I would have walked up to meet you. Did they have a teacher's meeting?"

"Who?"

"The teachers. You got let out ahead of time."

"Oh, there was a fire drill."

"And everything went all right?"

"Uh-huh."

"What's the name of that older boy?"

"Who?"

"The one I saw you talking with right now. That teenager."

"Elgin."

"Hang up your pants and that shirt. It has to do another day yet."

"Okay."

Tommy's mother had a strict system for his two white school shirts. The first one did Monday, Tuesday and Wednesday and the second Thursday and Friday. They got washed and ironed on the weekend. The boy complied and neatly arranged the two items on a wobbly wire hanger, wooden ones being extremely rare and protected.

When he was completely disrobed, he reversed the process, starting with a striped tee-shirt, blue dungarees, gray socks, blue-and-white sneakers and a beat-up zipped jacket that his mother didn't mind him getting dirty. When he was finished, he grabbed his red motorcycle policeman and waited on the sofa. Soon enough, a glass of milk appeared and was put on the lamp table next to him. But as to what was on the plate behind his mother's back, he would have to guess.

"Twinkies?"

"Pretty close. They had a box on sale today."

"A Devil Dog!"

"That will hold you until supper."

He quickly finished his snack and got to telling the policeman all about the hilarious fire drill fiasco and how Muldoon got away with acting the eejit again. The policeman, although sympathetic to harmless horseplay, stressed the importance of taking fire drills seriously. Tommy wasn't completely convinced but nodded in agreement to humor him. What he did agree with was taking the motorcycle on a spin through the big valley of the living room floor. He was just approaching the huge steamer trunk in the corner of the room when he noticed a pair of shiny saddle shoes blocking his way. It was Deidre.

"I thought we could practice some dancing."

"I'm going out to find a ball with the boy across the street who sticks his head out the window."

"Where?"

"I don't know."

"Then I better come along to make sure you don't get lost."

Putting the policeman into his jacket pocket, Tommy went into the kitchen to receive a kiss on the forehead and instructions:

"Be a good boy and be back in time for supper."

"Okay."

Once outside, there was no sign of the neighborhood boy so he cautiously approached the fire alarm box and waited. He was only there a few minutes when his mother leaned out from the kitchen window and waved. Waving back, he knew there would be another check on his whereabouts shortly thereafter and certainly didn't want to still be standing there. That would require answers as to what he was up to. He had just turned towards the alley looking for a possible arrival when he felt his head being rubbed. It was Eileen coming back from school with her girlfriends.

"Why are you standing here?"

"I'm waiting."

"For who?"

"A boy."

"Oh, that's nice. Which one?"

"Him."

Tommy pointed to a boy running across the street. Arriving out of breath, he politely lifted his ball cap as a greeting, causing the girlfriends to giggle at the boy's old-fashionedness. Eileen stared at the wire hanger the boy was holding and wanted a little more information out of Tommy.

"Aren't you going to introduce us to your friend?"

"I don't know his name."

"Hi, I'm Mark Levine!"

"Hello, Mark, this is my brother Tommy. Don't I know you?"

"He's the boy across the street who's always sticking his head out the window."

It was Eileen's friend Cyrilla, who knew everything. Mark was delighted for the acknowledgment.

"That's me! Tommy, we gotta hurry before it floats away.

Good-bye everyone."

He took off down Naples Terrace in a sort of hop and run. As Tommy turned to go, Eileen rubbed his head and told him to be careful. He gave her a hug.

"See ya."

OCTOBER 1935

"He seems to have brought you a wee minding, Bridie."

There were no flies on Gavina as far as boyfriends and presents were concerned, but since neither one was officially confirmed yet, Bridie remained uncommitted as to a response. She did respond to Tom's waving by directing him to the Schrafft's cloak room. They weren't open for lunch until eleven so they wouldn't be disturbed there. As she opened the half-door to enter, she couldn't help but notice his pants. A more shabby looking pair she had never seen.

"Good morning, Tom. Now what brings you here so early in the day?"

"Morning, Bridie. Looking lovely as ever. I hope you don't mind but I figured I could catch you before business started. You see it's like this: I got a touch of mending to do, but the thing is I'm no good at it."

He pawed nervously at the package wrapped in brown butcher paper, but waited for Bridie to give her nod before opening and explaining.

"The knees got a bit of a rip in them."

She laid the pants out on the counter and put her hand through the hole in each knee.

"More of a cow's mouth than a rip. Let me guess, the ground came up and hit you?"

"Something like that. I need them for work this afternoon as they're the only decent dark pair I have."

"I'll have to put a patch of dark material on the inside before I sew them. There's not enough fabric to hold the stitches together. Wait here."

Gavina was right on Bridie as she walked swiftly to the ladies' locker room.

"Candy?"

"Trousers."

"Oooh, how stylish! How did he ever know your size?"

By now Bridie had found the sewing box in her locker and was on her way back to the cloak room.

"*His* trousers. He's gone and put holes in both knees. Dear girl, do me a favor and make sure my tables are all tidy-looking for lunchtime in case the manager checks. It shouldn't take me more than twenty minutes."

Gavina smiled and nodded. Cutting through the kitchen on her way to the dining room she gaily commented on Tom's torn knees to one of the cooks winking at her.

"Mibbie he was practicing proposing."

"Come here, babe. I don't need any practice."

Gavina was giggling and ducking his pursuit when she ran straight into Bridie's sister.

"Have you seen Bridget?"

"Nae, I haven't."

The sister made a quick assessment of Gavina's face and thanked her before heading toward the ladies' lockers. The cook, chopping a head of cabbage, laughed when she left the room.

"Gavina Lochhead, you no good at telling lies!"

"I didna want her to know Tom was here. She thinks him a corner boy."

"Well, then, you better go off and warn her."

She blew a kiss off her palm and took the long way 'round through the dining room. When she opened the door of the cloak room, Tom was perched high up on the counter reading *The Racing Form*. Gavina was impressed.

"My Granaidh had a pair just like them."

Bridie, sitting down low on the attendant's stool, looked up from her sewing just long enough to cause the both of them to break into a fit of laughter. With a naïveté that was to become legendary, Tom stuck his head around the paper and asked, "What's all the laughter about?"

"That's what *I'd* like to know!"

It was Bridie's sister.

Gavina, caught in the lie, quickly excused herself. It was left for Bridie to explain as she spun the thimble on her thumb.

"We were having a bit of fun about Tom's sock suspenders."

Tom, finally catching on, raised one leg slightly higher to showcase the plaid garters.

"They belonged to my late cousin."

The sister never acknowledged Tom but instead focused her stare on Bridie.

"With half the country out of work and you getting paid good wages, I'm glad you're able to have such great fun on company time. I'll make it my business to look after your tables."

When she left, Bridie waved Tom off from talking and quickly got back to her sewing. It was only a few minutes more when she re-wrapped the pants in the brown butcher paper.

"I did the best I could. The patches shouldn't be too noticeable unless you're looking for them."

"I got you into trouble."

"It'll be all right."

"Let me make it up to you. I know just the thing! A double feature. How about tomorrow night? I'll come by for you after work."

"That would be lovely."

She meant it, but there was something else on her mind. A doubt, brought on by her sister's sharp appraisal of how uncertain things were and how protective of each other they needed to be in this new and unpredictable country. As she considered, Tom went on rubbing his head until he finally remembered something.

"Oh, that's it. What would your last name be?"

"Kiernan."

"With a K?"

"Yes."

Tom gave her a small peck on the cheek and was about to leave when Bridie grabbed his arm.

"How *did* you tear those pants?"

And he told her. He didn't know why, but there was something about her way of asking, and when he was finished, he was glad, and she knew he told the truth.

She would record his face at that time as the standard. A time when he didn't try to get away with things. And, as the first layer of the onion came floating off, she was surprised at the same shared insecurities, but instead of being frightened, it gave her a new confidence.

"You're not able for the likes of Johnny McCabe."

"And why not?"

"Because he's made a bargain I hope you never make. Now, you better be off and get to work on time. Or maybe you didn't hear how scarce jobs are?"

Tom smiled and gave Bridie a hug.

"I heard."

"But I didna hear. Could you tell me?"

It was Gavina sticking her head back into the cloak room. Tom's wink as he rushed to leave only made her more convinced that she had to know and got right to asking Bridget.

"Did you say yes?"

"I did—to the moving pictures!"

* * *

And off they went, Tom, Bridie and the sister. And on Saturday they all met again at Roscommon House. Tom understood that she was part of the package for now and it was Bridie's way of standing her ground. And the old girl—one year his senior—wasn't so bad when she was off duty and had a whiskey and soda in her hand. She had that same Leitrim fierceness, of course, but it was tempered with a charming wonder of all the new things the country had to offer and an admiration of the learning that was needed to understanding such things. This respect for education led young Betty Kiernan to register for night school right away when she landed, at the age of sixteen. She was no doubt the family trailblazer and Tom knew early on he would never be up to the standard she had set for herself, so he didn't try. Instead, he enjoyed the differences between the two sisters and was glad that they had each other. A bittersweet reminder of something he had once with his own brother in Ireland. He would not be the cause of any separation, and the sister in turn responded by cautiously including him in a new circle of family. She was even starting to act as lookout.

"Tom, that fellow over there is trying to get your attention."

It was Nicholas. As soon as Tom recognized who it was he

quickly excused himself from the sisters and followed on out of the room. Betty was impressed.

"*He's* not one of your regular dance hall lads. Looks quite distinguished. What's Tom's business with him?"

"I don't know."

Betty knew that frozen-face look of her sister meant she had dug her heels into something and getting it out of her was never easy. The two whiskey and sodas under her belt eased her into the more agreeable approach.

"Have you met him before?"

"No."

"He seems to have an interest in Tom, taking him off like that to talk."

"I guess."

"Well, why so down in the mouth about it?"

"Yes, heavy is the head that wears a frown. I believe this is a waltz, Bridget. Shall we lift our spirits together?"

It was Johnny McCabe popping into the conversation and looking quite excellent in his light gray wool and silk suit. But Bridget left his hand dangling in mid-air and made her intentions quite clear.

"Not tonight, Johnny. Perhaps my sister, Betty?"

With a deep bow Johnny took Betty's arm and gracefully led her out to the dance floor. They were only gone a few minutes when Tom reappeared.

"Well, look at them. She's a fine stepper, your sister."

No answer. Tom could feel the coolness and shook out a cigarette. He was just about to offer one to Bridie when he caught himself. She didn't seem to be in the mood for jokes. After taking a few puffs and commenting on the size of the crowd and how the weather was finally beginning to be more seasonable he realized small talk was not going to cut it.

"What's the matter?"

"You know very well what's the matter."

"Me leaving? I had to. That's the feller who gave me the delivery job."

"I figured as much. I guess he thinks he's Santa with the false whiskers."

"Oh no, the whiskers are real enough. He takes great pride in them."

"Something that you could try having about yourself."

"He owed me money which I needed to collect. Here, if you don't believe me, look."

Tom twisted away from the crowd and showed the top of the cash roll he had in his pants pocket. Bridie's blue eyes shone brightly in the dimmed lights of the dance hall.

"He paid you all that?"

"One hundred dollars."

"For just driving the truck?"

"That was the second payment. He had given me another hundred before that last week."

"Two hundred dollars! What are you going to do with all that money?"

"I can't tell you."

That was it. She resumed her frozen state and he was not going to get another word out of her. He was more of a schemer than she realized and wouldn't be worth the watching. As she turned toward the direction of the bar, Tom grabbed her arm.

"Why so glum? I would have thought you'd be happy since I told the man I'm not interested in any more jobs. Quite disappointed he was, too."

"A likely story."

He knew better than to try to hold her but luckily there was no need since he was rescued by the exuberant arrival of Gavina, forcing Bridie to delay her exit long enough to not make a scene. And that was long enough, for at that moment everyone's attention was directed to the commotion on the dance floor. Clyde Bowman, the newcomer from the rooming house, had just delivered a wallop to the jaw of Johnny McCabe, forcing his dancing partner to keep him upright. Gavina was fascinated.

"They be quite strict about cutting in at this dance hall."

"I don't think that's it, Gavina."

Bridie raced out to help her sister, who was being relieved of her burden by Clyde. He now had Johnny face down on the floor. She was shocked at what came next.

"Handcuffs?"

"Yes, miss. I'm sorry, but necessary."

Clyde helped his captive up onto his feet. Facing Betty and Bridget, Johnny was not to let unfortunate circumstances diminish a gallant farewell.

"Well, it seems I must retire early for the evening. As always, ladies, it has been a pleasure to see you again. Adieu."

And off he went. The band immediately went into a lively version of *Finnegan's Wake*, knowing from experience that no matter how big the row and the ruction things will be quickly forgotten when you have a song about rising from the dead. Tom, however, was not satisfied and went running out to see the Giant. He had stayed on his stool the whole time and never got involved. That meant he knew something.

"Hello, Tom. How's your evening going?"

"That was Johnny McCabe that just got hauled out of here."

" 'Twas."

"Do you know why?"

"I do."

"Would you mind telling me?"

"It's like this, Tom. That other fellow had a badge and a piece of paper that had Johnny's full Christian name on it. It also had the seal of the Immigration and Naturalization Service giving that other fellow the right to haul Johnny out of here."

"Immigration? That means he did something back home and they're looking for him."

"I would say so. And it's a shame. He was a very generous chap, but there was nothing I could do about it."

Tom took a look down the hall at the office and the Giant picked up on it.

"That one. He took off too. As soon as Johnny was out the door."

"I took your advice. No more jobs for me."

"Glad to hear it. You're not able for the likes of him."

"That list is growing longer all the time. I wish someone would tell me who I *am* able for!"

The Giant laughed and slapped Tom on the back, sending him halfway back to the dance hall. Looking out he saw Bennett wheeling Bridie around the floor, quite elegantly. He needed a bit of time to think things out and, since Bridie was mad at him anyhow, he decided to call it a night.

Bennett made one complete turn of the dance floor before he got down to business—after all, it was Saturday night.

"Well they rolled him up in a nice clean sheet
And laid him out upon the bed
With a bottle of whiskey at his feet
And a barrel of porter at his head."

"I believe your full name is Bridget Kiernan."

"Yes, that's correct."

"Well, I have some papers for you to sign."

"What kind of papers?"

"You are to be the beneficiary of a very valuable life insurance policy."

"Biddy says she, you're wrong for sure."

"Who would make me a beneficiary?"

"Tom Marshall."

Bridget fell out of step to the music and apologized before catching up again. Once in rhythm, she asked:

"*When* did he take out this policy?"

"A week ago tomorrow."

"A week ago?"

"That's correct."

"Then it was before he ripped his trousers."

"What?"

"And before he brought them in to me to fix—and *before* we talked."

Bennett, always a bit doubtful of the intellectual capacity of pretty women, chalked up these irrelevant comments to senseless whimsy. They would never make it in the insurance game. Nevertheless, he pushed on.

"Of course, I can't reveal the amount required to secure such a valuable investment."

Bridget smiled as she extended Bennett's arm so she could twirl underneath.

"It was two hundred dollars!"

Bennett was impressed. Maybe the red-haired ones were different.

"Wasn't it the truth I told you?
Lots of fun at Finnegan's wake!"

TUESDAY 6:30PM

"Those were very tender. Where did you get chops like that now?"

"Same place as always, the Grand Union."

"Early in the year for them. The lambs aren't even born yet."

"They're from New Zealand. They have a different season from us."

Old Tom pulled the widow curtain aside to have a look out at the weather. When satisfied, he let go and watched as the curtain slid silently back into its usual position. It reminded him of a horse that knew the way home.

"Dandy."

"I enjoyed them myself."

"Willy McNiff's old horse."

"The one pulling the milk wagon?"

"The very same. Many a time poor old Willy fell asleep on the bench and Dandy would bring him back to the barn."

"He was one of the last to have the horse and wagon. The war put an end to all that."

"But not before he paid to have the horse sent up to a farm

in Saratoga. His ol' pensioner, he called him."

"Imagine that. And him never having the price of new soles for the shoes."

"I saw him take them off once. He must have had the whole Sunday edition in there to keep out the sidewalk. That didn't matter; the horse meant everything to him. Never got to collect the pension himself. He was gone before it."

Bridie got up to put the fire under the small white kettle. He was staring straight ahead and she wasn't sure if he would want it now or later.

"Will you have tea before you go?"

"Go where?"

"Down to the church. Wasn't that why you were looking out the window?"

"No need. The snow's turned to rain. We have all night to have our tea."

OCTOBER 1958

"I can't reach."

Tommy waited for Mark to lift his head from the grating of the storm drain to grab hold of the wire hanger. The last thing they wanted was for it to fall into the sewer. Then they would have no chance.

"I see it."

"But I can't scoop it!"

Tommy examined the hanger. The triangular structure had been disassembled and the wire had been straightened to its full length with the hook being reshaped into a circular hoop so the ball could be snagged. Since the hanger could clearly not be made any longer they would have to come up with some way to stretch the attached arm. Tommy, still suspicious of neighborhood friendships, wanted to introduce his suggestion in a roundabout, non-threatening way. It was, after all, Mark's hanger.

"Monkeys have long arms."

"You've seen real ones?"

"Eileen and Cyrilla took me on the bus to the zoo."

"Our class was supposed to go, but the teacher got sick."

"My arm is longer."

"Than a monkey's?"

"Than yours."

Mark got shoulder-to-shoulder with Tommy and they both stretched out their arms. It was true!

"Don't stick your head in all the way or it will get stuck."

Mark waited for Tommy to lie out flat against the storm drain before handing him the hanger. The first thing he noticed was how bad the sewer smells and how much other junk was floating around! But he was focused and used a partially submerged hunk of newspaper to prod the ball closer to him. In no time the ball was within easy reach and it floated softly into his wire hoop. Now the trick was hoisting it up slowly and… whoops!

"Garbage truck."

The driver had seen the two boys lying in the street and gave a warning blow of his horn as he passed. The reverberated sound in the sewer made Tommy jump and he dropped the ball. Mark however was encouraging.

"Try again."

But the ball now seemed to understand the game and although you would think it would be keen to escape this ignominious dungeon, it teased itself onto Tommy's hanger several times, only to slip off just as Tommy reached for it. It would require teamwork.

"I'll scoop, you grab."

Mark understood and laid out flat on his stomach right next to Tommy. The ball once again floated easily onto the loop but this time Tommy slowly lifted the hanger hand over hand and, when it got to the sewer opening, held steady as Mark skillfully snatched the sphere before it had a chance to slide off.

"We did it!"

* * *

"What's that you have?"

"A ball."

"And where did you get it?"

"Mark and I found it."

"Who's Mark?"

"The boy who sticks his head out across the street."

"Is that his name? I'm always afraid he'll fall out like one of the Joyces' kids. Well, wash your hands before you have your supper. Never know where that thing's been."

For once, Tommy showed great enthusiasm for his mother's hygiene requirements and ran off to the bathroom. While examining the black circle the ball had obtained from floating in the sewer certain perplexing mysteries presented themselves. Why was it exactly half of the ball? How does the ball know how far down in the water it should float? What else floats like that? These were questions that he would have to explore someday, but for now, the concern was how much of the dirt would come off after a more-than-appropriate application of Bon Ami cleanser and a powerful blast of hot water from the tap in the tub? Much cleaner, but its recent digs could not be completely whitewashed. It would always be recognized as a sewer ball.

Nevertheless, Tommy was happy to have a ball in his pants pocket that he could take out and bounce any time he liked. Once out of the bathroom his father, who had just arrived home, noticed the bulge right away.

"What's that you have? A big bankroll in your pocket?"

"No, a ball."

"Let's see that now."

Tommy tossed the ball to his father who bounced the ball

back to the boy to see if he could catch it on one rebound. It was great fun with Tommy laughing and egging the father on to make it go higher and higher. The ball had just taken a wayward bounce and knocked the picture of Bridie's mother off the wall when she walked into the living room with Tommy's supper.

"I don't know which of you is the worst. Put that away before you have the food knocked onto the floor."

The father made a better-do-as-she-says face at the boy and snuck off to the kitchen. As directed by his mother's nod, Tommy took a seat on the sofa.

"I can eat out here?"

"Yes, Betty Ann gets home early tonight. We'll put the television on when you finish. But first, show me those hands."

Tommy stuck out his hands as if he was blessing the five loaves and two fishes.

"You did a great job. Never seen them so clean. Enjoy that now. The mashed potatoes have plenty of salt and butter."

It wasn't long after his mother disappeared back into the kitchen when Tommy had company.

"You didn't really wash your hands. It was just from trying to get the ball clean."

"It made it fun."

"What are you eating?"

"Meat loaf. Would you like some?"

"Yes, please."

Tommy snuck into the kitchen and took a saucer from the dish rack. No one saw him. When he returned to the living room he put a small portion of meatloaf and mashed potatoes on the saucer and placed it on the serving tray for Deidre.

"Thank you, that looks lovely. Well, we certainly had a busy day."

"You were with me?"

"Of course! Who do you think gave you the idea of the monkey's arm?"

"Oh."

"Besides, I always find traveling exciting."

Tommy thought about it and it was true. He did travel. Today he left Naples Terrace on his own and went two whole blocks away from home. The tiny circle of experience that started from his courtyard steps had been expanded.

"I wonder how big I can make it."

"As big as you can imagine."

Tommy laughed and took out his motorcycle policeman to share the good news. The two of them would ride together through the wide valley of the living room floor.

* * *

When you have a ball, the place to be is the alley. Mark had told Tommy to meet there after school the next day and he would teach him one of the games. But Tommy had to get through the afternoon classes at St John's first. He was busy daydreaming and fingering the ball in his pants pocket when Mrs. McGowan asked the class to identify the letter she would write on the blackboard. She had just finished a very calligraphic W when Muldoon shouted out:

"Dub blu."

"That's correct, Michael. Very good."

Muldoon immediately stood up and chastised the Cleary kid sitting behind him.

"See, I'm no dope."

"Michael! That will be enough of that. Thomas, can you tell us a word that begins with W?"

"What?"

"Excellent! A very important word when some—"

The bell! The class jumped up and Mrs. McGowan led them in a Hail Mary. By the time they had reached *the hour of our death*, Tommy was heading out the door. He was considering staying in his school clothes to play, but when Mark wasn't in the alley yet he decided to go home and change. And he was glad he did.

"Twinkies!"

"What was said at school today?"

"How did you know?"

"How did I know what?"

"That I said it as soon as she asked me. Can I have more milk?"

Since his mouth was full with half a Twinkie his mother knew that she wasn't going to get any more of an answer. He was becoming heedless like the father. She was just at the ice box when she heard the front door opening. It was Eileen.

"You're home early. Do you want milk or tea?"

"Tea, thanks."

Eileen went into the living room and rubbed Tommy's head.

"Whatcha got?"

Tommy showed her the empty Twinkies package.

"Oh good, let me get one too."

She took off for the kitchen. Tommy was still tying the laces of his blue sneakers when she returned holding a plate. She looked as though she was going to be shot.

"What is that?"

"A cold lamb sandwich."

"Oh no!"

"Don't worry, it's not for you. It's supposed to build me up."

Tommy stayed as far away from the gray meat as possible while Eileen arranged it this way and that way on the plate hoping it would somehow be reduced in size.

"I'll bring out your tea."

Panic! Eileen hadn't touched a bite! Tommy ran over grabbed half a sandwich and hid it in his pants pocket. Just in time, too!

"Here you are, and I see you're enjoying that lovely lamb."

"I think I've had enough."

"Well, you made a good start. I'll save the other half."

When she left Tommy came over to put it to rest.

"Somebody else will eat it."

"What are you going to do with the half in your pocket?"

"I don't know."

They went out together but Eileen soon joined her friends who were on their way to the candy store, leaving Tommy at the entrance to the alley.

"Have fun."

"See ya."

Since there was still no sign of Mark, Tommy decided to wait in the courtyard of his own building where he arrived just in time to see a boy being toppled over by an old-fashioned bicycle he was trying to bring down the steps. As a spinning wheel encircled his face, the boy remarked that the bicycle was too heavy to get off him. Could Tommy help?

"Okay."

Tommy grabbed the handlebars and pulled as the boy pushed upwards. He was soon able to crawl out from underneath and the two of them got the bicycle standing upright.

"My name is Philip. What's yours?"

"Tommy."

"Thanks for helping me!"

"Is this your bicycle?"

"It belonged to my brother, but he went away and my dad said I could have it, but I had to get it out of our hallway and it came down the building stairs okay, but when I got into the courtyard the steps were too steep and it fell on me."

"The wheels are flat."

"My dad says that's from being in the house a long time. They lose their air."

"What are you going to do with it?"

"I was told to put it into the carriage room. I need a pump to put air back into the tires. Do you have one?"

"No. Where's the carriage room?"

"In the cellar. Do you live here?"

Tommy pointed to the left side of their building.

"Oh great! I live on the right side. Do you want to come with me?"

Tommy nodded yes, ran across the street, saw Mark, and brought him along to join up. Philip was delighted.

"Hi, my name is Philip. What's yours?"

"Mark Levine. Your wheels are flat."

"He needs a pump. Do you have one?"

"No."

"We're going to our carriage room. Do you want to come with us?"

"It's in the cellar."

"Sure."

Philip guided the bicycle as it thumped its way around the building with Tommy and Mark walking alongside as honor guards. The cellar entrance was all the way in the back of the yard where the garbage cans were kept. It was also right next to the ground floor apartment of the super who couldn't walk right. Tommy liked the super. He would often come to the apartment to fix the toilet or some other thing that wasn't working. Sometimes Tommy would even lie on the floor next to him and see how things were coming along. The super didn't mind. But other kids thought the super was mean and called him cripple legs and were scared to go by his apartment. Happily, the bicycle trio got past his door without being noticed.

They went down the long, dark passageway, coming to a stop at the one washing machine and one dryer. Here the solitary light bulb was directly overhead, so Philip was able to point out the door to the carriage room. Tommy immediately noticed that it was padlocked and was amazed that Philip had a key! That's something he'd never had and he immediately volunteered to hold the lock once it was off. Opening the door revealed a large, orderly room where baby carriages and baby buggies of every description were neatly parked. Once inside, it was easy to tell the ones in current service by their position near the door and the shine on their chrome wheels and handles. But moving further back, models more popular when high shoes were in fashion lingered; layers of dust indicated that they had not been on a stroll for many years. Mark was peering into a vintage wicker pram when he suddenly jumped back.

"Look out!"

It was a spotted tabby disgusted that his nap was disturbed by the likes of them. He gave each of the boys the once over and made his way unhurriedly out the door to who knows where? Mark said cats made him nervous.

"Why?"

"They seem sneaky."

Philip laughed and bumped his lame bicycle into the room and propped it up against the opposite wall. There he found an old candle sitting on the ledge with box of wooden matches next to it. He couldn't resist and, once lit, asked Tommy to close the door shutting out the light from the passageway.

"This could be our fort!"

Philip set the candle on an old fruit crate and invited his pals to sit on the floor around it. The scene reminded Tommy of something but before he could remember the door flew open and an apparition yelled:

"What are you doing in here?"

Mark and Philip shot up from the floor and ran past the figure in the doorway. As he turned to allow them to leave, a face was revealed that Tommy had seen before. He was the man his father would speak to when he came to mop the hallway of their building. The kids called him Mike the Bum. Tommy blew out the candle and walked toward the door.

"We put a bicycle in here."

He pointed to the bicycle against the wall and showed Mike the padlock to the door. In the passageway Mike recognized him.

"You're Tom's boy?"

"Uh huh."

"That's all right then, but you should be careful with matches. I could smell that candle."

"Where?"

"In my room. In the back."

"Can I see?"

"If you like."

The passageway to the back was a continuation of the one the boys took coming in but much longer and darker. At the end Mike made a left and you could see a lighted area a few yards ahead. It was Mike's room. The first thing Tommy noticed was the smell, a combination of whiskey and dirty socks. There was a small, unshaded lamp with a forty-watt bulb set on a wooden box and when Tommy's eyes became adjusted he could make out the mattress on the floor with the one top sheet crumpled up next to a flattened-out pillow. Further on, two large cardboard boxes were set neatly against the water-stained wall.

One acted as his wardrobe, sheltering three half-clean work shirts and a pair of blue coveralls. The other was the library, displaying a discarded encyclopedia—volumes alphabetically arranged—and a dictionary. A bible with a memorial card acting as a bookmark somewhere in the Old Testament lay on top.

Tommy soon became aware of a shower curtain that was blocking the light from a very high window.

"What's that?"

Mike pulled the shower curtain back enough that Tommy could see. It was the courtyard! The window looked up from the cellar and gave a good view of the people coming and going into his side of the building.

"I keep it covered so people won't look in on me."

Mike put the shower curtain back in place.

"Would you like this? My mother made it."

Tommy handed the lamb sandwich to Mike.

"That's very kind of you, don't mind if I do. Mmm, that's a lovely leg of lamb your mother makes. You take after your father. He's always trying to look after me."

"Are you Irish too?"

"Me? No, I'm like you. A narrowback."

Tommy saw Mike reaching for his pint of Fleischmann's to wash down the sandwich and suddenly became nervous.

"I better go."

"You're welcome to come by any time. Say hello to your father."

Tommy turned and ran down to the long passageway. The open door to the cellar was his goal and he was running so fast that he bumped into Mrs. Hyde who was bent over pulling her wash out of the machine.

"Sorry."

"Oh, Bridie's boy. What were you doing back there?"

He didn't answer but turned and kept on running. The fresh air never felt so good! Mark and Philip were waiting and ran towards him as soon as he left the yard.

"We thought you were killed!"

"Huh?"

"Mike the Bum can be crazy."

"Why?"

Philip echoed his father's assessment of hopeless cases.

"He goes crazy if he can't get whiskey."

Tommy looked to Mark, who nodded in agreement.

"It was okay. He showed me his room."

"He did! Boy, you're lucky to get out alive!"

Tommy didn't feel very lucky and had an urge to run home when Mark reminded him of their appointment in the alley.

"You got it?"

Tommy felt for the lump in his pants pocket and pulled out the sewer ball.

"Great! Let's go!"

* * *

The alley was jumping! Almost every inch of playing space was taken up forcing Mark and Tommy to go all the way to the back near the low stairs. A chain of eight teenage girls had a very intense game of King-Queen raging which forced the newcomers to squeeze into the one remaining space right across from the local tailor shop. They were warned early on about any intrusions.

"Don't step in my box!"

The admonisher appeared particularly fierce-looking to Tommy and his estimation was immediately verified by Mark:

"Irma goes to my school and she's nuts."

Mark asked for the ball and turned Tommy to face the wall with the exposed bricks.

"This is what you do. You throw the ball against the wall and if it comes back on a fly and you catch it you get a point. If it doesn't come back on a fly but you don't drop it, you throw again."

"What happens if you drop it?"

"I knew you were going to ask that! I'll start."

Mark threw the ball and right away it came back on a fly. There was a bobble—but he caught it.

"That's one point for me."

"Okay."

"Whoever gets to ten first wins."

"Suppose I don't go."

"Ha ha! When my brother goes first, I never get a chance."

"You have a brother?"

Mark ignored Tommy and threw the ball more fiercely this time. It returned on a mean hop, careening towards the next box. Mark tried to grab it, missed and flinched as it bounced off Irma's head.

"I told you to look out!"

She gave Mark a shove and kicked their errant ball toward the stairs. Tommy was just able to capture it before it was sent down to 231st Street. When he returned he was told the rest of the rules.

"I missed. You go."

The Gorgon was waiting. Tommy tried bouncing the ball a few times to ward off her stare, but he knew she was still watching so he was very careful as he stepped into his allotted space. Once there, however, he noticed a great commotion in her game. Their ball was on its way down, towards her box! This was his chance while she was distracted! He threw the ball and it came back weakly to him. Mark didn't hide his opinion.

"You throw like a girl."

Impulsive criticism is always ill-advised and, even more unfortunate in this case, Tommy wasn't the only one to hear. Irma, now on her way to the top of the chain, made it clear that Mark's gender disparagement would not be forgotten.

"I'm king! But I'll be back to show you."

Off she went and a much friendlier teenager took her place in the box next to Tommy. He noticed immediately her black and white saddle shoes.

"My sister has shoes like those."

"Who's that?"

"Eileen."

"Oh, I know her! She has red hair and braces."

"No."

"Is she the one who fainted in church on Sunday?"

"I don't think so."

Mark grabbed the ball out of Tommy's hand.

"Are you going to play or not?"

"Okay."

"Then I'll show you how to throw."

Mark raised Tommy's arm parallel to his ear and pushed it forward.

"You let go of the ball when your arm is all stretched out. Forget about the game and just try it."

Tommy threw several times and after each attempt Mark came over to adjust the position of his arm, all the while keeping an eye on the King-Queen game. It was now time to put it all together.

"You're too stiff."

Mark pantomimed a boneless chicken and Tommy understood. On the next try he got his body behind the throw and the result was immediate. The ball came straight back at him from the wall—and he managed to catch it on a fly.

"That's a point for me."

"Let's get out of here!"

The game of King-Queen was over and here comes Irma racing down the alley! Tommy stood to the side and watched as Mark took off down the low stairs. Irma gave it a good try but came to a screeching halt just at the top step. Oddly enough, on her way back she rubbed Tommy's head.

"Hey Squirt, you were lucky for us. We won!"

Tommy watched as the whole chain of girls assembled and dashed off together. From there, they would invade a small candy store at the bottom of 232nd Street where a brother of the friendly one was the soda jerk. He was very generous with the scoops of ice cream. Tommy left the alley and waved to his mother watching from the kitchen window. She wanted to tell him something so he positioned himself just below on the sidewalk.

"We'll have supper in a half hour."

"Okay."

He had turned to go when he heard:

"Is Irma gone?"

It was Mark's voice but Tommy couldn't see him.

"She's gone."

Mark crawled out from underneath a blue and black station wagon.

"You still have the ball?"

Tommy took the ball out of his pocket and bounced it a few times.

"What grade are you in?"

"First."

"How come I don't see you at school?"

"I don't go to your school, dummy. I go to PS 7."

"Why?"

"I'm Jewish. Wanna meet tomorrow?"

"Okay."

Mark grabbed the ball and tossed it quickly to Tommy. After fumbling it a couple of times, he finally scooped it up before it started to roll down the hill.

"I was right!"

"What?"

"You catch like a girl, too."

"See ya."

* * *

As warned, the supper was set when Tommy got upstairs. Eileen and the father were already seated at the kitchen table but Eileen's untroubled appearance told Tommy it must be something she liked.

"Hamburgers!"

"And that's lovely ground steak I made them with."

Tommy didn't understand his mother's gastronomic distinction but he did enjoy putting too much ketchup on the meat and squeezing the bun tight. His father never liked the idea of a hamburger so his meat was served on the plate with two boiled potatoes and some green beans. He also required a generous portion of Coleman's English mustard freshly made up in a whiskey shot glass. While he was slathering his ground steak an old Irish expression came to mind.

"They say Coleman made his money with the mustard people leave on their plate."

There was that uncomfortable silence again. It was bad enough for Eileen when he brought up old stuff from Ireland that she couldn't understand but when nobody answered she might be asked for an opinion. Tommy stepped up to help.

"What does that mean?"

"It means people's eyes are bigger than their belly."

"Oh."

"And you have the jam on from ear to ear."

An aphoristic double play! Bridie was on her game tonight, although Tommy was none the wiser as to mustard or ketchup. Eileen told him to wipe his mouth and calmly ventured:

"I guess people really don't know how much mustard they are going to use and put a lot on their plate. Is that it?"

The father smiled at Eileen's astute analysis.

"That's it! And old Coleman laughs all the way to the bank."

Eileen was happy that was settled and concentrated on her hamburger. When finished, she asked if it was okay to go over to Ellen Riordan's to study. Told it was, she waved to Tommy and took off. Without his eating partner, the act was over for Tommy and he plopped the remainder of his hamburger on the plate.

"I'm full."

"See, your eyes were bigger."

"But I didn't leave any ketchup on the plate!"

He laughed and was told to sit out in the living room to make room for both older sisters who were expected home for their supper. He probed for the possibility of something sweet.

"Wait and see if one of them brings in anything."

There was nothing on the TV at this hour except the news so Tommy didn't even ask if he could watch. Besides, he had some thinking to do and was wishing Betty Ann's Bob was around. He was good at all sorts of ball playing.

"Pat-a-cake, pat-a-cake, baker's man,
Bake me a cake as fast as you can.
Roll it, pat it, mark it with a "T"
And put it in the oven for Tommy and me!"

It was Deidre.

"What's the matter?"

"I catch like a girl."

"And what's wrong with that!"

"They make fun of me."

"Well, I guess then I'm no help. But maybe someone else we know…"

Suddenly Scarecrow was standing next to her with a dilapidated catcher's mitt on one hand and a wreck of a ball in the other. He lifted his moth-eaten ball cap just enough to wink at Tommy. The boy saw some possibilities.

"Okay, but we'll use my ball."

Tommy got to the far end of the living room and waited. Scarecrow threw the ball on a bounce and Tommy caught it by cupping his hands together. Scarecrow nodded his approval enthusiastically. He waved Tommy in a little closer for a ball on the fly. Tommy waited, cupped his hands, caught it, but couldn't stop it from popping out. Scarecrow waved him in a little closer. The next throw was softer and this time Tommy held on to the ball. He was excited that he was getting the hang of it when he noticed his mother standing there watching.

"You'll knock down the grandmother's picture throwing the ball against the wall like that. Go out to the courtyard to play."

"Okay."

Tommy put the ball into his pocket and ran down into the courtyard. He was just about to resume his catch with Scarecrow when he remembered: the window into the cellar! He saw the shower curtain had been pulled to the side so he got down on his knees to peek in. The only light coming into the room was from the cellar passageway, making it scary and sad at the same time. He had seen enough, but as he turned to stand up, he came face to face with the freckled face of a red-haired hellion.

"Mike the Bum lives there."

It was Kevin McCormick—the one who always tried to pull Eileen's hair as he ran by.

"I know."

"When he mops the hall, I sneak in there."

"Why?"

"For matches. Wanna see?"

Tommy nodded yes and was shown a damp-looking, small box of matches.

"What are you going to do with them?"

"I light stuff on fire. Hey, what's that in your pocket?"

"A ball."

"Let me see!"

Tommy was suspicious but pulled the ball out.

"It's a sewer ball!"

"Uh-huh."

"Can I try it?"

It was only a rhetorical question since Kevin grabbed the ball out of Tommy's hand and started to throw it against Mrs. Brannigan's courtyard window. It wasn't long before her window went up and her head popped out.

"Don't throw that ball at our window. My man is trying to sleep."

She had no sooner shut the window when Kevin was at it again. He did it enough times to anticipate her return and then dropped the ball and took off down the courtyard steps. Tommy was left scrambling to corral the bouncing ball when the window went up.

"Tommy, I'm surprised at you! Stop throwing the ball at the window."

"Okay."

Not being able to play now in the courtyard, he went down the steps only to be met by Kevin once he turned the corner.

"She doesn't like me."

"No one does."

The effect was immediate. Kevin was six and a half—a full year older than Tommy—and it would have been easy enough for him to get the slightly smaller boy in a headlock and wrestled down to the ground, but instead he smiled and gave Tommy a good-natured push against his shoulder.

"I know."

Tommy put the ball back into his pocket and walked to the end of the block to look up at his window. Good; his mother wasn't looking out. He was standing next to the ornate fire alarm box when Kevin said, "Hey, watch this!"

He jumped up and pulled the handle. He had an odd expression on his face as he waved to Tommy and took off down the block. The loud ringing of the alarm soon had nearby windows being raised and Tommy knew his mother's would be next. He ran across the street, melted into the assembling mob of kids alerted by the alarm and waited.

"Here they come!"

It was the pumper engine, siren blaring, leading the way and pulling far up into Naples Terrace. A couple of firemen jump off the back of the truck and waved to the kids as they scanned the buildings for any sign of smoke or fire. The supporting hook-and-ladder was having trouble making the turn at the bottom of the hill because of a double-parked car and blasted its horn for the driver to get that thing out of its way. When it did arrive, Tommy noticed the steering driver sitting way up in his little seat atop the ladder assembly. What a job to have! Tommy snaked his way up to the front and snuggled between two chatty grammar school girls to get a better look at the equipment attached to the side of the big truck. There were axes and long poles with hooks and a big heavy hammer that you could smash things with and a huge roll of thick rope and all sorts of neat stuff.

The lieutenant in his white cap shut off the alarm and received word from his scouting firemen that it appeared to be a false alarm. He made a note in his little book and walked straight toward the gang of kids Tommy was secluded in.

"Anybody see who pulled the alarm?"

Silence. The lieutenant started to leave only to suddenly turn around and randomly point at potential witnesses. "Did you see?"

"See what?"

"What about you?"

"I got bad eyesight."

"And I guess you didn't see anything either?"

He was pointing at Tommy! The chatty girls had stepped aside, leaving him exposed.

"Uh-uh."

The lieutenant made another note in his little book and this time did leave, getting into the cab of the pumper engine. The two fire trucks were just on their way down the Terrace when Tommy felt the friendly push of someone standing behind him. It was Kevin McCormick, smiling.

JULY 1936

The long coat that the mother always wore was new then, Bridie having brought it over from New York especially for her. It naturally had to wait for Sunday mass to be worn for the first time where, besides the priest's blessing, all the neighbors were given the chance to see how well Bridie was doing in America to afford a coat like that for her mother. But for that praise Bridie would have to pay the additional price of hearing the question she was trying to avoid.

"Do you have a fella yet?"

The old woman was very calculating in her timing and location. It was said loud enough that the mother would naturally hear—herself never to ask it—but also for Michael Connelly, standing nearby, of whom it was well know him having a particular fancy for young Bridget.

"No time for that. Too busy."

Her brother laughed and grabbed her by the arm to escort her back to the waiting horse and wagon for the return trip home. Michael Connelly, however, was not so reassured by Bridie's answer and kept staring at the mother hoping for further confirmation.

"You heard what she said. There's nothing written on my face."

And that was all the information he was going to get.

* * *

She had saved up two months' paid holiday for her return to Leitrim that summer and her boss, appreciating his dependable Irish waitresses, agreed to hold the job for her at Schrafft's. It was a journey she looked forward to but was nervous about at the same time. And it wasn't just the traveling aboard ship again. Being much the wiser, she had gotten some tablets from the doctor and everybody said they were grand for the seasickness. No, it was the inevitable leaving again and not knowing if she'd ever be back. It made her stay around the old house the whole time in spite of all the urging to visit this place and that. She would draw the strength needed in the new country from these memories. It was only on the day the hired car was to take her up to the moorings of Donegal that she opened the door to her new life and handed the photograph she had been carrying to the mother. He was never very good at standing still so she wanted her to understand it was taken with a Kodak and not a studio portrait.

"It's a snapshot."

The mother brought it over to the window and let the morning sun warm her hand as she held it up to the light. Bridie remained by the cold ashes of the fireplace and didn't quite know what to make of it, her taking so long. Finally, when she was satisfied, she handed her back the snap.

"What's his name?"

"Tom."

SEPTEMBER 1960

"It's okay."

That was it. All the information his mother would get whenever she asked Tommy how he liked being in the third grade. And forget finding out anything about the teacher, Mrs. O'Reilly. He couldn't tell you one thing what she was like. She would have to wait for the teacher's meeting next week to see if the woman had two heads.

You couldn't blame him. He was officially institutionalized now and knew he had five more years to go. Different room, different teacher, it didn't matter. It was all the same. The important thing was he understood the system, knew who to soft-soap and who to ignore. The religious were the ones you had to be on your toes with, and it paid to have multiple story lines. The lay teachers like O'Reilly were easily snowballed. Especially if they got regular telephone calls at school during class, you knew that things at home were messed up and they were easily distracted. He also established a coterie of trusted advisors, kids who actually paid attention in class. He would rely on them to tell him when the test was or where to line up and other pointless details that he never heard being said in class. He had other stuff to think about.

The school may have been the same but Tommy was different. He was taller now; almost five foot five and he lost the last of any little-kid chubbiness. Bob on his last visit home from the navy showed him the latest haircut—a flat-top. Essentially a modified crew cut, the top was a little longer and there was this little fringe of hair in the front that you could stick straight up with a dab of Vaseline. A "scut-tail" his mother called it. It was cool.

Once school was over, he was on automatic to get home and exchange his required uniform for play clothes and head out onto the street as fast as possible. His mother watched as he reappeared in his gray plaid short-sleeved shirt tucked in tight to blue dungarees and held securely with an elasticized belt featuring a cowboy silver belt buckle Betty Ann bought for him from Grants. Blue-and-white Keds sneakers gave him the support and traction he would need to climb, jump, and run away from authority.

His mother checked to see if he hung up his good pants and shirt—he did—and gave him a kiss on the forehead.

"Where are you off to?"

"Just out."

"Remember, we'll have the dinner at five."

"Okay."

Not that Tommy ever told where he was going, but this afternoon he was supposed to meet Elgin at his pigeon coop on the roof across the street and he was certain that any such disclosure would elicit extreme cautionary guidance from his mother and maybe even a direct command not to do it, which he would have no choice but to ignore. He was happy that the interrogation today was relatively short and benign.

It was a beautiful autumn day, and as Tommy ran across the street he could see the pigeons' synchronized ascent high above the roof of Elgin's building. But his climb up the five flights of stairs was interrupted when the apartment door on the top floor swung open and Richie Faye popped out.

"Follow me!"

"Where?"

"I'll show you!"

Without waiting for a response, Richie was already going headlong down the stairs to somewhere. Tommy was unsure but decided to follow on and ran after him. Once outside in the courtyard, Richie turned the corner and scrambled down the metal steps that led to his cellar, a place of high intrigue which Tommy had only explored once before. But he didn't go in. Instead Richie jumped the small retaining wall onto the store roof of Sweeney's Bar and showed Tommy how to lean perilously over the edge to catch the action on 231st Street.

"It's a parade!"

"No, it's not! It's a motorcade."

Tommy watched and got it. It was a parade of cars, most of them open tops with people sitting high up on the back seat and waving.

"Why are they having this?"

"It's for the election in November!"

Richie was a relatively new acquaintance, one grade ahead of Tommy and up-to-date on all sorts of neat stuff. That was the attraction to the budding friendship, but Tommy had to pay the price of Richie's sharp rebukes anytime he displayed a lack of cultural sophistication. And to correct Tommy was seemingly very important to the physically bigger boy. For now the benefits gained from the new experiences outweighed the put-downs, but later Tommy would even things out by making up stories about events that Richie could not possibly have any first-hand knowledge about and enjoy his discontent. Fair enough.

"Who are those fat guys?"

"Big shots from the Democratic Club."

With the traffic from the motorcade picking up, they were going to need some supervision down there and who would be more appropriate than the red motorcycle policeman? Tommy took him from his pocket and set him up on the ledge. This was the first time Richie saw the policeman and Tommy sensed a strong urge that he would try to knock his toy onto the street below. Like a gunslinger, Tommy had his hand ready to snatch him away before the other could draw. But Richie released his stare and nodded, and somehow they both knew that the episode had passed. Tommy understood that this was also a part of Richie and a sympathetic but unspoken accommodation would develop between them. In exchange for an acceptance of Tommy's make-believe world there would be a tolerance of Richie's intense, periodic outbursts. It worked, for now.

"It's him!"

Tommy wasn't going to ask but could tell he was a big deal. All the patrons from Sweeney's rushed out to cheer the long, black Lincoln Continental Mark V Convertible as it crested the hill of 231st Street. Tommy looked straight down and, sure enough, there was his father in a long, white apron standing next to the door of the bar and waving. He scanned the street and some of the spectators crowding the sidewalks were holding big, blue-and-white signs: *A New Leader for the '60s—Kennedy for President.* So that's who it was! He had heard his name raved about in the house, something to do with being Irish and Catholic.

A red light at Broadway stopped the motorcade right outside Sweeney's and Tommy got a good look at the young senator as he reached out and shook hands with the mob of young boys who ran over to his car. When the light changed, a beaming Irish-American policeman came over to release the candidate from the grip of his admirers and wave the motorcade across Broadway and out of sight toward Bailey Avenue. Tommy looked straight down again and tapped the side of the roof with his red motorcycle getting the attention of his father before he went back to tending bar.

"Good job! You got the best seat in the house!"

Tommy smiled proudly and waved enthusiastically to him. As he turned back to his companion he could tell Richie was impressed.

"Who's that?"

Not knowing the most popular bartender in Sweeney's? Talk about a lack of cultural sophistication!

"That's my father!"

APRIL 1939

For a month that had only thirty days it was packed with Sundays—five of them. But even with all that abundance, when the priest took down his big black book from the shelf in the rectory there was only one with an open time slot, the next to the last.

"Three o'clock on the twenty third."

The priest looked sharply at Bridget to see if there was any sign of distress. He knew that these working Irish had only Sunday off and many of them were in a terrific rush to get married and not for the most ecumenical of reasons. A "hurry-up job" they called it. But then, if he thought he was going to get any information from the face of the Leitrim woman sitting across from him, he could think again. Without anything even resembling a facial expression, she steadily wrote the date and time down in her little pocket diary and said, "That'll do."

Disappointed, the priest told Bridget he would have to have a chat with this outstanding prospect and she promised to bring him by after mass on Sunday, them being new parishioners at the Church of the Annunciation. She thanked him and dipped a slight curtsy to keep on his good side. When she turned the corner on Convent Avenue her sister Betty was waiting for her.

"Did he put horns on your head?"

"No, he's looking to put the horns on Tom. Wants to see him next Sunday."

"Wants to see what kind of shape he's in after Saturday night."

Bridget didn't respond, but she didn't disregard the remark either. Her sister was usually correct when it came to human nature. She would ask Tom for them to skip the dance hall the night before. With that settled, she decided to accentuate the positive.

"We got the date. The twenty-third at three o'clock."

"Let's hope the weather will be getting nice by then."

"Will you bring Pat?"

The actual phrase she had in her head was "Will you be dragging Pat along?" But she was accentuating the positive.

"We'll see."

Was that an answer? She took it for one, and went on to put a nickel in the subway turnstile for each of them. Before the train arrived, Betty had fished about in her change purse and refunded her the nickel.

"Don't be sloshing your money around. You'll soon have your hands full running the house for the two of you."

"We'll be all right."

APRIL 1961

"He daydreams."

"That's what you said the last time."

Tommy was next to the schoolroom bookshelf examining an old checker set that had half the pieces missing. He was far enough away that he couldn't hear what Mrs. O'Reilly was saying but close enough to see if his mother's face was getting red. So far, so good.

Anyway, it turned out to be a very short meeting because how many times could Tommy's mother say she was well aware of that? He was called over and given an encouraging rub on the head by Mrs. O'Reilly.

"To his credit, he's always respectful to me and the other teachers."

Tommy shot her his best grin and his mother thanked the woman and they were on their way. Since the school hallway was crowded with other parents and kids waiting to see teachers, Tommy knew there would be no yelling here. When they were alone, out on the quiet sidewalk of Godwin Terrace, that's when he would hear it. But he didn't. His mother never said a word.

He was taken aback, disappointed actually, as he had carefully contrived complex excuses that would repudiate any flimsy accusations proffered by O'Reilly. However, he was soon buoyed by the idea that he would be able to exchange these gems for favors from some of the more dim-witted dumbbells in his class who had their teacher's meeting next week. Once that was settled in his mind, he sensed something was troubling his mother for her not to say anything.

"What's the matter?"

"Thinking to myself. I have a lot to do to get ready for Saturday."

The wedding! Tommy almost forgot about it. Kathleen was marrying Billy this Saturday. He wasn't sure how he felt about it. It was different and, for him, different was always good. But as they crossed 231st Street and the unobstructed afternoon sun shone brightly on his mother's face, he knew. She was sad and that had to change.

"I'm a narrowback."

She laughed.

"Who told you that?"

"A person."

It was risky for Tommy to throw out that line since it was his mother's; an artful ploy designed to conceal the identity of her informant. But his calculation was correct. It made her laugh again.

"Well, whoever said it was correct, although I was called worse."

"What?"

"A greenhorn."

"Huh?"

"When the horns are just coming out and the sheep is too new to know anything."

"Now you know everything!"

They were in the alley and she gave him a hug—disastrous! Some of his friends were playing ball! But when she released him he was relieved to see nobody was paying attention and happy that her mood had changed.

"*You* better smarten up and pay attention in school if you want to go to college some day."

She was back to her old self.

* * *

Having successfully dodged a bullet at the teacher's meeting, Tommy had the rest of the afternoon to hit the streets. And it was with a budding confidence that he did so. No more tiptoeing about and peeking around corners. That concave circle focused at his courtyard steps was now a full-fledged panorama of unlimited adventure. He bounced down his building's steps and enthusiastically looked around to see who was out and what was up. And due to the bizarre and threatening situations that went on all the time, he was learning to fit in. Tommy used these occasions to sharpen his survival skills and to judge the relative strength and weaknesses of his companions. These insights were carefully guarded and silently forged within his brainy crucible into unexpected comebacks and embarrassing put-downs appropriate to the occasion of either being verbally or physically attacked which, because of their effectiveness, became less and less. He had provided himself a shield of protection, much like a poisonous plant, and gained the advantage of being the permitted observer. Without an older brother, the experience became his mentor.

"Hi Tommy!"

It was Philip standing in front of his building. He was all

excited.

"Wanna come with me?"

"Where?"

"To the bicycle shop. I saved up to buy a pump."

The Terrace was jumping with all sorts of ball and street games, but Tommy was intrigued by this idea of a bicycle shop and Philip having money to spend. That was always a good thing.

"Okay."

They headed off under Tommy's window and he instinctively shot a glance upward to see if his mother was watching. No, the window was shut. Normally thrilled to be unspotted, he remembered that look on her face today and hoped everything was okay. He would have a few routines ready when he got home to lighten things up—just in case.

The name of the bicycle shop was called The Wheel and it was down on Broadway across the street from Williams Funeral Home. The first thing Tommy noticed was the smell. Some sort of combination of old wood and rubber. He liked it. The second thing he noticed was the mysterious dimness of the place. A small picture window in the front of the shop provided the only daylight with the rest of the illumination coming from a scattered array of unshielded light bulbs hanging from the ceiling. It reflected sharply off the row of chrome handlebars belonging to the bicycles lined up on along the unadorned brick wall of the interior. The third thing he more than noticed: it was the person running the shop, dressed in a plaid shirt, Lee dungarees, and heavy work boots. He was glad that Philip had to do the talking. This gave him the opportunity to decide.

"Hi, my name is Philip."

"Yes, what do you want?"

"I was here once before with my brother."

"I don't remember."

"I was a lot smaller then. He had this bicycle, but he went away and my father said I can have it. But it was left in the house a long time and the tires are flat."

"Do they have a puncture?"

"No, they just need air."

"Then you want a pump?"

"That's right!"

"Come over here."

He was led to a wooden counter and told to wait. When they were alone Tommy volunteered:

"That's a woman."

"Sure. My brother calls her the Woman in the Wheel. She's good at fixing busted stuff."

She came back holding three different types of aluminum pumps, all in one hand. Tommy was very interested in how she had her hair arranged. It was all piled high in a sort of spherical bun. When she leaned over the counter it looked like a bicycle wheel.

"This is the strongest model. Pump up a tire in no time."

Philip took the pump and stared at it.

"How much?"

"Nine dollars."

"Whoa!"

Taking that as a no, he was handed the second model.

"This one has a very smooth action. Even a girl can do it."

She winked at Tommy and he smiled back. He wasn't sure what was going on but he knew that there was something funny to it. Philip again stared at the pump in his hand.

"How much?"

"Six dollars."

"Uh-uh."

She exchanged the pump again.

"This last one has less power, but will get the job done. It's four dollars and fifty cents."

Philip didn't bother to hold it. He just shrugged his shoulders. There was obviously a problem.

"How much money do you have?"

"I'm not sure. I returned four bottles to the store today and put the twenty cents with the other money but I forgot to count it again."

"Put it all up on the counter and we'll see what you have."

Philip did what he was told and the Woman quickly announced:

"Three dollars and twenty cents."

"Oh, that's right I had three dollars before. But it's not enough."

"Not for a new one. Wait here."

When she disappeared, Tommy examined all the coins spread out on the counter. He was impressed with the two half-dollar pieces.

"Who gave you these?"

"This one is from my uncle for my birthday. I found the other one."

"Where?"

"Under the pew at church. Probably fell out of a fat guy's pants."

"You would hear it!"

"You can't look for money if you drop it in church. My mother said it's bad manners."

Tommy hadn't heard that one and was thinking of all the fat guys that must be at Sunday mass when the Woman returned holding a slightly dented bicycle pump.

"This one is used, but it works fine. I just tested it."

"How much?"

She looked over the money and swept it all into her hand. She then looked at Tommy and put two dimes back on the counter.

"We'll call it three dollars even. That's your change."

Philip picked up the pump and started pumping it enthusiastically.

"Gee, thanks so much!"

"When you fill the tires, ride by here and I will check the bike for you. Make sure it's safe."

"I will, I will. Thanks!"

Tommy scooped up the two dimes that were left on the counter, Philip being so excited with his slightly dented pump. The Woman told him to come back again too. Tommy smiled.

"See ya."

* * *

They had ten cents apiece to spend and that meant snow cones from Moe's candy store. As soon as they were outside, they started to run but stopped just as abruptly when they realized the subway train was on its way towards the 231st Street station. They saw it all the time, every day, but when you are on Broadway, right underneath the elevated tracks, you always came to a standstill and watched it go by. It was a full two blocks away and going strong when suddenly the train blew its horn. As it passed by Tommy could clearly see why and waved to the man sticking his head out of the motorman's window. Uncle Pat had good vision to spot Bridie's boy among all the kids dashing about. It was his last run of the day and he would surprise the boy again by being at the house with Aunt Betty when Tommy got home.

Philip was awestruck that his friend knew a train engineer and, maybe even more impressive, that he never said a word about it. He also noticed Tommy was no longer in a running mood and wanted to check out things along the way to the candy store. The first stop was the RKO Marble Hill movie theater. Being ahead of its time in sensual marketing, they always kept their front doors wide open allowing the tantalizing aroma of freshly-popped corn to drift out onto the sidewalk. The boys stopped to take in big gulps of the sweet-smelling fragrance and to examine the movie billboards.

NOW PLAYING! One Great Big Onederful Motion Picture

"I saw it with my mother. She likes movies in color."

"What's it about?"

"The puppies with the spots are Dalmatians. They get stolen so a woman can make a coat."

"Is that the end?"

"Oh, the mother and father dog get other dogs to rescue the puppies and a whole bunch of other Dalmatians, too."

Cartoons were okay with Tommy, but he could watch them at home. When he went to the movies he wanted to see big screen action. They moved on to the next billboard.

THE EVENT EVERYONE IS WAITING FOR!
West Side Story

"Looks like mushy stuff."

"A lot of singing, too."

The big poster in the corner was more to their liking.

COMING SOON! King of Kings

"Gladiators?"

"Maybe. My mother said Jesus is in it, but they're not allowed to show his face."

This was much more encouraging and it sent Tommy checking the prices up on the board at the ticket booth. A kid was still twenty-five cents in the afternoon, but seeing the woman in the booth reminded him of one of the worst times in his life. Eileen and her friends went to see *The Tingler* and he was dragged along. Of course, he was too young for that type of movie, just six at the time, but it got him out of the house for the day. So, while sitting there munching away on his allotted half of a Nestlé's Crunch, here comes this scene where the centipede-like monster is in a movie theater. The idea was you were supposed to scream to keep it from harming you. But was it in the movie or actually in the RKO? Eileen and Cyrilla were screaming away and poor Tommy didn't know where this thing was. It was all so confusing! Finally, he couldn't take it anymore and buried his head into Eileen's sweater. It was horrible, but he was made to promise not to say anything. Fortunately, back at home, nobody noticed he was scarred for life.

They moved on and pressed their faces up against the glass window of the store next door that sold mink coats and other fur stuff. There was something about the yellowed manikins and dated display that amused them. This cheeky nosiness was a far cry from the days when young women waiting in line for the movie would look longingly on the glamorous styles and, shortly thereafter, chivalrous sweethearts would arrive to place deposits on romantic daydreams they could ill afford. But today, the old owner of the shop was only busy chasing boys and complaining about smudges on his window. When he returned to his place behind a counter that hadn't been visited in weeks, a cup of tea waited to soothe the sting of the boys' derisive laughter. Nearby, his wife stood silently among the manikins, ready to redress their fading daydreams.

Taking their defenestration in stride, the boys now stood in front of the most modern store in the neighborhood: Progress Radio & TV. An electronic emporium, its center window displayed the most talked-about must-have feature of 1960s consumer life: an RCA Victor color television, exhibited with a promotional picture of the most popular cowboy of the day.

"That's Hoss from Bonanza!"

"He's even bigger in color."

"Twenty-one inches, diagonally measured. My mother wants one, but my father said no."

"Why?"

"It's too much money. Look!"

Tommy couldn't read the small white card at first, being so discreetly placed to the side of the stylish, simulated-wood cabinet, but when he squinted:

"Four hundred and ninety-five dollars."

"My father says that's over three weeks' salary."

"Oh."

"How much money does your father make?"

"A thousand dollars!"

Tommy laughed and impulsively entered the store to rummage through the boxes of 45s that ran along the center counter of the store. He knew all about them from tagging along with Betty Ann. Philip sheepishly followed him in and listened attentively as Tommy announced:

"I like this one."

"*Runaway*? I never heard it."

Tommy kept rummaging.

"Here's one for your mother."

Philip was handed Patsy Cline's *I Fall to Pieces*."

"Why?"

"No color TV for her."

Tommy landed a good one, but Philip didn't understand what he did to deserve it. Too bad. He shouldn't have asked how much money Tommy's father made. None of his business. Anyway, it was just a practice shot to stay sharp. He figured correctly on Philip being a harmless lamb and rushed back out onto the sidewalk to assess the next situation. They had to get past the high stairs.

Another step street abruptly appearing at the dead end of Naples Terrace, the high stairs was the main thoroughfare leading down to Broadway and 231st Street. In the morning it was a torrent of commuters rushing off to school or work. Depending on the weather and the condition of your eyesight from the night before, the top landing provided a panoramic view as the sun started to peek above the jumbled assortment of apartment buildings. But aesthetics aside, this commanding height also provided a practical reconnaissance point as to the location and speed of an approaching subway train or cross-town bus. Hurling themselves downward like an eagle from a jagged crag, the recently arisen would fearlessly confront the treacherous, unevenly-spaced steps, keeping an ever-watchful eye for broken bottles, slippery swatches of cigarette cellophane, gobs of gum and other remains of the night. Once safely landed and their confidence in their athletic agility reignited, they enthusiastically merged into a pedestrian flow brilliant with the buoyancy of a new day.

However, in the afternoon, when school was released, this soaring stairway ceased to function as a mundane utilitarian passageway and magically became a dizzying wonderland providing danger and amusement to children of all ages. This was possible because of a city building design which called for a cement border just beyond the railings, creating a buffer from a shallow dirt yard on one side—the little deep—and a very high void on the other side—the big deep. This seemingly innocuous architectural trifle was cleverly transformed by the addle-brained youth of the neighborhood into a treacherous test track for all sorts of jerry-built, preposterous transports. Today it was stolen trash can lids reforged into flying toboggans.

"Look out!"

There was no way Billy Whelan could stop since at this point he was airborne, so he had to be ruled out from taking any responsibility. It was clearly up to Philip to get out of the way, but Tommy could see that he was frozen in place. He instinctively pushed him hard enough to the side that they both fell down in opposite directions, the soaring sled narrowly missing both of them. When Whelan hit the ground on his metal saucer he skidded across the crowded sidewalk, raising sparks all the way up to the curb of the busy street. Ignoring the admonitions of passersby he just missed sending to the hospital, he came straight over to Tommy and Philip waving his toboggan high in the air.

"Wanna try?"

As Whelan wiped the blood from his scraped elbow, a badge of courage received from the cement border, Philip examined how the handle to the lid was hammered flat to give it a smooth surface. He seemed lost in thought admiring a tinker's handiwork. When challenged again to try the run, he replied no and handed the lid back to Whelan. Tommy watched carefully as a sneer was drawn across Whelan's lip.

"Afraid?"

"I'm not allowed."

"Who says?"

"My mother. She says they're dangerous."

This logical explanation of following good, orderly direction from one's parent seemed to enrage the defiant daredevil and he quickly shifted his attention to the shiny object sticking out from Philip's dungaree pocket.

"What's that?"

"It's a bicycle pump."

"Let me see."

Once in his possession, Whelan stuck it into his own back pocket.

"I could use this. Thanks."

"Give it back!"

"Maybe tomorrow."

"No, now!"

"Make me."

Philip smacked Whelan with an open hand across the face, so hard that he fell down to one knee. While he was down there, Philip took back his bicycle pump and Tommy dragged him to the side. Another tobogganist was flying through. This one skidded all the way out to the center of Broadway, making the Number 20 bus come to a screeching halt.

"Pretty good, eh? Next time I'm going to make it all the way across."

It was Patty Morgan, the tomboy of the Terrace. No simple trash can lid for her. She somehow commandeered a section of straight sheet metal which not only allowed her to approach escape velocity but would instantly decapitate anyone in the way of her descent. She was glad to see Whelan down on the ground because it gave her the opportunity to kick him in the ribs.

"That's for teasing my little sister. She hates you!"

Whelan scrambled to his feet to chase Patty, who was already on her way up the high stairs. But not before he gathered up his trash lid and turned to Philip.

"I'll get you for hitting me."

Philip didn't answer but watched as Whelan ran off. When seemingly satisfied, he turned to Tommy and yelled, "Snow cones!"

They ran again with Philip taking the lead. The corner of 231st and Broadway was mobbed; forcing them to weave around this one and that and then make a sharp turn up the street to head to the candy store in the middle of the block. Tommy threw a sideways glace as he passed Sweeney's to see if his father was in there but couldn't tell it was so busy. Betty Ann said all the men in Sweeney's look alike and from the street it was true. Tommy kept on running and met up with Philip just outside the store. It was jumping.

Moe and Hilda Rosenberg ran the candy store situated near the low stairs and, as usual, had their hands full with the afternoon drove of Catholic school boys and girls all cramming into their little shop—each one in various states of staring, sighing, laughing, shouting, spinning, and crying. Moe, standing stoic at his soda fountain, tried to decipher the hodgepodge of requests:

"I'll have a vanilla Coke."

"Me too, but no vanilla."

"Then you want just a plain Coke?"

"How much is a seltzer?"

"Hey, what happened to my chocolate egg cream?"

"I'm making it now."

"But I don't want an egg cream."

"Not you, her."

"How much for a strawberry malted?"

"Fifty cents."

"For a seltzer?"

"Not you, the malted."

"Hey, where's my chocolate egg cream?"

"I changed my mind. I'll have vanilla coke too."

"Large or small?"

"How much is large?"

"Fifteen cents."

"For a seltzer?"

"Not you, the malted, I mean the Coke."

"I've changed my mind about the egg cream."

Hilda, a few feet away, was in charge of small purchases and traffic control. She especially kept a strong watch on the garrulous group perusing comic books with no intention of buying. "The library is closed. No reading here."

"How much are the bubble gum cigars?"

"Two cents each."

"I'll take two blue."

"Take one more. They're three for a nickel."

"Okay, make it one yellow, one pink, and one green."

"What happened to the blue?"

"Oh yeah, one blue."

"That's four cigars."

"How much?"

"Eight cents."

"Okay."

Tommy and Philip edged their way into the store and stood impatiently in front of the snow cone machine. Unfortunately, it was located right between Moe and Hilda, forcing them to keep turning their heads this way and that until they finally caught Hilda's attention.

"And what can I do for such nice boys?"

"Two snow cones, please."

Hilda took a paper cone cup from the stack and pressed the lever to start the descent of the shaved ice. After filling the cup carefully to the top, she gave the frozen concoction two generous squirts of chocolate syrup and handed it to Philip. He seemed amazed.

"How did you know I wanted chocolate?"

"You come here every day."

"Oh, yeah!"

"This one I don't know as well. What flavor would you like?"

"Lemon and lime."

"If you get that magazine all sticky, you'll have to buy it!"

Tommy turned to see a tall, freckle-faced girl goggling over the cover picture of Ricky Nelson, seemingly forgetting she was holding a fast-melting orange Popsicle. Regaining consciousness at the sound of Hilda's decree, she hurriedly stuffed the magazine back into the rack. It was there, however, that Tommy saw Kevin McCormick lurking.

"Now, something nice for you."

"Thank you."

Tommy gave Hilda the twenty cents for the two snow cones and immediately buried his mouth into the flavored ice to get the full effect. It didn't take long for him to lose all feeling in his lips. Following Philip out of the store, he gave an over-the-shoulder look at the girls spinning on their soda counter stools to see if Eileen might be with them. She wasn't, but he did notice the new DC Comic with Jimmy Olsen as Elastic Lad and that would require coming back again and trying to grab a free read. Philip and Tommy were just at the low stairs when they heard:

"Hey, wait up!"

It was Paulie Valletta running across 231st Street. When he caught up to them, Tommy tipped his cone in his direction so he could get a mouthful of ice. Paulie was still in his school clothes. Tommy figured why, but with Philip, everything had to be spelled out.

"You're only getting home now?"

"Got punished, had to stay late."

"Why?"

"Fighting."

"With who?"

"Don't know his name. Some jerk in the seventh grade. We were playing cards in the schoolyard and he said I was cheating and started to fight. Brother Michael saw us and made us stay after school to sweep the gym."

"Did you cheat?"

"A little bit."

Tommy laughed and offered Paulie another hit from his snow cone, but he declined. Instead he pulled out a half-eaten Mounds bar and popped it into his mouth. As they went up the low stairs he noticed the bicycle pump in Philip's pocket and asked to see it. Now Paulie was good at mechanical things so Philip had no qualms about letting him have a look. He was always generous with his advice.

"It's a nice one. Where did you get it?"

"The Wheel."

"How much?"

"Three dollars."

"Stupid! You should have stolen it. I would have."

It was Kevin McCormick eating a double-scooped ice cream cone. Paulie gave him a push and confronted his conviction.

"You couldn't steal from the Woman. She's too smart for you."

"Maybe, but I can steal from Moe's!"

Kevin took out a spotless Spaldeen from his pants pocket and started twisting it this way and that in the air. He let Tommy bounce it a few times and there was no doubt: it was a brand-new ball and a good one. He handed it back to Kevin and they resumed their ascent up the steps. Once in the alley, Paulie challenged Kevin to a game of points with his new ball. Tommy wasn't interested.

"See ya."

But Philip wanted to make his own point with Kevin before he left.

"You shouldn't steal. It's a sin."

"No, not when you steal from them. They're Jews."

* * *

"Wait here, let me check."

Philip disappeared into his top floor apartment while Tommy was left in the building hallway. He was used to it. There were some apartments you were immediately invited into, but there were also others where prior authorization had to be obtained and then there were those where you were not let in at all. This time it was a relatively short period for the all clear.

"Come on in."

The top floor corner apartment looked out over Broadway and was flooded with light. It took Tommy a few seconds to adjust his eyes coming in from the dark hallway but when he did he saw a woman in a large sitting chair waving him towards her.

"So, you must be Tommy."

"That's me."

"Ha! It's good to know oneself. Philip tells me that you are a great friend."

"I guess."

"Take my word for it, you are."

Just as quickly as Philip had disappeared after inviting Tommy in he suddenly reappeared, vigorously drying his hands on his dungarees. He ran over to his mother and gave her a kiss on her forehead.

"Look what I got!"

She took the bicycle pump in her hands and gave him a smile. Tommy had seen that type of smile before and knew she had no value in it.

"You'll need the key to the carriage room."

"It's in my pocket!"

"Do you know how to ride a bicycle, Tommy?"

"A little bit. I don't have one of my own."

"Then the two of you should be careful."

She returned Philip's pump to him and reached behind her chair. Tommy watched carefully as she balanced herself awkwardly on two black canes and hobbled fiercely over to a windowsill where a well-worn cushion was waiting.

"I can watch from here."

As Philip gave her a hug, Tommy took a long look at the face of the woman staring at him.

* * *

Tommy waited until Philip was fiddling with the key in the lock to the carriage room before asking him. He wanted Philip to be distracted, in case it was sensitive. He also had learned it was a way to get a more honest answer.

"What happened to your mother?"

Philip never changed expression. He still had the tip of his tongue resting on his top lip as he twisted the key trying to spring the lock. His eyes widened as he heard the click.

"It's getting stuck more and more. The super has this grease you can spray to keep stuff loose. He might let me use it. She was in a car accident. Her brother was driving. He was drunk and smashed it all up."

Philip was now on his knees running his hand along the rim of the front tire of his brother's bicycle trying to find the air valve. Tommy needed more light on the subject.

"Take it outside where we can see."

They bumped it along the cellar passageway and out into the front part of the yard where they kept the garbage cans. Philip immediately reached for his pump and went to work.

"Here they are! Hold the handlebars while I fill 'em up."

"Was he killed?"

"Who? Oh, my uncle. No, nothing happened to him."

"He was lucky."

"I guess, but my father hates him. He's not allowed in our house."

Suddenly the Patsy Cline record came spinning back into Tommy's consciousness.

"I didn't know she couldn't walk."

Philip was admiring how nice and plump the tires looked and the new adventures they would bring. Tommy was still holding the handlebars when his friend grabbed him around the waist.

"It's okay. You try her first!"

"Her?"

"My father was in the navy and he told me anything that moves is a she."

"What's her name?"

"I… I don't know. She should have a name."

Tommy did a walk-around, taking in the Schwinn brand logo on the flashy red tank and the name Panther on the two-tone mudguard. When he swung his leg over to get onto the brown leather seat he noticed the speedometer winking at him like a big class eye. He laughed.

"She just told me!"

"Really? What is it?"

"Polly. Polly Panther!"

With Tommy aboard, and freshly inflated tires, Polly was ready to go! Where she was going, Tommy wasn't sure because he really hadn't figured out the steering thing, but for now it looked like the high stairs. He had only sat on a bike once before and that was just to get the feel of the balance. It never moved. Now he was picking up momentum and if he was going to take this shortcut down to Broadway, Polly better have wings as well. Fortunately, he was tall enough to keep his feet firmly on the pedals. Fortunate because that was where the brakes were, this Schwinn edition not yet having any fancy hand brakes. Facing imminent doom, he first gave the pedals a half turn to get a feel of engagement, then he slammed into reverse just as the front wheel hit the top step. As the bicycle came to an abrupt halt he fell over sideways. Like a capsized tortoise, he was trying to right himself when he saw his sister's face peering through the spinning spokes.

"Whatcha up to?"

"Riding."

"Whose bike?"

"Mine! She's called Polly. Tommy named her. Oh, and I'm Philip."

"Did Tommy name you, too?"

"What?"

"Never mind. I'm Eileen, Tommy's sister."

"Very nice to meet you!"

With Philip's help, Tommy was soon out from under and standing tall. He pointed to the big cardboard box with the fancy ribbon under his sister's arm as a way of extracting some information. Eileen was clearly excited about it.

"Guess what's inside!"

"A leg of lamb?"

"No, my dress for the wedding."

Philip, who had been staring in awe at Eileen up to this point, became positively ecstatic.

"You're getting married?"

"I'm fourteen."

"Oh, you look older."

"Do you have any sisters?"

"No."

"I didn't think so. Anyway, you two have fun."

"See ya."

As Eileen happily headed home, Tommy noticed Philip waving to someone. Looking up, he could see Philip's mother watching from her window seat.

"We better go. It's making her nervous, us being so close to the high stairs."

Philip swung onto Polly and started off across the Terrace. He tried to make the turn to go down the hill and ran straight into the fire alarm box. Patty Morgan, who was sitting up on top eating an apple, was waiting for an adventure.

"Can I get a ride?"

The crash didn't dislodge Philip from his bicycle, but he was discombobulated and didn't know who was talking.

"Up here. Can I get a ride?"

Tommy caught up to them and watched as Patty came within inches of setting off the alarm on her descent. She tossed her apple core aside and settled herself onto the handlebars.

"All set, let's go!"

Tommy shook his head no. Philip, his cavalier nature surrendering to the challenge, remounted and started off down the hill. They did great, flying down the center of the street in majestic style. But instead of turning for Broadway, the bicycle continued straight and wound up smashing into the shrubbery in front of the big building at the end of the block. Feeling now like an ambulance chaser, Tommy ran down after them. His first job was to disentangle Patty from the azalea bush. Not yet being in bloom, it was a jumble of rough limbs holding Patty at bay. She held out her hand and Tommy gave her a great yank upward. He knew that sound well enough, and when Patty stood up, there it was—a big tear in her cotton jumper.

"My mother's going to kill me. Thanks for the ride!"

It was her building, so she just nonchalantly strolled inside; like she just got out of a taxi or something, and totally ignored the newly assembled crowd of people. One member, an old lady, was admonishing Philip, who was sitting on the sidewalk rubbing his forehead.

"You ought to be more careful, recklessly riding all over the place. A person could be killed!"

Tommy retrieved Polly from the garden and dislodged the mud stuck under her fender. When he got her rolling, Philip was standing. His forehead was red and bruised, but not bleeding. When his eyes met Tommy's he was given all the reassurance anyone would ever need.

"It's okay."

Without saying a word, Philip started rolling Polly down the hill toward Broadway. Tommy followed. He knew where they were headed—The Wheel.

* * *

"You got a screw missing."

Tommy laughed and the Woman winked at him. Philip didn't get the joke. He was too busy sticking his battered head under the handle bars.

"Where?"

"Right there, where the frame connects. There's a screw missing. That's why you can't steer."

"Oh."

"I think I got one that fits."

Philip starting squirming around, going through his pockets. The Woman picked up on it.

"Don't worry; we'll put it on your tab."

She was off to the back of the store. Tommy was investigating the odd collection of bicycle lamps and electric horns that were laid out on a table when Philip came over, rubbing his head.

"I could steer it when I brought it down the stairs."

"When?"

"The day we met, remember? We brought it into the carriage room and it steered okay."

Tommy nodded yes but was looking at the Woman as she returned to the counter. She was carrying a big brown ice bag.

"I found one that should fit, but first let's have a look at that head."

She bent her gooseneck lamp towards Philip's forehead and asked if he was dizzy. He said he thought so and was immediately taken by the arm to a big leather chair near the work bench. Once she got him seated, she put his head back and gently balanced the ice bag on his forehead. He was told to stay put. She would look after the bicycle.

"You! Give me a hand."

Since Tommy was the only other person in the store, he figured she meant him.

"How may I be of assistance?"

"What's your name?"

"Tommy."

"You got a good sense of humor. I like that. Hold the front

steady while I refasten the frame. What happened to his head?"

Tommy related the wild ride down Naples Terrace, while trying to keep the front wheel steady from the violent twists coming from the Woman's screwdriver. She certainly had powerful hands. When she was finished, she told Tommy to sit on the bicycle while she turned the handlebars this way and that. Polly had her steering back.

"That's a nasty bump your friend got. Tell his mother to keep an eye on him tonight. If the dizziness gets any worse, she should take him to the doctor."

Tommy remembered the look on the mother's face and it must have reflected back on his own.

"What's the matter?"

"His mother's a cripple."

"Oh. Maybe I should go with you in case she needs help. Where does he live?"

"Just up the high stairs."

"Okay, it's time to close anyhow. I'll get ready."

Tommy stared as she rolled down the sleeves of her plaid flannel shirt and undid the spherical bun on the top of her head, causing the hair to cascade down both sides of her face. She took out a comb from her back pocket and raked it furiously. She laughed at Tommy's facial expression.

"You don't know what to make of me, do you?"

"No."

"That's okay; most people don't."

"Doesn't it bother you?"

"When I was your age it did, but not any more."

"What happened?"

"Something I hope that never happens to you. But I will tell you a secret, just between us for now because it'll upset his mother even more. There's no way that screw comes out by itself. It's done in the factory by a machine and takes a deliberate effort to unscrew it. Someone did it on purpose."

Tommy didn't say anything more, but just walked slowly behind with Polly as the Woman and Philip made their way up to Naples Terrace. At the front of his building Philip gave Tommy the key to the carriage room and asked Tommy if he would put Polly away for the night. The Woman nodded that it was okay. She would bring Philip upstairs to his mother but also wanted to know where Tommy lived.

"What apartment are you?"

"D."

Tommy gave Philip a good-bye look and rode Polly right into the cellar. It felt even spookier than usual and he wanted to get out as fast as possible. He felt like he was being watched and sure enough, as he turned around from securing the padlock, there was Kevin McCormick standing under the hanging light bulb.

"I know who did it."

"Did what?"

"Ooh, you're a smart one. You know what I mean. Hey, look what I got."

Kevin took a long screwdriver from his back pocket and started twirling it. For some reason Tommy thought of Philip's mother and went for blood.

"They say there's something wrong with you."

"Who says?"

"Everybody."

The single hanging bulb provided a grotesque element to Kevin's facial contortion and Tommy was pleased. The follow-up was instinctual.

"They say it all the time."

"No, they don't!"

"Yes, they do! All the time! All the time!"

Tommy's shouting provoked a sudden roar of "who's there" from the back of the cellar. It caused the boys to take off running toward the street. When they got to the gate by the garbage cans, Kevin grabbed Tommy's shoulder.

"That was Mike the Bum!"

"So? He's my friend."

The remark seemed to settle Kevin, who let go of Tommy and started to walk around in a circle with his head down.

"I never touched his bike."

"I don't believe you. Why do you have that?"

"I stole it from the super's toolbox today when he came upstairs to fix our toilet. But look at it!"

Kevin pointed to the tip of the screwdriver and saw that Tommy was confused. It didn't look like the one the Woman used to fix the bicycle.

"It's called a Phillips head."

"Philip's head ain't doing so great right now."

"Ha! This kind of screwdriver won't work for the screws on his bike."

"Oh."

"See, I told you I didn't do it. But look what else I stole."

Kevin excitedly produced a big roll of black tape.

"It's electrical tape. You can wrap the handle of a stickball bat or tape up an old baseball."

"Can I see it?"

Tommy was impressed at how strong and elastic it was. He was thinking of all the busted things he could tape back together when Kevin, sensing his importance increasing, slid over and whispered:

"I know a lot of stuff."

"Who messed up Polly's steering?"

"Billy Whelan."

He was all teeth; like the Coney Island smiling guy, but his bizarre expression helped Tommy to remember.

"I'll get you."

"What?"

"That's what he said to Philip."

"He thinks he's slick, but he never saw me.

"Where were you?"

"I was hiding behind the washing machine. I thought I could open the coin box, but I couldn't."

"Why not?"

"It's the other type of screwdriver!"

They both laughed and Kevin appreciated an attentive audience. It didn't happen too often. It gave him confidence to continue.

"Do you know the woman with the ugly baby?"

"Which one?"

"The one who's always calling down when the ice cream truck shows up."

"Oh, yeah."

"She locks her stroller in the carriage room. Whelan was waiting outside for someone to open it for him and when she showed up, he went in, too. Said he had to fix his bike. She left him alone in there, but I saw."

"Why didn't you tell Philip?"

"Why should I?"

Kevin sensed the good time he was having with Tommy slipping away and quickly added, "I would now—tell you, I mean."

Tommy studied Kevin's face, but didn't reply. It was getting dark and he should go home for supper. He also needed some time to sort this out. For him it was over, but not for Kevin. He wanted to seal the deal.

"I know something else, too."

"What?"

"Follow me."

He led the way into their side of the building and had Tommy wait in the hallway as he dashed into his apartment. He was out in a flash holding a shiny cylinder. It was Philip's bicycle pump.

"I saw him crash into the garden and went down later and found his pump. You give it to him."

"You could of gotten three dollars for it."

"I know. Friends?"

Tommy took the pump and shook the offered hand.

"Friends."

Kevin happily bounced back into his apartment. The door was barely shut when Tommy heard the shouting from inside and that meant there was nothing to be gained hanging around there. He took off and ran down the stairs into his own house. It was a big party!

His father was the first to see him. "There he is now. Tommy, come over here and have your picture took."

They were gathered by the window, with Kathleen standing in between her father and mother. Next to them were Betty Ann and Eileen, dressed in their fancy new dresses. Bob was a few feet back fiddling with a Brownie camera while Billy was off to the side kibitzing. Aunt Betty and Uncle Pat were there, too, hoisting a glass in a toast. Tommy took Kathleen's signaling to mean he should stand next to her and the father. As he snuggled in, some mysterious hand appeared from above to tame his cowlick. It stayed down long enough for Bob to get the picture. After that there was a lot of laughing and talking and it was decided to have the supper in the living room. Bob and Billy got to maneuver the big metal table through the door jamb of the kitchen and up against the wall next to the television. Tommy and Eileen were unsure just what kind of cuisine would accompany a festivity of this sort, since it never happened before, so it was a great relief to see cold cuts from the German delicatessen being strategically arranged on plates around a colorful centerpiece. They actually liked a lot of this food, especially the potato salad and pickles. Tommy's mother was just setting out the knives and forks when they heard the knock on the door.

"I'll get it."

Tommy swung the door open wide enough for a horse and cart to enter which, of course, drew everyone's attention. In an instant all the talking and laughing were replaced with staring at the newcomer standing in the doorway. Tommy's father finally broke the ice.

"Won't you come in?"

"Thank you, perhaps not. I can see you are having a celebration."

Tommy's mother swiftly came over to get to the bottom of things.

"What do you want?"

"I stopped by to let you know the doctor was on his way to take a look at Philip."

All eyes turned to Tommy.

"He hit his head riding his bicycle."

The interrogation was now officially started, with Tommy's mother lead prosecutor.

"Is that the boy with the mother trapped in the house all day?"

"She's crippled."

"I know the poor woman is! Now she has this. What happened?"

"He smashed into the garden at the bottom of the hill."

"Were you riding on the bicycle with him?"

"No."

Eileen jumped in with the sympathy angle, always a clever tactic to defuse the mother.

"But you fell on that bike too, by the high steps."

"The steering was busted."

As Tommy's mother started to check the boy's head for undetected bruises, the Woman from the Wheel added to his credentials.

"Tommy helped fix the bicycle and was a good friend to Philip. I better go. I wish you all a pleasant evening."

"It's a party. My sister is getting married."

The Woman responded by looking awkwardly at each of the sisters until she concluded that Kathleen must be the lucky one and offered congratulations. Kathleen smiled and thanked her, giving Tommy the chance to run and hold the door wide open again. As she left, the Woman told Tommy to come by to the shop with Philip when he's feeling better. Tommy said he would and she gave him a rub on the head. He had felt it in the room, but the Woman's face now confirmed it. She was embarrassed.

Tommy's father said a quick grace over the food and everyone was told to dig in. Bob was well on his way, heaping roast beef atop rye bread when he nonchalantly asked:

"Who was that?"

"She works in The Wheel. She fixes bicycles."

"I would say she was jealous of that new dress of Eileen's."

The father's remark and follow-up wink made Eileen blush. She tried to be nonchalant by positioning more sliced pickles around the perimeter of her plate. Everyone knew, however, that opinions on the matter were now open for discussion.

"I don't think dresses are her thing."

"More of an overalls kind of gal."

"Probably not the marrying breed either."

"She didn't seem to know what to say to Kathleen."

"With shoulders like that you don't need to say much."

"You play linebacker for the Giants!"

Tommy had made the sofa the place to eat his pile of potato salad. When he finished, he ducked between the adults laughing around the buffet table and grabbed a custard pudding. Jumping back up on the sofa, he took advantage of the momentary lull to quietly announce:

"I like her."

* * *

"I like her, too."

It was Deidre.

Tommy was in bed, kind of. He was straddling the chair that was placed next to his bed to keep him from falling out. It was an attractive dining room chair with a green padded seat. There was only one of them in the apartment and where it came from no one knew. And why they thought Tommy had subliminal inclinations to fall out of beds was not clear either. As far as he could remember he never did. Maybe the chair was where it was because there was nowhere else in the small three-room apartment to put it, so there it went. It was the seat section that was placed next to his bed, making it very easy for Tommy to climb aboard and make believe he was riding his bicycle.

"She has a lot of neat stuff for bikes."

"Where are we?"

"Going down a really steep hill."

It was up in Riverdale, someplace that he saw while driving around with Kathleen in Billy's car. It was not an exact location but a composite of images. He saw things as he wanted to and sped by on his bicycle as fast or as slow as he wanted to. Sometimes there were people he knew and he would wave and sometimes it was just him on the road or sidewalk peddling away. He was free on his bicycle and could expand his world in any direction. Deidre and Scarecrow had a hard time keeping up with Tommy, which was only natural since they were peddling on a tandem bicycle. Scarecrow's legs would get wobbly and Deidre had to do most of the work. It was Tommy's fiercest wish to have a bicycle and when he did get one it was great, but it never was as good as his rides on the chair that kept him from falling out of bed.

"We have a flat."

"Let's stop here and have a picnic."

Scarecrow took some straw from his stomach and put it into the hole of their tire as a patch. Tommy was skeptical but was reassured there was nothing better, and besides, it gave him more room in his belly for the tasty treats they had packed. Scarecrow untied the wicker basket that had been attached to their tandem bicycle and to his surprise Patchwork Teddy had been a stowaway the whole time! He was glad to see him.

"I'll make tea."

Tommy watched as a checkered table cloth was lifted from the picnic basket followed by a folding table, four chairs, and a full tea set. Scarecrow stepped far back as Deidre made a small campfire to boil the water and warm the custard puddings she prepared for dessert. Liverwurst sandwiches, one of Tommy's favorites, were stacked high on a center plate in an arrangement resembling the Tower of Pisa. It made Teddy giggle.

The tea and sandwiches hit the spot and Tommy was just scrapping the bottom of his second custard dish when Deidre suggested a little dancing might be fun. Scarecrow wobbled to his feet and got his accordion from the basket and a tambourine for Teddy. They were a little surprised by Deidre's sheet music, but soon got the rhythm going.

"It's something new and exciting!"

Deidre started to sway and twirl toward Tommy as she sang:

"I like to be in America,
Okay by me in America,
Everything free in America,"
"For a small fee in America!"

Tommy stood still with his arms folded until Deidre took his hand and started to get him to mimic her steps. Soon they were both stomping and sashaying all along the bedroom floor.

"I'll get a Terrace apartment."
"Better get rid of your accent!
Da da, da da"
"Life can be bright in America."
"If you can FIGHT in America!"
"Yee-ha!"
"Olé!"

"Why are you up?"

It was Tommy's mother.

"I have to go to the bathroom."

"Betty Ann's new record album has you all jittery. Well, don't dilly-dally. We'll have no ease to our feet tomorrow."

"Okay."

* * *

There was no school the next day and, since it was Friday and Tommy's father was off from work, that meant pancakes!

The boy's mother made pancakes, of course, several times for lunch. But there was something about the father and pancakes that made it special. He put an egg in the batter which she didn't and he put more butter on the pan, but other than that there was no difference, except there was. Tommy's father always had a fantasy of being a short-order cook, probably from working in and around saloons all his life. So when he got the chance to play with a skillet he made a whole make-believe world come alive.

"Okay Bub, what'll you have?"

"Whaddaya got?"

"Flapjacks!" The old-fashioned term always made Tommy laugh. He nodded his approval. "One order of flapjacks coming up!"

Tommy sat and watched as his father turned up the heat and loaded on the butter. The table had been set before Tommy's arrival with a plate and silverware all set out diner style. With the first sizzle of the pan Eileen would usually make her appearance, like a graceful egret at the sound of a splash. This would not go unnoticed and Tommy always enjoyed the announcement.

"We got another customer!

As she slid into her seat at the other end of the table, Eileen would quietly put in her order.

"I'll have some pancakes, too."

"We ain't got any pancakes. We only got flapjacks!"

The cook would reinforce that it was a limited menu.

"That's what being served: flapjacks. Take it or leave it."

Eileen went with it and repeated flapjacks which made Tommy laugh again. By now the skillet was steaming and smoking furiously, which inevitably would precipitate a visit from the local fire chief—Tommy's mother.

"You'd think the house was on fire!"

Most times Tom would acquiesce to Bridie's terse observations, but Friday mornings were different.

"Don't disturb the short-order cook when he's at his work."

Sensing that this was a world where logic was suspended, she would just shake her head and retreat into the living room. With his domain secured, the cook would proudly announce:

"First order of flapjacks, coming up."

Tommy would customize the hot offering with an excessive topping of sickeningly-sweet pancake syrup, thereby assuring a dangerous level of hyperactivity for the next four hours. When the predictable crash did occur he would simply recharge on Twinkies.

"Mmm. They smell good."

An intruder at the feeding pond! Betty Ann, whose usual morning nourishment consisted of a piece of candy and a glass of water, was being deviously drawn to the peculiar prospect of eating breakfast. Tommy waited for the announcement.

"We have another customer!"

Betty Ann angled in to the kitchen table as to not be in the way of the short order cook. She was no sooner seated when she started the instigation.

"Is there bacon, too?"

"Special order coming up. Flapjacks with a side of rashers!"

Eileen was still in the process of her very deliberate buttering process when she suddenly stopped. Tommy, looking across, knew why.

"Eileen wants bacon, too."

"Two sides of rashers!"

Eileen smiled at Tommy for speaking for her. She now had to concentrate on fending off Betty Ann, who was tearing off pieces of pancakes from her plate to taste.

Bacon meant another skillet and a well-worn, blackened version was loudly banged onto the burner. It was obtained from an out-of-business saloon and had more stories associated with it than the Book of Kells. The smoke from this new source brought a return visit from the fire chief. But no, this time it was the food inspector! Nothing was said, but she suspiciously examined just how much bacon was being tossed onto that pan and how carefully the short order cook rewrapped it. Annoyed but satisfied, she left.

Soon bacon and pancakes were served up along with cups of tea to wash everything down. Tommy had finished and was helping the cook dry his big skillet when they heard Charlie the canary squawking from the living room. Tommy was instructed by the father to go out and investigate. The boy arrived just in time to see Charlie in his cage being hauled off to the bedroom by his mother. He peeked in to see the cage being clamped up on a hook by the window. The bird seemed confused by the change of location. Tommy dutifully reported back to the father who was not at all pleased and took off to get answers.

"Where's Charlie?"

"I moved him into the bedroom. We have to get him out of the way for tomorrow. Everything on this side of the living room has to be moved."

"Why is that now?"

"To clean up and make room for the photographer to take pictures. We can all stand over by the window where the light will be good."

That such advanced preparations were required for pictures astonished the father of the bride but he was more concerned about Charlie and turned toward the bedroom. Kathleen, who had tried to sleep late to keep fresh, was reluctantly making her way toward the bathroom. There was too much commotion. Her father wanted to make sure she knew what was happening so she would be kept calm for the big day.

"They moved Charlie."

"I heard."

Well, at least someone was calm, because Charlie certainly didn't like this wedding business one bit. He was flying wildly around in his cage. He did regain some composure when he heard Tom's reassuring voice and clucking noises, but it was plain that some concessions had to be made for the displaced companion. The Venetian blinds were raised full up so the bird would have plenty of light. Next, Tom took off for the kitchen to get a piece of lettuce. With the leafy treat in hand he was quickly intercepted by Bridie.

"Where are you going with that?"

"The poor thing is upset about being moved about. He won't do any singing in there."

She stood aside and Tom proceeded. Kathleen was out of the bathroom and asked the mother what it was now.

"He's worried that the bird will stop singing."

Tommy, who had been watching this episode from the big chair under the cuckoo clock, suddenly remembered he had an important issue to clear up.

"How much money does Da make?"

"Don't ask!"

* * *

The boy did help out with some of the preparations, at least the cleaning up part. As furniture was being whizzed about, he dusted and polished the tables that were to remain in the living room. The spray polish was fun to overuse and he made the surfaces as shiny and slippery as possible. As a test, he ran his motorcycle policeman around the tables a few times and could really notice the difference. Some of the polish naturally went way beyond the table and onto the wooden floor, creating a surface comparable to black ice. People wearing fancy shoes tomorrow better be careful.

Getting bored, he used his technique of nonchalantly getting in the way as a reason for him to be dismissed from further duties. This time he was ordered to take out the garbage and stay out, but not to go too far away in case they needed him. Tommy knew they wouldn't. They had too much to do to get the apartment ready for the big day. He was free.

Like any unique talent, being the incompetent hindrance had its drawbacks. The boy really didn't know how to do anything practical. Oh, he could dust a few tables and dry a few dishes, but he didn't know how to fix anything or why stuff worked the way it did or what went with what. Nobody showed him. Maybe because they were all too busy or, more than likely, they saw that there was something completely impractical about him and he would always have someone to do things for him. How they were going to fund this dependency was never said, but the boy may have sensed it and subconsciously sought sponsorship through powerful institutions, hence his early interest in being an altar boy.

He had seen them at work during Sunday mass. They stood on the other side of the altar rail, making them obviously important. Tommy liked that. His cousin and the older brother of one of his street chums were to be the altar boys for Kathleen's wedding. They got to be up close to all the action and in all the church pictures. Tommy liked being considered important for nothing more than just standing around. Next September he would be in the fourth grade, the launching pad for an altar boy career. He could become an acolyte, the smallest of the boys who get to hold a candle. Tommy liked playing with candles and matches, so this was especially appealing. Given consideration, the altar boys had all the trappings of impracticality that fit a boy like Tommy perfectly. They didn't allow any girls to be members. They enforced a memorization of a dead language—Latin. And most impractical of all, they required the wearing of medieval garb. In spite of all this, or maybe because of it, there was the rumor that altar boys got paid for some of their duties. This added attraction of institutional subsidy made the position irresistible.

The boy, however, was considering none of this right now. He was free and out on the streets. Carrying his bag of garbage towards the cans in the yard he came across several slats of wood that were being discarded. They had been part of some piece of furniture, maybe a bookcase that had felt the weight of the ages and broke apart. Tommy dumped his bag and picked up the slats of wood. They must be good for something. Thinking Richie Faye would be the one to know, he was going to hide them in his cellar when he heard from across the street:

"We can use those."

It was Elgin. Tommy liked that Elgin always said 'we' when Tommy was around. He included him naturally because of his fondness for the pigeons. Anyone who liked pigeons was welcome. If you didn't, Elgin had no use for you.

"We can?"

"Sure, we can make some flooring in the coops. This way they won't have to stand on the tar all the time. We can take them out and wash them too. They're perfect."

Tommy was pleased by his serendipitous contribution and, after grabbing an armful of the slats, happily followed Elgin up the six flights of stairs of the building across the street and onto the roof. It was an early spring type of day with light blue skies and buttery sunshine trickling through playful, puffy clouds. The air was fresh and clean and, looking north, you could see all the way up to Van Cortlandt Park. Going to the other side of the roof, you could watch as the stubborn Harlem River struggled south, toward the East River and the great bay of New York. Over to the east were the patient waters of the Jerome Park Reservoir and to the west was that impenetrable citadel of the affluent, Riverdale. What a place to be—on top of the world!

It wasn't at all cold, but Tommy zipped up his blue gabardine jacket right to the neckline, because that's the way Elgin had his horsehide bomber jacket and there was nobody cooler than Elgin. Tommy once asked about that jacket and was told it belonged to Elgin's uncle who fought in Europe and even had some blood stains on the inside lining where he got wounded. Of course that was from a fight over a girl in a Dutch saloon, but that didn't matter. It was still blood. Girls seemed to be Uncle Teddy's thing, because he was currently the bachelor about town and would relay all sorts of exploits to Elgin, which to any sixteen-year-old were awesome. He also had a frothy collection of girlie magazines, a couple of which Tommy got to see because Elgin had them pushed down the side of the upholstered sitting chair that was next to Coop Number One. Their contents presented a mixture of exotic sexual crimes with absurdly-posed pictures of unattractive woman. Tommy had no value on them and Elgin didn't try to get the younger acquaintance improperly interested. Elgin didn't push any cigarettes on Tommy either. He smoked Viceroys because they were dentist-recommended and he had nice teeth, but he never offered or tried to get Tommy to take a puff, unlike many of the sociopathic teenagers on the Terrace. He knew Tommy was only eight years old and told him he should stop growing before starting to smoke. Elgin waited. He was almost fourteen.

"They moved Charlie."

"Your canary? Why?"

"We have to move everything around for my sister's wedding. To clean stuff."

"That's not good, birds don't like change. How's Orphan Annie today?"

Tommy went over to Coop Number Two and put his face up to the wire. There were ten pigeons in this hutch and most were half dozing after just coming in from their morning flight. Tommy made a small clucking noise and one pigeon, the black one with just a touch of white in her tail feathers, looked up and hopped over. Tommy reached in and brought her out to give her a rub on the head.

"She's good."

Elgin was laying out the boards on the roof to get a rough estimate of the size needed for the pigeon coop but stopped to look up at Tommy and smile.

"She's your bird, that's for sure. Remember when you found her?"

"Over two years ago on the low stairs."

"She never forgot. Now she's a big shot when they go out to fly. Always takes the lead."

Orphan Annie had decided to climb up Tommy's arm and hang out on his shoulder. This gave Tommy the chance to walk over to the other coop. He was being cagily watched by a large, all white male pigeon.

"Dick Tracy wants to know where I'm going with her."

"The protective husband. I'm keeping them apart for a while. We have two eggs on deck now and it's starting to get crowded."

"Maybe Coop Number Three?"

"I don't know. The super had conniptions when I built the

second one. He's threatening to make me take both of them down."

"With no home, the birds would be all scattered and wouldn't know how to find each other."

Elgin had a pattern to the boards that he thought would work so he tapped out a cigarette from his pack. He bent his head to get a light sheltered from the breeze, but when he stood straight his face had a real hardness to it.

"That does not happen. I won't let it."

Elgin and Tommy moved all the pigeons from Coop Number Two into Number One so they could set out the new flooring without disturbing everybody. The boards fit nicely all around except for sticking out quite a bit in the front. The door to the hutch wouldn't close. It was during this period of contemplation that Tommy saw Elgin's girlfriend, Rosalind, sneaking toward them, but since she had a finger on her lips he kept quiet. Elgin was still bent over examining his handiwork which gave her the perfect chance to jump way up on his back and throw her arms over his shoulders. Elgin shot straight up with surprise but got right into it and took his new passenger on a short trot around the roof with Rosalind laughing all the way. Tommy appreciated an unpredictable piggyback ride and liked that Elgin took her real close to the roof's edge. The tease produced the most high-pitched screams he heard yet from Rosalind and she was hanging on tighter than ever when her silly steed returned back to base. She slid down graceless but grateful from Elgin's back and gave Tommy a slight push as a greeting.

"Hiya Squirt. I bet you thought he was going to throw me off?"

"Uh-huh."

Rosalind tried to land a noogie on Tommy's head but her arm lock was weak and he was able to twist out. It was Elgin's appearance that got her to finally lay off. He was holding one of the flooring slats.

"It's a good thing you showed up. We need your father's hand saw."

"Is that all I'm good for?"

"What?"

"We were supposed to go over to Fordham Road today, remember? And you were only supposed to come up here to check on the birds."

"Tommy found these boards and they make great flooring for the coops. But they're too long and I need to saw off about four inches from each. You better bring his measuring tape too. We can mark all of them so they're even."

"Gimme a cigarette!"

Elgin tapped out a Viceroy and gave her a light. She snapped her head back very dramatically and stared to walk around the roof. Tommy also appreciated pouting and knew when to stay clear. She made a complete solo journey around the perimeter and returned to stomp out her cigarette in front of Elgin.

"I'll get them!"

She was in mid-step when she noticed the girlie magazines stuck in the side of the sitting chair. She reached in and pulled them out. Tommy was in the range of the question.

"Whose are these?"

"They're mine. I found them."

She quickly flipped through a few pages and turned to Elgin, who was regarding her reaction.

"He's too young. I'm going to throw them away."

She flung open the door to the roof and disappeared down. Elgin got to counting the number of boards to see if there was enough for two coops. When he was finished he stood up to ask Tommy, "Why did you tell her the magazines were yours?"

"I dunno. Just thought of it."

"Thanks. I didn't need any more heat."

"How old is she?"

"Fifteen."

"That's old enough to have them?"

"I guess. I never saw a girl look at that type of magazine before."

"Maybe it's okay by the time you stop growing."

"What?"

"You know, like smoking."

Elgin laughed.

"Yeah, that's it!"

They fed the pigeons, all in Coop Number One now. They seemed to enjoy being bunched up together and having sweet grain early in the day. It made it a type of party. Elgin and Tommy were just sweeping up when Rosalind finally arrived with the hand saw and measuring tape. Elgin's initial impulse was to grab and get to work, but he resisted and tried being the gentleman.

"Thank you."

"You're welcome."

"It's a big help."

"That's me, always helpful."

"Did you have trouble finding them?"

"Oh, no, Father is very neat where he keeps his tools."

"Then what took you so long?"

"I'm sorry! I guess I should've ran all the way from Peter Reeves!"

"What do you mean?"

"When I went downstairs my mother was out of vinegar. She never has enough and she knows my father and grandfather use a lot. Grandad was going to have fried fish for lunch, so she was in a panic. I had to go to Peter Reeves. Oh, by the way, Squirt, your sister was looking for you."

"Which one?"

"Eileen, she was in the store with me. I'm glad I bumped into her—because you didn't tell me!"

Rosalind again tried an arm lock on Tommy with better results. She was able to get in two noogies before he escaped. Elgin was confused.

"Why are you picking on him?"

"His sister is getting married tomorrow and he didn't tell me!"

"Why would he?"

"So I can go to the church."

"For what?"

"To see what everybody's wearing! What's the matter with you? Luckily, my mother pays a lot of attention when they announce the banns of marriage and knew that Squirt's sister was tomorrow. Do you want to come with me?"

Elgin by now had marked off a board for reduction and was sawing away. It was clear he was finished answering. Tommy, hoping to avoid more punishment due to lack of wedding information, jumped in with an update.

"I had to get new blue pants to go with the jacket that someone gave us."

"That's nice. Do you like them?"

"No, they're itchy."

"Then why did you get them?"

"They were on sale."

Wearing a horsehide bomber jacket with a strong sun shining is not the thing when there's a pile of work to get done. Elgin took it off and threw it across the sitting chair. In his white, sleeveless tee-shirt and slim jeans, Rosalind thought he looked like a young Marlon Brando, but with better teeth. Tommy's itchy pants suddenly became unimportant.

"Gimme a cigarette."

"They're in my jacket. Bring me one too."

Rosalind took the pack with matches and stood in front of Elgin as he cut a board while holding it against a roof buttress for support. She put two in her mouth and lit them. She then reached across and put one in Elgin's mouth. He stopped sawing.

"Where did you learn that?"

"From a movie."

"Which one?"

"I don't remember."

They both laughed and soon the end piece fell off. Elgin checked the freshly cut board in the coop and held it up for Tommy.

"It fits perfectly."

Tommy came over and ran his hand lightly across the board.

"It has rough spots."

"Probably had nails to hold whatever it was together."

"It might hurt their feet."

"You're right."

Elgin waved Rosalind over.

"Rosie, we need sandpaper. It won't take long, I promise. Tommy can do it while I cut."

He took the cigarette from her mouth, gave her a kiss and put the cigarette back. She took a few quick drags and threw it away.

"My mother doesn't want to see me smoking. I'll be right back."

True to her word, Rosalind was only a few minutes this time. Tommy was sitting on the roof watching Elgin cut wood when she came over and balanced three pieces of sandpaper on his head. He laughed and started to work on one of the boards. Of course, since he had no idea how to do it, Elgin gave him the technique.

"Do it in one direction. A light touch is enough. There, that's it."

As the boys were busy, Rosalind tried to kill time by snooping around Coop Number One. She found one bird in particular very odd.

"How come this gray one has no feathers on his head?"

"Sandpaper."

"You know Elgin; this kid is a wise guy."

"Why don't you give him a hand? We'll finish faster."

"I don't want to ruin my clean skirt sitting on the dirty roof."

Elgin stopped sawing, went over and got his horsehide bomber jacket, and spread it out on the roof next to Tommy. He bowed very low and she gave a reasonable representation of a curtsy. When she sat down and folded in her skirt, Tommy handed her a board and a piece of sandpaper.

"Do it this way."

"Gee, thanks. What are these pink spots on the inside of Elgin's jacket?"

"Blood."

"What? You know, I should have gloves on doing this."

"His name is Henry."

"Who are you talking about?"

"The bird with no feathers on his head. He was born that way, so it doesn't bother him."

"I bet the other birds are nasty to him."

"Only the females."

"Wise guy! How come you don't get beat up all the time?"

"We like guys who are funny."

Tommy smiled but said nothing. Praise like that from a cool sixteen-year-old didn't need any comment. Even Rosalind knew she was shut down. She resigned herself to sanding and spying on Elgin sawing wood in that tee-shirt. True enough, with everyone pitching in they were soon on their last board when Rosalind remembered.

"Oh, my mother told me that boy who lives on the top floor across the street was taken away in an ambulance last night."

"Who?"

"I don't remember his name. He's about Squirt's age."

"What happened?"

"He smashed his bike and hit his head."

"Probably didn't see something in the dark."

"No, it happened during the day. He went home and his head got worse during the night."

"I hope he's okay."

"Yeah me too, but that's not the excitement. This kid told his mother that someone fooled around with his bike and that's why he crashed. His mother now wants to know who did it and told the police."

"Wow, the cops."

"Yeah, that's big trouble. My mother says if the kid croaks, they won't stop until they find out who did it."

"And anyone else involved. I wouldn't want to be those jerks right now."

Rosalind finished sanding her last board and was just about to jump up when she turned to Tommy.

"What's the matter, Squirt? Run out of wisecracks?"

* * *

They installed the newly-sanded boards in Coop Number

Two, and not only did they fit perfectly, they looked beautiful; like a parquet floor in some fancy Inwood apartment. Then they moved all the birds from Number One into Number Two and laid down the remainder of the boards in there. The dance floor of the Rainbow Room never looked better. Elgin said they could all stay together in one coop for a while because he would separate them when they came back from their evening flight. Whether this was to please Rosalind by not spending any more time with those pigeons, Tommy couldn't tell. She definitely was determined to get to Fordham Road to window shop and Elgin was resigned to take her. Tommy had a last look at the birds and took off first.

"See ya."

There was a police car on the Terrace when he went downstairs! Tommy took the horseshoe-shaped sidewalk back to his building instead of cutting across the street. He hoped this route would give him a better assessment of what was happening, but what he got instead was being shouted at by the policeman getting out of the patrol car.

"Hold on there, sonny!"

"Yes?"

"Do you live in this building?"

"Yes."

"Where is the super's apartment?"

"It's around back, through the yard with the garbage cans."

The cop was struggling to reintroduce his pants to his waistline after a most protracted effort to exit the vehicle. Tommy noticed all the stuff he had on his belt: gun, flashlight, summons book, and two busy key chains, all fighting to stay as far below an emergent beer belly as they could. Finally, the cop had everything brought up to regulation level and pointed toward the yard.

"Yes."

"Thanks, kid."

Tommy walked nonchalantly to his building's steps and gave a quick look back. It was true. The cop was on his way to grill the super about Philip's bicycle! He could hear it all now. Who's been seen fooling around in the cellar? Who's a friend of Philip? Who went with him when he took the bicycle out for a ride?

"Betcha they won't ask that."

"Ask what?"

"Who told him not to ride down the hill with Patty Morgan on board?"

"Who won't?"

"Cops. I've seen what they do on Dragnet*."*

Eileen passed it off to more of Tommy's imaginings and asked him if he was hungry. The little brother looked around for the first time and noticed no one was home except him and the sister. If they were all arrested, he had to play it cool.

"Where's everybody?"

"They went to church for the rehearsal and to have lunch with Billy's relatives."

"Oh."

Eileen was being very motherly explaining to Tommy that she could make sandwiches, or soup, or boiled eggs, or—there was someone knocking at the door. She went straight for the peephole, having endured a particularly disturbing version of *The Twilight Zone* the previous night. Betty Ann always said crazy things can happen.

"It's the super."

"Don't open the door!"

"What's the matter? You like him. I'll let you talk."

Eileen swung the door open wide and pushed Tommy forward. The super nodded to Eileen as she left and turned toward Tommy.

"Hi, tell your father I'll have the hallway mopped early tomorrow so it will be clean for the wedding party."

"The cops were looking for you."

"Yeah, I just got rid of them."

"Did you tell them?"

"I told them I can't help it if the lids to the garbage cans keep getting stolen. Kids use them to slide down the high stairs. They wanted to give me a summons. The garbage men complained because they got no tip at Christmas. They'll be back when the weather gets hot to see if they're covered."

"That's all?"

"That was enough for me. Oh, by the way your pal Philip is home from the hospital. He's all right, just a bad bump. Go up and see him."

"Okay."

Tommy closed the door and sat at the kitchen table. Eileen, with no previous meal commitment from the boy, took it upon herself to make boiled eggs and cinnamon toast. It was one of her favorites and she knew Tommy would like it, too. She put a freshly boiled egg in a whiskey shot glass for Tommy and let him cut off the top with a knife. That was the part he enjoyed the most and today he imagined himself as Elgin with that big saw. He had just completed the job when two freshly-buttered pieces of toast landed on the plate next to him.

"Thanks."

Eileen sat nearby and sprinkled his toast with the cinnamon and sugar concoction their mother always had on hand in a small glass jar. It made the toast almost a dessert. Everyone now was happy. Tommy started to saw the top off his second egg.

"What did the super want?"

"I forget."

"Well, it couldn't be too important. Our toilet is working.

Mom was worrying about the hallway being dirty when Kathleen goes out in her dress tomorrow. It has a long train. I'm gonna have to make sure doesn't get dirty."

"That's it!"

"What?"

"The super said the hallway would be mopped in the morning."

"Oh, good! See, you really didn't forget. You just don't listen very well—do you?"

"Was the super born that way?"

"You mean not being able to walk? I think so."

"Then it doesn't bother him."

"He seems okay."

"That's the way Henry is. He was born that way, too."

"Is that where you were this morning? On the roof with the pigeons?"

"Me and Elgin. You should have come up."

"Wasn't Rosalind there, too? I met her and that's where she said she was going."

"She was there."

"I would've been in the way. She's very protective of her Elgin."

"He almost threw her off the roof."

"What?"

"She was riding piggyback."

"They musta been only fooling! Which bird is Rosalind's favorite?"

"She likes Brenda Starr."

"Ooh, that rose-colored one. She's pretty. But I like Dondi the best.

"He's shy. Elgin found him on a ledge last year all alone. I give him Social Tea crumbs."

"Why are you worrying about the super?"

"I'm not. I was thinking about Philip's mother."

"What about her?"

"She wasn't born that way."

Tommy finished his lunch and went out in the living room to take his motorcycle policeman out of the cardboard toy box. He hadn't played with him in a while, but when the boy checked, he still didn't have any beer belly. He ran him through the old familiar valley of the living room floor until he came up against the fancy patent leather shoes of Deidre.

"We're all prepared."

Tommy looked up and saw Scarecrow fidgeting in a black robe, trying to keep a curly white wig to stay put on his straw head. Next to him was Patchwork Teddy, slouching proudly in a three-piece, knitted orange suit and holding an enormous law book. Deidre, sporting a black ensemble and white blouse with a black string tie, led the legal team over to the sofa for a conference.

"Prepared for what?"

"For your murder trial, of course. We prepared a defense."

"What is it?"

"You're to run far away and hide."

"Where?"

"We haven't figured that out yet, but Scarecrow suggested a haystack."

"What about Teddy?"

"He says keep your eyes closed and everything will disappear."

"Philip didn't die."

"That's wonderful! Then your legal team suggests you visit him right away."

"Okay."

* * *

"Oh, look who's here!"

Tommy wasn't expecting Philip to answer the door and was surprised by the energy he showed in leading him into the living room. He was also surprised to see the person Philip was shouting out to. He was expecting his mother.

"This is my father!"

He was a tall man with a weathered face and a big head of white hair. Tommy's hand got lost in his, but the handshake was restrained, so as not to intimidate his son's guest. Wherever Philip got his loquaciousness, it wasn't from his father. The man just stood there politely and let his son run the show.

"Tommy was with me yesterday when I crashed and helped me to get back home."

"I thought you would be wearing a big white turban."

"I don't need any bandages. They put me in this gigantic X-ray machine to examine the inside of my head and they didn't find anything."

The father let out a little chuckle and went off to the kitchen, returning with two small bottles of Pepsi. As the boys got comfortable on the sofa, the father told them he had to get ready for work and not be too boisterous. Philip quickly explained, "My mother's resting."

"How is she?"

The father stopped abruptly and turned to Tommy.

"That's very nice of you to ask. This took a toll on her. She worries about Philip getting hurt."

He threw Philip a fake air punch which Philip easily countered. Tommy could see it was a well-practiced routine. The father then rubbed Tommy's head and winked at his son as a way of retaking his exit. Philip seemed to shrink into the sofa, quietly drinking his whole bottle of Pepsi without saying another word. Tommy thought maybe he should leave. Maybe his friend's head hurt, but it wasn't that. It was the subject Tommy wanted to avoid.

"How's Polly?"

"She's safe in the cellar. Here's the key to the carriage room."

"I don't know when I can ride her again."

"Oh, I forgot to bring the pump."

"Where was it?"

"Right where you crashed. Kevin found it and gave it to me for you."

"McCormick!"

This conundrum made Philip frown. He knew Kevin could have gotten three dollars for that pump and no one would have known. Before he had him branded a bad person and that was that. Now things were a little more complicated.

"Tell him thanks."

"Okay."

"He's always sneaking around. Maybe he saw who sabotaged Polly."

"You know, Philip, the bike wasn't new and sat up here in the apartment unused for over a year. Things can get loose and slip out. That's much more likely than someone removing that screw on purpose."

Philip's father was dressed in blue coveralls with the logo of two criss-crossed pipes sewn on his jacket pocket, the symbol of the plumbing company he worked for. He suggested to Tommy that it might be best for Philip to get some rest now and, after Tommy said good-bye to Philip, he walked Tommy to the front door.

"His mother gets very upset about this idea of someone deliberately trying to hurt Philip, so I'm trying to discourage any talk of it. As a matter of fact, we don't know if that is the case or not. It's not like anybody saw someone do it."

Displaying excellent coordination, Tommy shook hands with the father and shook his head no at the same time. Once free, he raced down the building stairs and wasn't surprised to see Kevin McCormick waiting for him in the courtyard.

"What did you tell him?"

"Who?"

"Philip! You didn't tell him who did it?"

"No."

"I'll betcha he'll pay to find out."

"I'll betcha he won't."

"Why?"

"Because nobody did nothing."

Kevin's head jerked sideways.

"What are you talking about?"

"The screw was loose and fell out."

"Who told you that?"

"Philip's father."

"Don't you remember? I saw Billy Whelan."

"That's just another one of your stories."

"It's true! Why are you saying that?"

"Because we're friends."

"Huh?"

"Your story would upset his mother."

"So?"

"I told Philip about the bicycle pump."

"Yeah?"

"He's your friend now, too."

"But that means… I don't want to upset his mother either?"

"Nope."

"I knew there's no money in telling the truth."

"Patty Morgan would like to know. She ripped her sweater."

"Her father would kill Whelan!"

"Especially when he comes from Sweeney's."

"But everybody would hear about it that way too."

"Yep."

Kevin took to walking around in a circle, like a dog looking for the head of his bed. When he was satisfied, he stopped abruptly in front of Tommy.

"I'm no snitch. But we'll fix Whelan somehow, right?"

"See ya."

* * *

That April was certainly a busy month for big events. The early part of the month saw Yuri Gagarin and his smile take an orbital spin around the globe, instituting a new phase in the space race with the Russians. Then, only a week later, a pretty beach in Cuba named Playa Girón took over the headlines and soon every kid in the alley was shouting about the Bay of Pigs. That only lasted a few days, as the whole invasion was quickly reported a bust. The resulting scorecard showed two stinging defeats to national pride back to back. The country's competitive blood now boiling, the president would quickly address the first setback by proposing to land a man on the moon and ensure his safe return before the end of the decade. Asking why it would take so long to get him back would ensure a noogie for being a wise guy. This noble quest would engender an engineering and technological renaissance soon to be the envy of all geeks everywhere. The second defeat was not so magnanimously handled and culminated in the terrifying climax known as the Cuban Missile Crisis, where it came pretty close to having no world for our brave astronauts to return to. Sometimes batting five hundred is not so great.

By the fourth Saturday in the month a relative calm had descended upon the nation, assuring a reverent atmosphere appropriate for Kathleen's marriage to Billy, who, in the opinion of many, had been hanging around long enough. The neighbors got to the church early to take in the whole show and, depending on your outlook on life, their attendance could either be interpreted as the warm support of well-wishers or nosy old biddies looking for something to criticize. This early arrival also provided onlookers with a good opportunity to evaluate the level of enthusiasm displayed by members of both families towards the proposed union. Their caught-off-guard body language could tell you a great deal about its likelihood of success, either resorting to candles being lit for the couple's happiness or I-told-you-so's being safely stored away until news of the breakup was made official.

Just like the wedding cake, there were successive viewing layers to be enjoyed before you got to the top—the entrance of the bride herself. Family members, some never before having suffered the vulgarity of the spotlight and painfully aware that everyone was looking at them, were a spectacle not to be missed. First up and always a crowd pleaser were the outfits on the small girls and boys dressed up like imitative ladies and gentlemen. In this category Kathleen was lucky, having only one younger brother; with two or more there would be the inevitable punching and jostling that attended any occasion where they would be on display and had the chance to ruin things. Tommy, having no fraternal rival, had the cuteness category sewn up in his borrowed blue blazer and itchy blue pants. His pocket handkerchief with the letter T proudly displayed along with his patriotic flattop haircut indicated that this was a lad of great promise. Next, Eileen would furnish the required up-and-coming younger sister. Nicely presented in her new light green spring dress and grown-up high-heeled shoes, she navigated the center aisle very correctly, just slightly behind Tommy, but far enough back to let her own personality be admired and not just be regarded as the chaperone of her younger brother. Her eighth-grade classmates had piled tightly into two pews to gawk and gossip and were proudly reminded by Cyrilla that it was she who helped pick out the dress. No greater approval was needed.

While the appropriateness of the young people's outfits was assessed with general open-mindedness, no such latitude would be given to the next category descending the main aisle of the good parish church. The mothers of the groom and bride would be held to strict standards. Billy's mother was an older woman and, of course, that should have allowed her the option of something very simple and suitable. Nevertheless, quite a few comments were passed as to whether the woman was dressed for a wedding or for a funeral. To make matters worse, her husband was deceased and she had to endure the critical stares on the arm of a handsome young usher whose rakish appearance unwittingly made her dowdiness all the more apparent. To her credit she didn't seem to care, and she marched mechanically up to the first pew on the right. In quite the contrast was the appearance of Bridie, outfitted in a lovely knee-length aquamarine chiffon dress. She looked very stylish—but not flashy—as she gracefully took the arm of her escort and made her way confidently to her seat in the first pew on the left. The consensus on her appearance was generally very favorable, gearing up the crowd for the big entrance of the wedding party.

Meanwhile, the organist, seated comfortably high above in the choir loft, was busy numbing the congregation with the usual repertoire of well-worn, unimaginative favorites. From his rear-view mirror mounted above the keyboard, he was pleased to see the mother of the bride being safely parked in her pew. This generally increased the odds that the dearly betrothed would show up and he would get paid. Relieved, he kept loose by repeating the same schmaltzy sequence and waited patiently for the curtain-raising buzzer. Kathleen had already been warned to be on time since hers was the first of three weddings that Saturday morning and if she was late it would throw the whole schedule off, the composure of the clergy being paramount. True to her responsible nature, she arrived a couple of minutes early and met the wedding party waiting for her in the rear of the church. The first to greet her was her father, as comfortable in his black-and-gray morning suit as a dog in an Elizabethan collar. Earlier, it had taken three members of the household to help him with the studs, waistcoat, and cuff links required, more time than the bride herself to get ready. However, when Kathleen stepped out from the wedding limousine all that hardship was forgotten as he ran to give her a great big hug. Once free, Betty Ann and the other bridesmaids quickly huddled around her, their secret ritual setting off silly grins on the faces of the attending groomsmen.

It was now show time and the sacristan got to it by telling everyone to line up as they had rehearsed. Then a buzzer to the sacristy informed the officiating priest that the bride had arrived and the groom was instructed to walk out from the side room to meet her at the foot of the altar. With the priest properly positioned at the communion rail and the wedding party having completed their procession into the church, another buzzer was pressed and the organist immediately threw himself feverishly into the first notes of the majestic Wagner Bridal Chorus. Almost on cue, everyone turned to the rear of the church and whispered:

"Here she comes!"

* * *

"One down, two to go!"

Tom tensed his lips at the old timer's remark and picked up the glass for a refill. When he returned, he first wiped up the spills and set down a clean cardboard coaster before delivering the fresh beer to his only customer.

"I was in no hurry to see her gone."

"Still, having three daughters is quite a burden."

Sweeney's had just opened and the Sunday rush from the twelve-fifteen mass had not yet arrived. Give it another half hour and there would be standing room only. For now, it was just old Dolan, teetering half-bent on his stool. He always reminded Tommy of Patchwork Teddy. Tom didn't reply to his filial assessment but instead went over to the table Tommy was sitting at to deliver the handful of cashews he got for him out of the nickel vending machine.

"Another soda?"

"Okay. Can I play the shuffleboard?"

A dime was produced from a pocket hidden behind the long white apron his father was wearing and, after starting up the game, he went to the bar to retrieve his soda. Dolan took note of the boy and continued his denunciation of daughters.

"I'll bet you're glad. More room for you in the house."

"She was no burden. She was the best!"

* * *

It was not long after Kathleen got married that Tommy was able to go to the movies alone. "Alone" meaning with a gang of ten to twelve other kids from the Terrace. But it did mean that he didn't have to go with Eileen or her friends any more. This was real independence, but like everything else this freedom had its price. There was a whole new set of group behavior rules to learn. If you understood that going to the movies on a Saturday afternoon was more like a camping trip than going to the movies, you got the idea of the thing. First there was the outfit. You would be sitting and fidgeting and fighting and spilling all sorts of syrupy, sticky stuff on you and your friends so your clothes had to be comfortable and durable and look exactly like everybody else's. The result: dungarees, striped polo shirt, sneakers, and a sweatshirt that would be lost. Next was food. On Saturday they showed two movies, run time about two hours each. You would also stay to see the first movie again, making the whole afternoon a six-hour outing. Very few boys from Naples Terrace could afford to feed themselves exclusively from the fare offered at the vending counter. A hot dog would run twenty-five cents at least. Then there was a soda for a dime and ice cream costing fifteen cents and finally candy which could be anywhere from twenty-five to forty cents, depending on the size. That would mean you would have to have at least a dollar to spend on this nutritionally-challenged junk. Not going to happen. At the most you got fifty cents to cover admission and a box of popcorn, bringing up rule number two: the need for a packed lunch. Peanut butter and jelly on Wonder Bread was the perennial favorite among those piling into the theater, but it was not Tommy's ideal choice. He liked toasted sandwiches, which of course was impractical, so after an initial try of a boiled egg on a roll, which he was made fun of for having and was not allowed to eat in relative peace, he conformed and brought along two peanut butter sandwiches in a brown paper bag, always concealing the mint that his mother had included. Arrangements now all set, Tommy would meet the pals out on the street at noon.

Saturday afternoon at the movies was not only a break for the kids but for their mothers as well, where two, three, and even four siblings could be unloaded at a time, enabling something to finally get done around the house. Also, like a general amnesty, it provided a much-needed respite from the countless violations of good behavior that were carried on continuously by the unruly street mob that was off from school, bored and looking for trouble. Superintendents could relax, the elderly and easily toppled could walk without worry, and local firemen could take a break from the frivolous false alarms sent from corner call boxes. This temporary tranquility would, in a generation, become a permanent silence when the hordes of kids on Naples Terrace disappeared during the great migration of Irish-American families from the Bronx, old Tom and Bridie being among the last to remain.

But in that *Tossin' and Turnin'* summer of 1961, when the movie gang assembled at the high stairs to descend on the RKO Marble Hill, there was plenty of noise and unruly excitement. They were going to see *Spartacus*!

Punching and pushing each other down the steps, they were already disheveled and out of breath by the time they hit the ticket booth, where they continued to feign fighting as they fidgeted in line. However, after squeezing their quarter through the glass slot and grabbing a ticket, their hilarity was quickly doused as they came face to face with their dreaded nemesis in the lobby: the movie matron.

Standing threateningly in a crisp, white uniform, she would continuously slap a large metal flashlight into the palm of her hand to remind everyone of her unchallenged authority. Who she was or where she came from, no one knew. She had no discernible age or ethnicity and couldn't conceivably have had any childhood of her own. Rumors swirled as to her previous line of work and the general consensus among the teenagers was either a prison guard or a Soviet sniper during the war. Endowed with keen eyesight and sharp hearing, she would at first sense some irregular behavior in a theater seat. Then, with leopard-like moves, she would quickly be upon her prey, utilizing her flashlight in a well-disguised left-handed smash that would have made Rod Laver jealous. Sitting next to the victim at this time was bad luck, because if there was to be a second assault you could easily become collateral damage. Once she had her culprit bent over rubbing his head, she would spotlight any companions for face recognition, followed by a quick sweep of the floor with her deadly beam to see what kind of contraband was to be found. Tommy still remembers sitting next to Kevin McCormick when she made her discovery.

"Matches!"

"They're not mine!"

"They better not be. This is the no smoking section."

That was all. She was suddenly called away by the sound of screaming coming from the balcony. The teenagers were at it again. Kevin reached down and retrieved his matches. Setting the seat in front of him on fire was too risky now. He would wait until the second showing when the old battleaxe was getting tired.

Tommy naturally was cautious on entering the lobby because he wasn't sure if she would remember him. A good three weeks had already passed since the fire alarm went off and everybody started running out the emergency exit, but he wasn't taking any chances and hid behind the giant promotional poster of Kirk Douglas until she was distracted. Fortunately, a fight at the concession stand over a dropped hot dog gave him a chance to sneak into the theater and get a seat next to Sonny Boy.

"What do you got to eat?"

"Peanut butter and jelly."

"I'll trade you for a meatball."

Sure enough, when Sonny Boy opened his lunch bag there they were, each one wrapped in excessive layers of tinfoil. A Fabergé egg couldn't have been better protected.

"How do you eat them?"

He took one out and tossed the bag to his sister sitting two seats over in the aisle. This is the first time Tommy saw her. He never knew her name because he never heard Sonny Boy call her anything, at least not in English. They spoke Italian in their house. Tommy liked visiting because it was mysterious and different from the usual Irish households. It was always dark with the shades drawn and votive candles lit under the two shrines in the living room. His grandmother liked Tommy and would always call him over to rub his head and say what a good boy he was. She would then go on to say what a wicked boy Sonny Boy was and recite some recent incident where he was in trouble. Sonny Boy, small, dark, and wiry, was always in trouble, but as much as he would initially protest the charge against him, once it was made irrefutably clear that he was caught, he would soften the imposition of any penalty with an endearing wink and a grin. You liked him in spite of himself.

"Like an apple. Look."

Having carefully unwrapped the meatball, he held it in his hand and took massive bites until it was gone. He then reached over and tried to wipe the sauce from his hands onto his sister's white sweater. Never taking her eyes off the coming attractions, she adroitly dodged him and handed him a cloth napkin that was in another bag next to her. She had several. Tommy got the idea of how the thing worked.

"Okay."

As soon as Tommy handed over his plastic-protected peanut

butter and jelly sandwich, Sonny Boy ordered up another meatball from his sister, like a waiter in a pizzeria. Tommy was expecting a fastball delivery, so he was surprised when she got up and personally handed it to him, along with a sliced roll and a cloth napkin.

"You don't have to eat it out of your hands."

"Thanks."

"I have to stay with him at all times."

"Because of Pollyanna*?"*

"Uh-huh."

Tommy nodded and Sonny Boy told her to get out of the way because she was blocking the screen. He didn't want to hear that all over again. Everyone knew about it anyway. It was almost a year ago, when *Pollyanna* had just hit the theaters. During the first showing, everything was pretty calm except for the occasional lewd remarks being shouted from the balcony by teenage boys. Maybe too calm. Anyway, it was always during the second showing when trouble started. Halfway through the movie, Sonny Boy got a dare and that's all it took. The RKO Marble Hill, originally The Marble Hill Theater, was built for live performances, having a real stage with a set of stairs at each end. The screen was simply hung from the ceiling downstage, but there was plenty of room in front of the screen, on the stage apron. An unavoidable mistake. Because when Reta Shaw went waving that wooden spoon at Jane Wyman for the hundredth time is when Sonny Boy took off, literally. He ran up the staircase, house right, took center stage and pulled down his pants, revealing no underwear. As the movie continued to play on behind him, with not even a frown on the cheerful Pollyanna, Sonny Boy treated the audience to some kind of demonic dance where he spun around wildly and accentuated private body parts. This cheekiness was all that was needed, because pandemonium, always simmering just below the surface at the afternoon movies, was set loose, with yelling by the boys and screaming by the girls and cheering by the teenagers up in the balcony. Sonny Boy was pretty proud of himself by this time when all of a sudden his sister started racing toward the stage, shouting at him. He forgot she was there! Trying to run and pull up his pants at the same time, he fell, repeatedly, ever mindful that his sister was getting closer and closer after scrambling up the same stage steps. She finally caught up to him just as he was at the front fire exit and started beating him with her fists. With the house lights now on and the movie paused, everyone jumped up on their seats to see. And they weren't disappointed because… here she comes! The house matron, looking like she was going to explode. Well, an Italian sister is not going to let just anybody batter her brother, that was for her and her family. So, when she heard her friends yelling "Run!" she did, and hauled Sonny Boy out the fire exit with her. With the door slammed shut in her face the matron had to endure taunts and insults as she marched back to the lobby empty-handed. Soon the movie restarted and everything was back to normal again.

But at home things were just getting started for Sonny Boy because his sister couldn't even get halfway through her report before her mother was grabbing the sauce spoon out of the pot and the chase around the house had begun. Cornered in the bedroom, Sonny Boy rolled the dice and blamed it on the Irish kids. They put him up to it! It worked. and soon the spoon was back in the gravy, but Grandma was still worried. The police might be called and that was something you always had to protect against. So it was decided that the mother and sister would take Sonny Boy back down to the RKO and appeal to the manager. As much as he was against the idea in the house, once in the manager's office Sonny Boy gave a magnificent performance of contrition and humility. The manager, who was known to take a drink or two, said no real harm had been done and was about to forget the whole thing except for the matron insisting that was not good enough. They finally came to the compromise that Sonny Boy would be allowed back into the movie house but had to be chaperoned by his sister at all times. No exceptions.

Tommy gave the sister his mint as a tip for meatball delivery and she just made it back to her seat in time because the coming attractions were over and the house lights went down. *Spartacus* was starting!

The overture was okay for a few minutes but then became a big bore with subsequent screaming from the balcony to get the thing going. Once the action did start, the gang was thrilled by the cruelty and savagery of the opening scenes, especially Kirk Douglas being chained to a rock. Sonny Boy, always stockpiling excuses for future bad behavior, wanted to get his terminology correct. He leaned over to Tommy.

"What's a Thracian?"

Now, Tommy didn't know, but since Sonny Boy kind of looked up to him because he was Irish and they always spoke good English, he didn't want to let him down. He was all set to say a guy who works with rocks when Sonny Boy's sister came to the rescue.

"It's a person who lives in Thrace, a country near Greece."

Sonny Boy, unbelieving, looked at Tommy for verification.

"She's smart."

A compliment! Sonny Boy couldn't understand why but when he looked at his sister all he got was a tongue sticking out at him. It wasn't long after Tommy had finished his meatball sandwich when an orange came his way. He didn't have to ask who sent it.

Well, the movie certainly delivered: gladiators, a guy being drowned in a tub of soup, running wild and robbing stuff, setting fires everywhere, and everybody afraid of you. Everything that makes a great movie. Owing to his tender age, there was naturally some stuff Tommy didn't understand, particularly the Roman guys taking baths all the time. Fortunately, he got clued in by the wise guys shouting up at the screen:

"Watch it, Tony. Olivier has ideas!"

Half time. Movies that had a running time of over three hours would provide an intermission, which everyone knew about beforehand, and you would think their bladders knew about it also. Because as soon as that curtain was lowered, everyone in the movie house realized all at once that they had to go to the toilet. Sonny Boy, waiting for this opportunity, shot out of his seat and quickly got lost in the gathering throng. Frantic by being caught off guard, the sister turned to Tommy.

"He's loose!"

"Is there a reward?"

She quickly reached for one of the paper bags she was guarding next to her seat. When Tommy looked in and saw this collection of tube-shaped fried pastry dough, he was unsure.

"What are they?"

"Cannolis. They're sweet."

"Okay."

Mark Levine was easy to find. He was at the candy counter.

"Gotta find Sonny Boy."

"Who's after him, the matron?"

"No, his sister. There's a reward."

"I don't like meatballs."

"No, not meatballs, she has these other things."

"Cannolis?"

"I think that's what she said."

"I love them!"

Now invigorated, Mark pulled Philip off the popcorn line.

"Sonny Boy broke out and we gotta find him."

"Let's go!"

Billy Whelan was spotted next, and although he was generally unwanted, his physical prowess could be useful and he didn't care who was lost. Anything to eat and he was in. When they got to the gents' toilet there was a line, so Mark went to work, talking just a little too loud.

"I don't feel too good! I think I'm going to be sick!"

Immediately, everyone in the line stepped aside, allowing Mark and the boys to race in. After yelling Sonny Boy's name about and getting no answer, it was Kevin McCormick calmly pointing to an open window that got them to stop shouting.

"He went out there."

Philip, ever suspicious of McCormick, wanted answers.

"He's not tall enough to get up there."

"He gave me a mint and I gave him a boost."

Sure enough, when Tommy looked at the evidence it was his mother's mint. Sonny Boy swiped it off his sister! Philip scrambled up and took a look out the window. His reconnaissance proved troubling.

"There's a ledge."

"Where does it go?"

"To the room where they run the movies."

"Uh-oh!"

Everyone knew the old projectionist and he was three urinals to the right. Sonny Boy was alone in there. The laughter coming from the lobby meant they didn't have much time. When they arrived at the projection room they found Sonny Boy in his element.

"Watch this!"

He had the projector turned on and was using the beam of white light to shadow hand images onto the closed curtain. So far it was just a duck and a chicken but he was still warming up. It was lucky Philip locked the door behind them because through all that pounding you could clearly make out the matron's voice.

"Open that door right this instant."

Without saying a word, Billy Whelan stood below the open window and cupped his hands. They all knew what he meant. He would give them a boost and pull himself up last. He was the strongest. They put Sonny Boy in the middle so he couldn't escape and up and out they went. Mark in the lead was the first to the toilet window and was helped in by Kevin McCormick who had hung around. Next was Philip, then Sonny Boy, then Tommy. They were still waiting for Whelan when Kevin told them to go ahead, he would catch up. As soon as they left, Kevin shut the window and locked it behind him. He stood at the door of the gents' toilet long enough to see the image at the frosted glass frantically pounding to be let in.

Back down in the lobby, Sonny Boy was handed over to his sister who smacked him repeatedly back to his seat. McCormick joined up just in time to see Whelan being hauled down from the projection room into the manager's office by the matron. It didn't look good for him. When asked by Mark what happened, Kevin replied that he waited but Whelan never showed up. They all agreed it was a tough break.

As the posse eagerly petitioned for their cannoli reward, Tommy invited Kevin, but he declined and Tommy knew why. He wanted to see Whelan getting thrown out.

* * *

"It was written by a commie."

Normally, on a Sunday, with Tommy sitting in the side booth sipping his soda, Tom ignored any instigating comment from old Dolan. He knew he only had to hold out for the relieving rush of the church crowd, where the stream of high spirits entering Sweeney's would be too cheerful for Dolan's taste. He would then quickly finish nursing the second of the two glasses of beer he allowed himself and dutifully retrieve the nickel remaining from the quarter he put up on the bar when he arrived. A few years back, when Christmas fell on a Sunday, Tom stood hovering as Dolan went for his change. After a moment's pause he relented and pushed it across the bar.

"Merry Christmas."

Tom thanked him just enough to be short of sarcastic, for Dolan was no fool, but made sure there was a loud clunk as he tossed it into the empty tip glass. Tom reminded the two other barmen who came on duty later that the wet coin at the bottom of the glass, now brimming with fives and tens, belonged to him. It became known as the Dolan Nickel and Tom brought it home that night and threw it into the drawer with his socks and underwear. Every once in a while, Tommy, at the urging of Deidre who said it might have taken root and grown into a quarter or even a half dollar, would take a peek inside the drawer. But so far, every time Tommy pushed aside the one gray sock with the gold toe it was still the Dolan Nickel.

But on this Sunday, Tom could be the disinterested observer because they had a newcomer sitting alongside at the bar. A young man in his twenties and he was up for the challenge.

"You don't know that he was a communist."

Old Dolan had a customer.

"Not only was but probably still is. He wouldn't cooperate, would he?"

"Why should he have? The whole thing was an unjust witch hunt."

"Who says so?"

"Kirk Douglas, for one. He was proud to let everyone know who was the screenwriter."

"Phooey! Actors can't be trusted."

"Can *he* be trusted?"

The newcomer opened his Sunday Edition of the *Journal-American* and pointed to a picture. Like a threatened turtle, Dolan stretched his old neck as far as it would go, took one look, and retreated back to his beer. Tom waited for Dolan's response and when none came went over to investigate. The newcomer smilingly swung the paper around, and once Tom saw the picture, he couldn't resist reading the caption aloud, as to officially declare the winner of the debate. In Sweeney's, there was one man you dare not say anything against.

"It says here, President John F. Kennedy crosses the picket line of the American Legion to attend the movie *Spartacus*. Well, I guess that settles it. The man is no communist."

Tom refilled the empty glass for the newcomer and understood when the young man tilted his head towards old Dolan.

"Will you have another beer on this young gentleman?"

"I will not. And I don't consider communist sympathizers gentlemen."

He took his nickel and slouched off. Tommy made sure he heard the door slam before he came out of the booth. He had started the whole thing by telling his father what movie he had gone to see the day before and was glad now that he could play a game of shuffleboard without being questioned about stuff he didn't understand. Scarecrow and Teddy were glad too because each had been busy boasting as to being the better bowler, but once under way, they immediately threw two gutter bowls apiece and complained to Deidre that it wasn't their fault. It was the machine; the sliding surface needed to be slipperier. Tommy was too busy shaking the canister of powered wax onto the board to noticed the arrival of the newcomer who came over to watch.

"Who are you talking to?"

"Myself."

"Here, I'll show you a trick."

Tommy moved aside, letting the newcomer face the simulated bowling alley. Taking the small, metal-cased hockey puck, he slid it strongly—not straight ahead as you normally would—but off the side of the machine with the resulting ricochet hitting the headpin on the nose.

"A strike! Do it again!"

"Sure."

He did and showed Tommy the exact spot on the side of the machine where the hockey puck would come back off and hit the head pin every time.

"Let me try."

"Sure."

Tommy slid the puck and hit the spot sure enough, but the ricochet wasn't strong enough to knock down all the pins.

"Bed-posts."

"Huh?"

"That's when you got the two corner pins, the 7 and the 10, left standing. It's tricky, but what you do is aim for the 10 and slide it as hard as you can. Try it."

Tommy threw a little more powdered wax onto the board and wound up, releasing a super-fast slide for the corner 10 pin. Both pins flew up simultaneously.

"A spare!"

"That was good. What are you looking for?"

"There should be the same type of spot on the other side too."

"Try it."

Tommy took a visual measurement and hit the spot on the other side but didn't quite get all of the headpin. The result, a 3 and a10 left standing.

"I threw it hard enough but it looked different coming off the spot."

"Interesting, right? Let's first clean up that baby split… and now try it with your left hand."

It was a bit awkward, but Tommy put good muscle behind it and was shocked.

"A strike!"

"You got a whole mathematics course going on here: the law of reflection, congruent triangles, not to mention linear momentum. Have you ever shot pool?"

"No."

"It's all the same principles. The way you figured out the spot on the other side tells me you're a pool shark in the making."

"What's that?"

"A guy who hustles for money. Whoa, look at the time. Gotta run. You know, talking to yourself is a sign that you got a good imagination. If it gets really good you can become a mathematician, thinking about this type of stuff all day long."

"What if your imagination just stays good?"

"Then you become a writer."

* * *

"They got Yankee tickets!"

It was one of the Maddens, an older one at that, so it was probably not only true but important as well. Tommy waited to see what group behavior would ensue from such an announcement before attempting any course of action. This reflexive modus operandi was by now a time-tested approach for physical safety as well as social standing when confronted by any new developments out on the street. Later, he would learn that Jewish grandmothers, drawing on their experiences, would encapsulate this philosophy with a memorable catchphrase, succinct and suitable for a wide range of situations: "Don't ask any questions."

He had been sitting on the sidewalk watching a game of curb ball being played on the corner of Naples Terrace. He was sitting and watching because he was not picked to be on either of the two teams playing. In the choose-up ritual it was determined that his curb ball skills did not rank as high as those who were chosen. There was no documentation of the actual skills they were deciding upon or the ranking system that they used. You just weren't good enough. This of course made it very difficult for you to ever improve, since you had to guess what it was that might sway the jury the next time. If you went as far as asking why you weren't picked it was routinely summed up as: "You suck." Hence, the Jewish grandmothers' advice.

Tommy, however, on this particular warm and muggy day in July, had reconciled himself to this spectator position quite comfortably because he was only eight years old and most of the kids playing were much older. He had no chance competing against them, or so he told Deidre when she asked why he was sitting there. But there were exceptions. Paulie Valletta was picked and he was in the same class in school. Tommy carefully watched to see if he could identify what characteristic he commanded to be one of the chosen. After a few innings it became clear, it was his ability to hit a point on the curb where the ball would automatically go over the third baseman's head and into the garden in left field, resulting in a ground rule double. After his recent experience with the newcomer and the shuffleboard machine in Sweeney's, Tommy concluded that Paulie had identified a spot on the curb where throwing the ball against it would give a known result. He had also seen several others attempt to throw the ball on a different pointed piece of the curb. The results here were interestingly mixed; sometimes the ball could go for a home run or sometimes it became an easy out. It depends, but on what Tommy didn't know. The spot and the effort seemed the same.

Tommy had a good chance to carefully examine the curb at home plate because the field was now empty. On hearing the Madden announcement, all the players went running down the hill toward the big building at the bottom. Tommy stood up to watch which direction they were going.

"Aren't you coming?"

It was Mark who appeared out of nowhere and was in a hurry.

"Paulie likes to play it safe."

"Huh?"

"He'll take his doubles over their maybes."

"They got tickets. Yankee tickets."

"Who?"

"PAL."

"Who?"

"The Police Athletic League. Follow me!"

Mark was on his horse and down the hill like the others. As soon as they turned the corner on Godwin Terrace, Tommy saw where everyone was headed: a disorganized line forming outside the cellar of the big house. Mark explained.

"That's their clubhouse."

"PAL?"

"That's right. They only got so many tickets so we better get on line."

They assembled with the others and finally got into the small room in the back of the cellar that was neatly outfitted as an office for this neighborhood branch of the organization. Tommy let Mark lead the way as they approached a desk with a sturdy off-duty policeman sitting behind it. They were assigned one ticket each and told what day and time to meet the bus for the game. Tommy spelled out his last name for the record book.

"Does your father tend bar in Sweeney's?"

"Yes."

"Be sure to mention that McMillan took good care of you."

"Okay."

Mark and Tommy thanked the cop and got ready to run the gauntlet out of the cellar and past the impatient patrons still waiting in line. Since they had their tickets and these others did not, that meant they would have to avoid the jealous punches and clumsy attempts to trip them that would be punishment for their good fortune. It was a relief to get out on the street where Mark's pent-up excitement could be released.

"Yankee tickets! I can't wait to go!"

Tommy, however, was glad for the wait. His father didn't watch baseball in the house and the only time Tommy saw the games on television was in Sweeney's and that was just for a glance or two up at the black and white screen. Judging from the resulting delirium surrounding the acquisition of these Yankees tickets here was another textbook case where he needed to keep his mouth shut, not to expose any humiliating ignorance. It would be miserable to have to spend the whole time at the game being on guard! So that afternoon, he walked silently up the hill to Naples Terrace and didn't say a word to anyone until he went into the house and showed his mother the ticket and asked:

"What's a twi-nighter?"

She didn't know. Neither did Betty Ann or Eileen. When his

father came home, he remembered someone in the bar saying such a thing and told him it was two games, a doubleheader, beginning early in the evening. It was a start but left him with just a week to learn all about baseball. It was like that episode of *The Honeymooners* where Ralph only had a few days to be a great golfer to play with his boss, Mr. Marshall, at the bus company. Tommy had no Norton to help but at least it was a good time to learn about baseball. Maybe the best time ever. He kept hearing about this Mantle and Maris and some old guy named Babe but didn't know what it all meant. He needed someone to teach him, but who?

"Now, Dee," says he,
"I'm glad to see, you're lookin' so fine and fat.
But all the while he was lookin' at
me old Skellara hat."

It was Deidre. Tommy had just finished his supper and was all alone, scrunched up on the sofa. It took him a while to figure out what Scarecrow was wearing. He finally realized he was an umpire. The chest protector was made out of straw. Teddy was dressed in a pair of old pants and a black striped vest, unbuttoned over a white tee shirt. When Deidre took off her floppy fedora and plopped it on Teddy's head, there was no mistaking Ed Norton. It made Deidre laugh.

"Ready?"

"For what?"

"To learn all about baseball."

"I have no one to learn from."

"What about Mark or Philip or Paulie or Richie or the Maddens? They know everything."

"I don't know what to ask."

"Then we need someone to start from scratch."

"Who?"

"Bob!"

"He's in the navy."

"Oh dear, that is inconvenient!"

"That's what Betty Ann says."

"Betty Ann says what?"

It was Tommy's mother telling him to go wash his hands and comb his hair. Why? Because it was a lovely evening and they would go visiting. On his way to the bathroom he saw the red motorcycle policeman and fished him out of the cardboard toy box. The wheels were all sticky because they hadn't been used in a while. He washed him in the bathtub and ran him around the rim of the tub. Much better. Tommy decided to bring him along in the back pocket of his dungarees and they were just about to leave when his father came rushing through the door in a great mood to see him.

"Just talking again to that young fellow who put old Dolan in his place. He said we need to get a billiards table in Sweeney's. That you'd be cleaning up a fortune in no time."

"A pool shark!"

That was enough for Tommy's mother. She already had to put up with racehorses and bookmakers and crooked card games, she didn't need to hear about any new shenanigans, especially for Tommy. She hustled the father into the kitchen for his supper and told Eileen to reheat the green beans if they were getting cold. Then they were off.

Tommy didn't ask where they were going but when they ascended the steep sidewalk towards Marble Hill he knew: Aunt Betty and Uncle Pat's house. They were always happy to see him and his mother.

"Look who here!"

Uncle Pat ran over to shake Tommy's hand and introduced him to his sister, Kitty, who gave him a big smooch on his cheek. Barely recovered, he was next led over to Aunt Kitty's husband, Uncle Andy, where he received a thunderous clap on the back. Now dizzy, he was told his cousins were at some summer event in the park, leaving him alone with the grownups. Aunt Betty, however, put things to right by setting down a big piece of chocolate cake and a glass of Pepsi at the kitchen table. He would make the best of it while everyone took off to chat away in the living room.

After he had finished his treat, Tommy noticed an edition of *Life* magazine left on the table, with a fascinating photo of Brigitte Bardot on the cover. He had never seen such a magazine and was just starting to look at the pictures when Uncle Andy wandered back into the kitchen.

"Better stick with baseball. It'll get you in less trouble."

"I'm already in trouble with baseball."

"Why is that?"

"I don't know how it works."

"It works just fine."

"You know about baseball?"

"Grew up with Murderers Row."

"What's that?"

"The name they gave to the 1927 Yankees. Maybe the greatest baseball team ever."

"What was so great about them?"

"Well, they won more games than just about any other team and swept the World Series, but it was the Babe's sixty homers that really made it special. Never thought anyone would break that one, but it looks like Mantle or Maris could do it this year. Maybe both!"

There were those names again and Andy seemed to know all

about it. Then it dawned on Tommy. Andy was *American born.* He remembered his father teasing Pat that his sister married an American! He brought out his twi-night ticket and showed Andy who became very excited and happily turned the kitchen into his lecture hall. He explained to Tommy the basic rules of baseball and the differences for a team being up at bat and being on the field. He described each position in detail and the main skills necessary to be good at that position. He talked about qualities like a strong throwing arm, quick feet, and being a heads-up ballplayer. Being able to hit the ball consistently and with power required another set of skills and most ballplayers couldn't play the field and hit equally well. The great ones can. He talked history of the game, recounting spellbinding stories of triumphs, near misses and big goofs—including the guy who came in as a game-tying, pinch runner with two outs in the bottom of the ninth, did five minutes of bending and stretching, took his place on first base and was immediately picked off! When Tommy laughed, Andy knew the kid was catching on.

He concluded with a big finish, the current captivation with the Mantle-Maris home run quest, and showed Tommy how to keep up-to-date by studying the box scores in the *Daily News*. It was a little textbook on the game where he could keep on learning. Finally, he asked:

"Do you really want to understand baseball?"

"Sure, I do."

"Then borrow a mitt and go get yourself a game."

* * *

Tommy spent the rest of the week studying box scores and reading baseball stories from all the evening papers. Being the only professional baseball team remaining in New York, everyone was focused on the Yankees, so Tommy had plenty of material. Every day there was a new picture of either Mantle or Maris on the back page of the newspaper, showing a homer or a strikeout. He was still uncertain as to who he liked better and decided to wait until he saw them live at the game. He even watched part of a game on Saturday afternoon and started to understand some of the stuff Andy talked about. It was there, sitting on the floor his Bronx apartment, with the warm summer sunshine streaming through the window, Tommy, like many immigrant sons before him, became a fan of the great American pastime.

* * *

"There's the bus!"

They were told to assemble on the sidewalk in front of the PAL clubhouse at 3PM, three hours before the start of the first game. Why so early no one knew, but they didn't care because they were going to a Yankee game. Tommy stood at the back of the pack with Mark and Philip, clutching his brown paper bag containing two peanut butter and jelly sandwiches. He was clutching because in the boredom of waiting for the bus there was a lot of grabbing lunches and holding them for ransom and Tommy didn't want any part of that. At 3:30, Officer McMillan and a buddy cop finally showed up and so did the aging yellow school bus. Filing in under the watchful eyes of the officers, they were soon on their way to the big ball park in the Bronx.

But it would be a circuitous route. Not allowed by regulations to take the Major Deegan expressway, their faithful transport was forced to contend with the oppressive heat and traffic of Fordham Road, only obtaining relief when it slipped under the shadows of the elevated subway line on Jerome Avenue. The open windows and slow speed of the bus did allow the boys the opportunity to inform all passersby where they were going and, in return, to receive the enthusiastic wishes of good fortune for them and the Yankees. Sometimes a gentler pace provides unexpected benefits. Once at 161st Street, they joined in a procession of school buses and obediently proceeded to an assigned area in the far parking lot. This was it!

They had to walk all the way around the stadium to the Grandstand entrance and the boys from Kingsbridge were soon confronted by their contemporaries from other parts of the city. After exchanging inane insults, the inevitable fighting was essentially ignored by McMillan, who firmly believed that it was good for the boys to stand up for themselves. Tommy, meanwhile, had sidestepped the skirmishes but started to dawdle, amazed by all the fans rushing this way and that. He was quickly warned by the buddy cop to not to get in the way of the bruisers heading toward the bleachers.

"With them, trouble's never too far behind."

Tommy caught up and followed on through the Group Sales gate, had his ticket split in half by an usher with beer breath, and ran up a bunch of stairs to their assigned section in the upper grandstand overlooking left field. The first thing that struck Tommy as he walked out from the pedestrian tunnel into the sunshine was the playing field. It was so green! Then, to look around and see this huge bathtub with rows and rows and rows of seats all focused on that field. What a feeling it must be to play here!

As soon as the boys sat down everybody went for their sandwiches. They were famished. Tommy had just gotten the plastic wrap off when he saw this big contraption being wheeled onto the field and positioned behind home plate. His baseball confidence was now secure enough to ask Paulie Valletta what were they going to do with that thing. Paulie, eyeing the four Mallomars that Eileen had included in Tommy's lunch bag, wasn't giving away information for free. He stuck his hand out and said, "That's the batting cage, so no one gets hurt with foul balls."

Tommy rewarded him with the rolled-up plastic from his sandwich. Philip and Mark laughed and eventually so did Paulie when he conceded that was a good one. Later, Tommy shared his Mallomars. He got half of a Baby Ruth and a bruised plum in return.

The Chicago White Sox took batting practice first and Tommy didn't know anybody on that team but listened attentively as the older boys yelled out who was in the cage. Tommy was impressed with the way they could hit the ball, several shots going into the lower deck below them. He also had the feeling of being watched by the wise guys waiting for the moment to test how sharp he was with the game of baseball. He expected a subsequent challenge sometime soon, but for now all petty provocations were suspended. The Yankees were coming into the batting cage.

The first one to hit was Bobby Richardson, followed by his infield teammates Kubek, Boyer, and Skowron. Bob Cerv, playing left field that day, didn't take any practice, but just hung around the cage to kibitz with the younger guys. Then there was a few minutes rest for the batting practice pitcher because Elston Howard had a hard time breaking free from signing autographs from the kids down in the box seats. Once at bat, he sent a bunch of pitches to deep left and center field. An impressive display of power for sure but you got the impression that he was just warming up the crowd because even the beer and hot dog vendors rested their buckets up against the railings to watch the next two batters.

They had been in the dugout and came out together. Maris stepped into the cage first, causing a bunch of kids running towards the grandstand in right field. He didn't waste any time, sending the first pitch deep into the seats. Then, the next pitch and the next pitch. He finally hit a pop up and Cerv, still hanging around behind the cage, made some wisecrack. It made Maris laugh and he missed the next pitch completely. The pitcher gave Maris a signal and he responded by hitting the next few pitches to the opposite field. His bat control was something else.

Next Mantle took to the batting cage and Tommy got a shove to his shoulder. It was Mark.

"Better get ready!"

Tommy looked around and saw everyone in his section standing. He didn't know why. Mark gave him another shove.

"He's batting righty!"

Tommy stood up in time to see a ball coming right at him! But, just at the last second, it started to sink and fell into the grandstand section below. Then, holy mackerel, here comes another one! And this one did make it all the way up, setting off a jumble of boys crawling between the seats to capture it. The victor of the scrum held the ball high in the air to show his prize and cautiously let a few pals touch it, but never letting go of it. Tommy was mesmerized.

"Sit down, we can't see."

It was a wise guy yelling at him. When he looked around he saw that nobody was standing any more. Why?

"Sit down, stupid!"

"Okay."

Once down he caught on. Mantle was hitting lefty now and sending balls up into the right field seats, just like Maris!

"Wow, how does he do that?"

"Mantle has more muscles in his neck than you have in your

whole body."

"So does a giraffe, but that doesn't make him a switch hitter."

* * *

They stood for the national anthem and cheered when the Yankees took the field. Whitey Ford was pitching for the Yanks so, according to the know-it-alls in the grandstands, the game was in the bag with Whitey on the mound. The White Sox didn't have a chance. Well, Whitey did cruise along, allowing no runs, but so did the opposing pitcher Frank Baumann. But in the bottom of the fourth inning Bobby Richardson started things off with a base hit. Kubek was unable to advance the runner, but that brought up Maris with just one out. He took a couple of pitches before hitting a rocket to deep right field. Number thirty-seven for the year and now tied with Mantle. The fans cheered as he rounded the bases. Baumann was a lefty so Mantle, who followed Maris in the batting order, was hitting from the right side. He took only one pitch before he hit a shot that looked like it was headed for the moon. It landed for a homer in the upper deck a couple of sections over from Tommy. The place went wild.

"Back-to-back homers."

"And Mickey got back the lead in homers again."

It was Philip, keeping score in his program. Tommy tried to figure out the marking system.

"Who taught you that?"

"My father."

"Do you want Mantle to win the home run race?"

"Sure, everybody does."

* * *

As predicted, Whitey did cruise along giving up no runs over seven innings when Luis Arroyo came in to mop things up. By then the Yanks had a four-zip lead but Maris wasn't finished for the game. When he got to the plate in the bottom of the eight against a Yankee hero of another time, Don Larsen, he sent another rifle shot into the right field stands. Mickey and Roger were tied for the lead again in homers at thirty-eight. Philip wasn't happy and when Tommy looked around it seemed the sentiment was shared by the crowd in the stands. Not wanting any more comments on his lack of muscle development, he kept his mouth shut but would inquire at home with his father. If it had anything to do with gambling, he would know.

The Yankees won handily at five runs to one and during the break between games Tommy got to follow some of the Maddens down to the field boxes and get a real feel of the distances between the bases and how far it was to the outfield. You could also look around and see how really big the stadium was and try to find your seat way up there in left field. The place was buzzing with activity, with autographs being signed and a few of the non-starters on the White Sox playing a game of pepper down near first base. Tommy was watching very closely when suddenly a ball popped over their way and Paulie caught it barehanded. He was about to throw it back when one of the players told him to keep it. A souvenir! Tommy rushed over to see and Paulie let him hold it. It was clean and smooth and didn't have any black electrical tape on it like the baseballs being played with on Naples Terrace. It was the best thing he ever held in his hand.

Back to their seats for the start of the second game. The Yankees got off to a strong start in the second inning with a homer by Clete Boyer to jump to a four-nothing lead. This is when Tommy found out the PAL doesn't stay for the entire second game and would be leaving after the fourth inning. In one way it was just as well for Tommy because he was starting to get hungry again and he had no money left to buy anything. Also, it was after nine o'clock and had no idea when they would get home. Naturally, since he didn't ask anybody, he couldn't tell his mother when they would be back. It was Eileen using her head putting the game on TV to see that they were still playing. She told the mother he would be all right.

They were all set to leave after the Yankees made the last out, when Maris said hold on a minute. Number thirty-nine and the lead in homers. Maybe seeing too much of a good thing can be numbifying because the cheers from the crowd were more subdued this time as he rounded the bases. Tommy thought he even heard some boos from the bleachers. Philip didn't say a word but going home in the bus the driver had an old scratchy radio tuned in to the game. The boys learned that Maris did it again in the sixth inning. He had forty homers on the twenty-fifth day of July, with more than two months to go.

The buddy cop was impressed.

"Wow, four homers in one day."

But the driver, an old Giants fan, reminded him that New York used to have another great home run hitter.

"That's nothing. In April, Willie hit four in *one game*."

* * *

Over that summer, the Yankee home run contest had attained Homeric dimensions, a battle between Achilles and Hector. Mickey's vulnerable spot turned out to be his hip where a flu shot sent him to the hospital in September and out of the race, leaving Roger alone in his pursuit of the unthinkable. Tommy was impressed that Philip, an unwavering fan of Mantle, switched his support to Maris immediately, displaying an allegiance to good sportsmanship that was not shared by all. By the time Maris did break the record on the last day of the season the fun had long ended for him and he would be shamefully shackled to a specious disclaimer in the record books because of the number of games he needed to achieve it. In the end, Maris may have hit more home runs but Mickey ended up being the winner.

TUESDAY 7:30PM

The seven o'clock news had just finished, allowing Bridie the occasion to sneak off into the bedroom to try on her new blouse. New in the sense that it was never worn, but not recently received. Kathleen's daughter had bought it for her at Christmas and, as was the grandmother's custom, she smiled when she saw what it was and then put it back into the box.

"Grandma, don't you want to try it on?"

"It's lovely, thank you very much. I'll try it on a bit later."

Whether it was being afraid of the fit or some other idiosyncrasy no one ever knew, and there was no point in your asking. You just waited to see if she would show up with it on. For some reason this night was picked as a good time to try it on. A test run with old Tom. Of course, he would be clueless as to when she received it or who gave it to her.

"How does this look?"

Old Tom was staring into the television, lost in the Potpourri category on *Jeopardy!* When he realized he was being spoken to, he looked at Bridie and proved he wasn't as heedless as he put on.

"Your pritty face would suit the dish-cloot."

Bridie smiled both for the compliment and the memory.

"That was Gavina talking."

"Your best buddy in old Schrafft's. Whatever happened to her?"

"She married the cook and they took off for somewhere. What about the blouse?"

"Don't need to be wearing so much orange."

Bridie took sight of herself in the full-length hall mirror and agreed that the orange trim on the collar and sleeves wasn't the best for her, although not because of the political connotations the color had for Tom. It just didn't suit her complexion. It would go back in the box and probably given in at the church's clothes closet when enough time had passed.

She changed into her comfortable old blouse and house sweater and took to her moorings on the sofa next to Tom. It was just eight o'clock and she would pick out the next show. Tom was not allowed to change channels without prior approval. She considered the acquisition of the TV one of her most insightful achievements, recognizing its entertainment potential and advocating for its place in the household shortly after Tommy's birth, a time when it was still a source of great controversy. Mrs. Earley, the upstairs neighbour, was particularly strident against it, holding out until the Kennedy inauguration, because it would keep the children from their homework. The television became Bridie's friend and companion during the intervening years—it never talked back to her and she could shut it off whenever she wanted. Naturally, she guarded the programming very carefully.

For her, television was a light and breezy affair: situation comedies, variety shows, and the seasonal specials where near-forgotten celebrities tried to revive their careers. Although the content may have been trivial, the relationship was not, and each offering was approached in a very professional manner. She would give herself honestly to the concept of any show but expected to be rewarded with quality entertainment. Open-minded to talented newcomers, formats and topics, she would not tolerate shows that were heavy on indoctrination or opinion. She had her own on almost every issue. What she wanted was the occasional laugh or smile and maybe forget a headache or two. She often engaged the television as she had formerly used the radio, concurrently reading the newspaper or walking in and out of the room to tend to some matter. She didn't need to be absorbed, just slightly touched.

Old Tom, on the other hand, liked mystery and drama, the same aspects of theater he had employed and enjoyed over much of his lifetime. The first bone of contention provoking Bridie about these melodramas was their program scheduling. They always appeared in the nine o'clock timeslot and would run for two hours. Unlike her variety shows, any disruption in viewing and you could miss the whole point of the thing. This necessitated a conversational blackout while these twisted tales slowly unravelled, often to the bewilderment of Tom, enveloped in some sort of hypnotic trance. Even though he was sitting right beside her, he was no company at all. Then, to make matters worse, every so often he would abruptly re-enter the world of the living room and ask Bridie, "Why would he do such a thing like that?"

Bridie, looking up from the evening edition of *The News* would simply reply, "How would I know? They're in there and I'm out here."

Tom, now trapped in some sort of Beckettian absurdity, would have to decide between resuspending reality and returning to his role as co-protagonist of the show or sitting on the sofa, safely behind the fourth wall effectively reconstructed by Bridie. Inevitably, like a moth to the flame, he would re-join the players and try to get to the bottom of things. Whether successful or not, the closing credits and accompanying music would shake him loose of his reverie where he would turn to Bridie and say, "Wasn't that something!"

No answer.

The second aspect of these nerve-racking tragedies that provided continuing disagreement was the amount of dramatic hysteria that was deemed necessary to convince viewers of the reliability of the storylines. Bridie said she had heard enough crying and screaming in her lifetime and didn't need to hear any more. Tom, understanding that he was undoubtedly included somewhere as the cause of much of that domestic discord, did not dare dispute her claim, otherwise episodes which he had wished long forgotten would be revisited in astonishing detail. No, those types of things are best ignored. Fortunately, these theatrical outbursts during the show did not seem to disturb him at all, and he shook them off like water from a duck. He would not be side-tracked in his quest to understand what was going on. This is not to say that Tom was not affected by emotion on the television. Not at all. Any tale where a dog or a horse was in trouble would be very troubling to him. And, worst of all, a story about some poor child who was disadvantaged in any way. This would be too much for him and he would leave the room for temporary relief. When he returned to resume viewing, he would soon realize that Bridie had changed the channel.

The one exception where all restrictions to Tom's viewing preferences were suspended was the weekly races presented on the local broadcasting station at four-thirty on Saturday afternoons. Consisting of a half-hour program, two races were shown live from New York racetracks. It was not a great sacrifice for Bridie to relinquish the television during this time since she was busy in the kitchen preparing the big meal of the week for the family. That's how it appeared, anyway. The truth was, Bridie enjoyed showing up for the post parade and seeing who was running and picking her own winner. This tradition had been carried on for many years, going back to the time when betting on horses in New York was illegal and Tom was forced to use that infamous enabler of desperate gamblers—the bookie. Like many other moral degenerates, the bookmaker conducted his business just over the city line in Yonkers and Tom would take the thirty-minute bus ride to secure his financial freedom. Since the father was supposed to be spending some time with his son on his afternoons off, the boy would often be brought along on these Runyonesque excursions where his education would be greatly enhanced in the art of deception. The bookmaker operated in plain sight, right on South Broadway in a supposed candy store, but it wasn't. It never had any candy and the few newspapers it had on its racks were days and sometimes weeks old. This intrigued Tommy. How does anything so fake be allowed to get away with it? Tommy would stand off to the side as his father conducted business and often be asked by the stream of customers entering the shop who he liked in a particular race. Tommy would look at the entries and pick out a name. The bettor would thank him and proclaim to no one in particular that kids are always lucky. Tommy didn't feel particularly lucky since there was no chance of getting a piece of candy or ice cream in this place. As much as he enjoyed a make-believe world, he would look forward to returning to the Bronx where there were real candy stores.

But this was Tuesday, an especially enjoyable television night for Bridie and, since she knew the schedule by heart, she had no hesitation in changing the channel for *Happy Days*. It was one of her favorite shows: cheerful, funny, and happy endings. The music also brought back fond memories of the 1950s when her own kids were that age. Normally at this juncture, Tom would retreat to the kitchen to study *The Racing Form* but the bad weather had cancelled all the horse racing for the next couple of days, leaving him with a nagging void. He decided to remain on the sofa and give Bridie's selection a try. It didn't take long for the questions to start.

"Who's that fellow?"

"That's the father."

"The father of who?"

"Richie and the sister."

"They have no mother?"

"Everyone has a mother. She hasn't been shown yet."

That satisfied him until the commercial break, but he picked a tough episode to launch into for the first viewing. It contained his old nemesis, the flashback. He could never keep up with the jumping back in forth in time. When the show resumed it wasn't long before he could no longer contain himself.

"Is that the same person?"

"It is. In the first part he was younger and in the gang."

"What's that they're calling him?"

"That's his name, the Fonz."

"He's a great one for having fun."

"He is. Reminds me of Bob when he first was coming around."

JUNE 1964

For Tommy, there was never a time when Bob was first coming around. He was always around. He was around when Tommy was five years old and sat patiently to have his head inspected with a flashlight after his first crew cut. He was around to give Tommy his first baseball glove, a black four-finger relic that had no padding in the pocket but plenty of wire holding the webbing together. He was again around to show Tommy how to pound the pocket of that glove into shape and how to catch grounders and fly balls. Then, when Tommy was nine, he was around to sign him up to play in the Kingsbridge Little League, and even around to help memorize the Suscipiat to become an altar boy. He was conveniently around to eat all the stuff that Tommy and Eileen didn't like and stayed around to make everyone laugh with his Italian jokes. He was around as far back as Tommy could remember and everybody always liked having him around.

Well, he was going to be around for good now, marring Betty Ann on the sixth of June. A lot had happened in the three plus years since Kathleen got married. She had her own child, a daughter, making Bridie the grandmother and Tom the grandfather. Bob finished up his hitch in the navy and got a job with Big Blue, so he was all set to settle down. Betty Ann worked in an office job downtown and took a few flighty trips with her girlfriends to Caribbean getaways, but essentially stayed Betty Ann, as always. Eileen got taller and went off to St. Simon Stock High School in the Bronx and made a whole new bunch of friends. She got an after-school job at Horn & Hardart at the George Washington Bridge store and would bring home their special raisin cake. She was finally in charge of what she got to eat.

Tommy was still stuck in the system, having two more years to go before being sprung from St. John's. But by now he was hardened to the routine, and even traumatic changes like gender segregation and switching from nuns to brothers really didn't matter all that much. His world was expanding so rapidly that the imposed parochial quarantine could sometimes be okay when things got too overwhelming on the outside. School also gave him the perfect place to fine-tune his chameleon technique—being one type of person in a certain environment, where he would evaluate and assimilate, then changing back into a more familiar persona when conditions allowed. This budding dissociative identity disorder was not to be undertaken by the timid. You had to engage completely. Otherwise, you might mix up impersonation number one, assigned to one set of school chums, with impersonation number two, assigned to another group. And that would appear insincere. All of this elaborate manipulation was thought to be essential in order to learn the dominant life skills of each pack of pals. Tommy wanted to be as well-rounded as possible.

He was almost eleven and a half and still on the skinny side, which was natural enough having added five inches to his height over the last three years. This vertical eruption had dictated two visits a year to Alexander's on the Concourse for a new set of school pants and shirts in sizes which never quite fit correctly. The salesman explained his proportions weren't standard and, at discount prices, it was the best you could get. On the bus ride home, his mother would console him with the prophecy that he would gain weight in the right places as the years went by, reassurance succinctly encased in the stirring aphorism that everything would be better by the time he got married. What this was based on was never revealed but luckily for him it was soon forgotten. It was only school clothes, and he didn't care how he looked there. What he did care about was baseball.

He finally made the majors of the little league in spring after two years playing in the minors, a rather slow development as compared to the other boys on Naples Terrace. Most were in the senior group by ten years old and sometimes nine! It was crucial that Tommy finally made a team by age eleven because it would have been much too embarrassing to try out again at twelve, that being the last year of eligibility. Selected to play for Williams Funeral Home, he got to wear the snappy yellow-and-black uniform of his sponsor. And it fit nicely! His father, however, was always a bit nervous to see the name of the team on the back of Tommy's shirt. He thought someone was trying to tell him something.

Tommy only got limited playing time his first year on Williams but at least he was on a team and was learning how to play by trial and error, the coach having only so much time to devote to teaching each kid. By June he was starting to catch on and got more chances to be in the line-up. He would be ready to have a big year next season, much better than anyone would have anticipated. A late bloomer! A pattern, or some would say a shortcoming, of which there would be many recurrences.

The other big activity where his Alexander's wardrobe was not a worry was being the altar boy. You would only see the cuffs of his pants below the black cassock. He joined up when he was nine and started off as an acolyte, holding a candlestick almost as tall as himself. He held it at funerals and weddings and on Holy Saturday and any other time someone thought it was a good idea to have a candle follow you around. The priest in charge of the altar boys liked him because Tommy figured out early on what worked and what didn't. He liked boys that were quiet and listened closely and Tommy could put that on easy enough. You also had to learn Latin responses to the mass and Tommy had Bob help him through some of the tough parts but he did most of it himself, studying a big card that had the responses all laid out for him.

He had incentive to learn and fit in because there were some big benefits to being an altar boy. There was distinction. You got to wear a special outfit and be up on the altar where everyone could see you. His mother took particular pride in carefully washing and ironing his gleaming white surplice and then showing him how to fold it and carry it across his arm without wrinkling. She also made sure his shoes were lacquered bright black with a liquid polish that she applied herself, garnering compliments from the priests themselves as to their brilliance. She always attended the services when he was up on the altar and, although she would never boast of his participation, she nevertheless would smile and nod at any compliments the neighbors might send her way on the appearance of her son. Tommy, idealistically protective of his mother, was happy that he was doing something that made her feel important. He had heard stories in the past where his mother's domestic skills were unfairly criticized by neighbors and, developing his own version of the Irish grudge, wanted to exact revenge. He would endure the weight of that candle to redeem her reputation.

Ambitious, Tommy quickly expanded his serving skills and ascended the ladder of liturgical prominence: candle carrier, cross-bearer, mass server, funeral server, and finally the big number, wedding server. Like any occupation requiring child labor there was some unpleasantness along the way. A particularly stifling service duty involved formal ceremonial blessings using a contraption called a thurifer which contained burning incense. An altar boy was assigned to hold the thurifer until the priest was ready to use it and then got it back to hold again after he was finished. With the amount of smoke pouring out of this thing if the kid had a canary on his shoulder it would have died. But you just had to put up with it until you got to dump the remains in a can outside the vestry door. Fortunately COPD was not known at the time, so there were no long-range ill effects to be concerned about. Other trifling burdens included getting up in the dark of night to serve 6AM mass, putting up with pretentious deacons who couldn't sing, and shutting up when the priest asked what was so funny, which was half the time waiting around in the sacristy. But the worst for Tommy was to serve at a funeral mass with nobody in the front benches to send him off. Who was this guy? Didn't anybody know him? Making matters more miserable was the haunting appearance of the bereavement woman—a stand-in griever! Lurking like a raven in the last pew of the church, she had somehow gotten word that there was a wretched soul with no friends or relations, and so she would duly attend. Did she look forward to the call? She always had the same drab outfit ready to go and Tommy would avoid her stare as he accompanied the casket down the main aisle to the church door always wondering, who would come to *her* funeral? The only silver lining was she received some sort of stipend for showing up. Tommy thought it might not be a bad gig when you got old.

Getting paid was a big part of things now for Tommy, and serving as the altar boy presented a perfect opportunity where he could earn his own money. Having money was important, he understood that from the conversations he would hear in the home, but recently it came to represent much more. It first changed his concept of time. He was always half hungry and having money meant he could go to Moe's candy store for a malted milkshake or for a slice a pizza at Sam's any time he wanted and didn't have to conform to mandated eating schedules. When he was younger, asking for the dime or quarter he needed was something that had no thought or energy behind it. But now he regarded this constraint as a tenacious leash tugging him back to the original half-circle of his front steps. The world was too big and he wouldn't go back. He liked to have his own options without anyone knowing or possibly interfering. Of course, having this new-found pocket money was welcomed by Tom and Bridie and looked upon as Tommy assuming some responsibility. But it was much more. It was independence and once tasted it would grow into a measure and a means of self-assessment.

Dovetailing with this new fascination for financial freedom was another awareness, so unexpected that if you told Tommy that being an altar boy would open up the world of social mobility he wouldn't know or care what you were talking about. But slowly he understood. Listening to the priests and monsignors and even the bishops when they visited, he learned there were famous schools you could attend and languages you could learn and books you could read and places you could visit and that all these exciting adventures were available to him. And when he was in the rectory, he saw fancy receptions and extravagant meals and a big dining room and people that cook and clean and answer the phone, and he understood that all these luxuries went along with an important profession where people looked up to you and treated you differently. Here were possibilities that were not spoken of anywhere: not in school, not at home, and not ever out in the street. And it created an uneasiness, a Promethean urge which should have been explored but which he kept to himself, and this entombment led to many false starts and disappointments.

* * *

"Hupp, hupp my little horse,
Hupp, hupp, again.
How many miles to Dub-l-in?
Three score and ten.
Will we be there by candle-light?
Yes, and back again.
Hupp, hupp my little horse,
Hupp, hupp, again."

Tommy was in the midst of a no-hitter when Deidre showed up. He had set up the bedroom to be his little league field with a pillow against the wall as home plate and the pitcher's mound just behind the second of the three beds in the room. He used a real baseball to throw into the pillow, and even though the full force was softened, it left marks on the wall. He never worried that his mother would complain because he somehow knew that when he went into the bedroom and shut the door to play she instinctively recognized it was important to him and left him alone. His father could repair the wall before it was painted the next time.

"Whatcha doing?"

"Working on my fast ball. Wanna see?"

Tommy reared back and threw the ball as hard as he could right into the center of the pillow. That one was going to leave a mark for sure.

"That was very fast!"

"Sure, I just struck out the sides. Where's Scarecrow and Teddy?"

"Oh, they're tired of baseball and stayed home to play funeral. What happened to your bicycle?"

"Nothing. It's in the cellar, locked up."

"Not that one. I mean your magical bicycle. The one that we would ride at night when the lights were out. We went to so many wonderful places."

"That was the chair that kept me from falling out of the bed. I don't have that anymore."

"I loved it."

"Da got me a used one. Not the one I wanted, but it's still okay."

Deidre looked around and saw the fanciful baseball field and the faux altar Tommy had set up on the dresser so he could visualize being the altar boy and practice his responses. He would imagine himself successful in both activities just like he imagined an actual bicycle to appear. She was happy for him, of course, but also a little sad knowing that between the make-believe and the reality falls the shadow.

* * *

Bridie got one look at the pants Tom had on and told him to change into the newer pair she had just brought in from the dry cleaners. Although she was told Bob's parents were not the fussy type, she didn't want him looking like a ragman at the rehearsal dinner. And there was no sense in saving the good pants. They may not fit him in another year or so anyway. The belly was getting bigger.

She had been looking through some old snapshots, taking advantage of the strong evening sunlight coming through the thin curtains of the living room. It was a habit from her mother. You would somehow see things you might miss if not looked at by the window. Betty Ann's wedding was now just two days off and she asked the mother to bring some photos of her as a kid so they could all have fun passing them around. Bob's mother was going to do the same. Bridie didn't understand when Bob said it was an "icebreaker" for the families. Wasn't having the dinner together enough? Anyway, it probably wasn't a good idea to go through them right before they were to be picked up in Billy's car for the journey up to Tuckahoe, New York. They got her thinking.

The first one showed Bridie and Tom standing in front of the small house in Yonkers that they shared with another couple for the first couple of years after getting married. Didn't everyone look so young! Kathleen was in the carriage and Betty Ann was on the way. It was a pleasant little cottage in a quiet neighborhood, but it was getting too cramped and too inconvenient for Tom to get to work at the A&P down in the Bronx. The War had just started and good apartments were very scarce, but by luck they were told of a nice one-bedroom on Naples Terrace in the Kingsbridge area, a classy section with good subway and bus service. After the move, they found many young Irish couples like themselves just starting their families, with the local bars and church providing all the necessary gossip required to adjust to the new neighborhood. The big topic, of course, was the War and how long it might go on for. The consensus was once Uncle Sam got involved, the thing would be over in no time—an optimistic opinion consoling young mothers with husbands in the prime draft age. By September of

1942 Betty Ann had arrived and the next picture showed them standing in front of the church after the baptism with sister Betty and her husband Pat; the big fedoras and long dresses looking so much out of style compared to the current fashion of no hats at all for the men and the girls wearing the short skirts.

"Are these the ones you mean?"

It was Tom modeling a pair of trousers he could hardly button.

"Where did you get them?"

"In the bedroom closet."

"Why would you go there looking for pants? The ones I just brought back from the cleaners are right here in the hall closet."

Without further comment, Tom quickly identified the correct pair by the plastic wrapping and took off again for the bedroom, letting Bridie resume her ice-breaking inventory. With a slight nod of the head, she put the one of the christening into the small white envelope she had available for safe transport. It would be good to let the new relations know they had value on the church.

Many of the snaps had both Kathleen and Betty Ann in the picture, reminding Bridie how she used to get them fed, dressed and taken out together for their afternoon outings. Betty Ann was now in the carriage with Kathleen walking beside and they would go down to Play Street and other areas of the neighborhood that were still semi-rural and wouldn't be developed until after the war. Predictably, there were none of the whole family, Tom never wanting to be in the picture himself and Bridie being the only one who knew how to work the old Brownie camera. She settled on the picture of Betty Ann on her first day off to school.

"Those years flew by."

Tom had re-emerged from the bedroom wearing the

presumed correct trousers. He was impressed by the sharp creases defining the pants legs. He hadn't seen them in a while. He was now ready for further instructions.

"Will I be bothering with a collar and tie?"

"I'd be expecting Bob's father to have one on."

Although such a comment could be subject to a number of responses, Tom played it safe and went straight for the white shirt. Once neatly tucked in and properly belted he asked Bridie for her opinion of a tie. She scrutinized the tie rack on the inside of the metal coat cabinet in the living room and picked out a nice blue one. It would go with her dress. He made the knot correctly but had trouble getting the collar over the tie in the back. Bridie was still folding it over when he asked, "What years were those?"

"When we were first married."

Bridie handed him the school picture of Betty Ann and saw his eyes getting red. She would worry about him at the dinner.

* * *

There were no pancakes on Friday mornings any more. At least not made by the short order cook—Tommy's father. He had a different job where he went into work in the afternoons and had to rest beforehand. It was just one of the many things that were different since the last sister got married.

There were two big blows to the Irish households of Kingsbridge during those intervening years. The first one had immediate local ramifications. Sweeney, the owner of the eponymous tavern, had a heart attack and died on a hot summer night in August of 1961. Tommy and Eileen had just run down the elevated subway stairs on their way back from another sunburnt visit to the relatives in Rockaway when they saw the ambulance in front of Sweeney's. They immediately froze, instinctively knowing the calamitous nature of the event and waiting for the parents to catch up. Tom, seeing his friend being placed into the ambulance, was quite shaken and it wasn't too long after the man was buried that the bar was sold and Tom would no longer be the most popular bartender in the neighborhood. This was on the heels of having to move on from driving the bread delivery truck. He had had an accident and it was suggested that it might be best to take a rest until he got back his confidence. Being at a bad age to start a new career he took a temporary position as a doorman in a swanky Riverdale apartment building. It would do for the time being.

The other big shock to the Irish-American community was the assassination of President Kennedy. It had only been a little more than six months since the tragedy and many people were just coming to realize how permanent the change would be. They would no longer have their lovely young and handsome president to look up to. The picture of him that hung in all the homes afterwards had deep meaning to the people who lost more than a popular politician. He was the embodiment of something finer, loftier, an inspiration to those who struggled, held to a disadvantage, first in their home country and then in America. And even after achieving his greatest triumph, he remained a companion to those still on the path, still striving, offering hope and encouragement and holding dear the values of compassion and understanding. Qualities that immigrant families desired for their own children. Many years later, when generosity and self-sacrifice were in full decline and the faded picture had become the butt of jokes for stale comedians, it would be impossible to understand any attachment to an ideal that did not promote self-seeking and opportunism. They took down JFK and put up Gordon Gekko.

So, on the Friday morning before Betty Ann's wedding, with all the skillets in the kitchen lying idle, Tommy shared toast and tea with Eileen and took off for the street. Or at least as far as the front door.

"Go get Mrs. Gins."

That was odd. It was his mother's voice but it was Betty Ann hovering over her as she sat frozen on a hard-backed chair placed by the windows in the living room. Tommy investigated and immediately noticed that his mother's head was tilted as far back as it could go. She also had her eyes closed. Like the child who thinks everyone disappears when they close their eyes, Betty Ann and Tommy acted like the mother wasn't there because she had her eyes closed.

"What's the matter with her?"

"She has something in her eye."

"What?"

"She thinks it's an eyelash."

"Did you try to get it out?"

"Of course, that's why I have her sitting near the window where the light is better, but I couldn't find it."

"Maybe it's not an eyelash but a piece of glass?"

"She's afraid if she doesn't get it out soon, her eye will be all red at the wedding."

"It'll look like she's crying."

"Luckily the pictures are in black and white!"

"Billy is taking the pictures?"

"No, we have a professional photographer. He'll be here early tomorrow before church."

Tommy was thinking about what kind of stuff the photographer will have with him when he noticed Bridie's head rotating back to its normal axis and the one good eye opening.

"Go get Mrs. Gins."

"Okay."

Tommy stood at the door of the apartment catty-corner to his on the same floor and waited. He had rang the bell twice and could hear movement inside but no action. Finally, the husband, known functionally as Mr. Gins, answered the door.

"Hello, young man. How can I help you?"

"My mother has something in her eye."

"Oy! You would want my wife, maybe?"

"Yes, please, she was requested."

The old man smiled at the boy's formality and, just as formally, invited him into their home and had him wait in their dimly-lit foyer. He would find her. Tommy edged in a little to get a peek at the kitchen which was small and looked out onto the courtyard. Their whole apartment was small, not much bigger than a studio but with three separate rooms. Speaking of size, Mr. Gins had disappeared now for several minutes with no Mrs. Gins. Just how many places were there to hide? Finally, a shout.

"I found her!"

She was as round as she was tall and came bounding into the dimness in a festive print housecoat and fuzzy white slippers. It was impossible to tell how old she was and Tommy often heard his mother say that she looked the same as the day she first saw her—over twenty years ago. They were the last of their breed, never wanting to move away like their Jewish friends and neighbors and would foreshadow Tom and Bridie's holding out as the last of the Irish on Naples Terrace. "Why should we move? We raised a family here," was the response Mrs. Gins gave to anyone who questioned their decision, and the sentimentality of the statement may have resonated with Bridie more than she ever knew or let on.

What the husband did for a living, nobody had a clue. When

he was younger, he left the house every morning around nine o'clock and came home every evening around six-thirty. Probably had a small shop somewhere. What was important was the man minded his own business, never had the smell of drink on him, and there was no loud yelling coming from their apartment. That was enough to know. And yes, he always tipped his hat when he said hello to Bridie and the daughters.

Mrs. Gins cupped Tommy's face in her hands and gave him a kiss on each check. She had two daughters and so a young boy was always a bit of a novelty to her, and she would enjoy seeing Tommy running in and out of the building. When his embarrassment from the display of affection had subsided she got down to business.

"So, your mother has something in her eye?"

"Yes."

"Maybe a sadness from one of her daughters getting married tomorrow?"

It was Mr. Gins from the kitchen. He was boiling an egg in a small saucepan. His wife had finished putting on a raincoat to make herself presentable for the journey across the hall when she stooped down to pick up her little black bag and said to Tommy:

"Let us go see."

"Ma, Mrs. Gins is here to look at your eye!"

He was about a foot away from her head and made her twitch with his announcement. She was in the same chair with her head still tilted back but now Eileen was the one hovering over her. Betty Ann got a phone call and needed a replacement. His mother regained her composure and excused herself for not getting up and for being such a bother. Mrs. Gins said it was no bother and don't even think like that. She was a neighbor. Tommy could hear the aspect of duty clearly implied in her pronouncement and smiled at Eileen. They were important. She got right to work opening her little black bag and took out a Q-tip and a cotton wipe. Gently rolling Bridie's eyelid back with the Q-tip, she announced she could see it and just touched the tip of the cotton wipe to her eye. Done! Tommy leaned over to see what it was and announced an eyelash. Mrs. Gins proceeded to put some drops in each eye and Eileen helped her mother over to the sofa to be more comfortable. When Bridie recovered, she thanked Mrs. Gins and asked if she would like a cup of tea. The woman was very happy for the offer but said she needed to get back home or her husband wouldn't know where to find the salt. Both women laughed and Tommy, being the young gentleman, escorted her back to her apartment door. But it was more curiosity than courtesy.

"Did you see any sadness?"

"Not a bit."

* * *

Tommy's quest to make it out onto the street was foiled again; because just as he turned from Mrs. Gins's door to take off down the hallway steps, he heard the voice of his upstairs neighbor.

"Just the lad I need!"

It was Mr. Moran, a small, wiry Irishman who, without so much as taking a deep breath, habitually raced all the way up to his top-floor apartment, earning him the nickname Three-Steps-at-a-Time Jerry. Always cheerful to Tommy, he was generous as well, once giving him an old retractable fishing pole which Tommy put to immediate use by catching an eel down at the Harlem River and proudly bringing it back home to show the mother. Eels were good eating to many people but Bridie, not in any way denigrating the boy's accomplishment, somehow got rid of it and never mentioned it again. So Tommy wondered what was up as he followed Mr. Moran into the apartment, the door being held open by Eileen, looking worried.

His father started vividly explaining to Jerry that the television was getting a lot of interference, making the viewing of some programs very difficult, most notably the Saturday afternoon races. Why this task had to be undertaken the day before Betty Ann's wedding, no one asked. Mr. Moran got right to it and after flicking through a few TV channels determined that the root cause of the problem was the improper positioning of the antenna on the roof. It would have to be adjusted, but first they needed position tracking. With so many antennas on the roof and the connecting aerials running helter-skelter down the sides of the building, it was impossible to tell from up there which one belonged to which television. Moran, always a step ahead, had devised his own tracking system and after disappearing briefly, he returned with the kitchen broom and stuck the business end out the living room window. Now he could identify their apartment and the connecting aerial by the window with the broom sticking out of it. Brilliant! But it was still a two-man job up on the roof and that's where Tommy would come in.

True to his moniker, up he went three steps at a time with Tommy following closely behind. When the heavy metal door to the roof swung open a beautiful June day was revealed, with plenty of sunshine and a nice cool breeze. Tommy noticed right away the pigeons circling above and knew they were from the coop across the street. Their number had been reduced over the last few years with Elgin having gone into the navy and his brother being in charge. He would go over later and check on things. He hadn't been there in a while.

"Tommy, see what you make out of that."

Mr. Moran stood next to a TV antenna and was shaking the connecting aerial wire. He wanted Tommy to see if it was the one going into his apartment. It was a lucky thing Tommy had some height for his age because he was able to lean over the edge of the roof without his feet leaving the ground. Yes, he could see the broom clearly enough and the aerial running into the apartment but no shaking going on.

"Uh-uh."

"Well, we'll move on to another suspect. How about this one?"

Tommy leaned over and saw this time it was the aerial going into the apartment next to them. They were getting closer.

"Kay Mitchell's apartment."

"Ah! Then this one should be yours."

And he was right. Tommy could see the aerial dancing outside their window and going into their apartment. Tommy was about to announce their success when he suddenly saw Betty Ann's head popping out from the window and smiling up at him. He smiled back but then turned away. She was making him nervous. He instead walked over to Mr. Moran.

"That's it."

"Grand. Take a look at your antenna then and tell me what's the trouble."

Tommy looked at the long aluminum pole and the array of prongs reaching out across the top. It looked like all the other antennas on the roof. Except…

"It's facing a different way."

"That's the lad! Whoever installed this on the roof has it going the wrong way. It should be facing south—that way."

He waved his flat hand up and down like he was giving a karate chop. He waved it in the direction of the Harlem River and Manhattan. Tommy knew what was coming next.

"Why should it point that way?"

Tommy looked up at the sky and saw his friends flying. They all flew together in the same direction. If they didn't, they would bump into each other. The direction didn't matter as long as they were together. The lead bird made the decision.

"Somebody said so?"

"They very well did say so. They put the television transmitter on top of the Empire State Building and that's south from here. You should always point your antenna towards the transmitter to cut down on the interference."

"Snow, that's what Paulie calls it."

"Right, and now you can tell him what causes it."

Tommy was pleased to have this practical knowledge that he could broker at an opportune time. He watched as Mr. Moran twisted their antenna towards the transmitting tower. He then pulled a screwdriver out of his pocket and tightened the connection to the roof. All they needed to do now was test it. Tommy could have run down the five flights of stairs into the apartment, seen the result, and ran back up but he had a shortcut in mind.

"Ma!"

He yelled down a few times, alarming passers-by on the sidewalk below, until finally she stuck her head out the window.

"What is it?"

"Try the TV."

While they waited, Mr. Moran showed Tommy his neat jackknife that he had in his other pocket. He always kept it very sharp and brought it along in case he had to cut any aerial wire. Tommy was still examining the handle when he heard his name being called and leaned over the edge of the roof.

"Yeah?"

"It's a lovely picture."

"Okay."

Tommy went back and reported the good news to Mr. Moran, who smiled and said nothing. On the way downstairs, he stopped on the top floor outside his own apartment to say good-bye to Tommy.

"You were a grand help. Now your father can watch the races!"

"Most of the time he can't stand to see the finish."

* * *

Her voice reverberating in the hallway was something to hear, and as soon as Tommy came through the front door of the building she gave him a big wink and waved him over to get a seat on the outside steps. She had a good crowd—especially for a Friday, Saturday being her normal schedule—with most of the windows facing the courtyard open and plenty of heads bobbing and smiling. She was just finishing up sweet-talking that ol' rascal *Bill Bailey* to get back home when she paused long enough to give Benny McGuire a chance to yell down:

"One more time!"

And she hit it again to a rousing finale. It was by now a practiced routine and everyone let out a cheer. She took a quick bow and went right into *Aggravatin' Papa*, Mandy Brown's promise of violence for her philandering boyfriend. This number was particularly satisfying to the women looking out and they showed their appreciation by starting the first wave of contributions. Tommy was on alert.

They came down in little bundles, wrapped neatly in a tissue. Some had a quarter, some a nickel or a dime, and, once in a while, there would be a half dollar. The audience would gently toss them from their window seat and most of the time they would land fairly evenly distributed across the courtyard. Tommy would gather them up for her and drop them into the big black pocketbook that she carried and left open for him. Tommy put them in as they were and never opened them but could generally feel the amount through the tissue. Once he was collecting and came across a lumpy one that felt funny. He unwrapped it and saw it had a peach pit. He hid it in his pocket. On leaving that afternoon she surprised Tommy by asking what was it. He didn't think she noticed. When told, she laughed and said that was nothing. Sometimes they spit in it. She saw the effect and quickly added:

"Not your people."

She was still gently patting the perspiration from her face when she saw Tommy had finished collecting and immediately got rolling with an upbeat version of *St. Louis Blues*. Then, keeping up her syncopated clapping, she seamlessly moved right into *The Hucklebuck*, really swinging now and showing some fancy footwork to go along with a serious sashay. Her signature closing number was *Sweet Georgia Brown* and this would give anyone who had not yet donated a final chance. When finished, she raised her arms, thanked all and moved on to the courtyard of the building across the street. Tommy did not follow, giving another kid a chance to collect for her. Maybe that was the reason, maybe not; because as much as he enjoyed the show there was something a little sad about it, too, and one performance was enough. During the summer months her little revue had been good business with all the windows being open, but she was no youngster and the number of consecutive courtyards was being reduced every year. Worse still, the dreaded air conditioner was cutting her off from her audience. People had their windows shut and you couldn't hear her sing over the hum of the machine.

As Tommy watched the singing lady waddle down the courtyard steps, he felt a tap on his shoulder. It was Eileen holding an umbrella.

"The spokes are bent."

She opened it slightly to show that it was true enough. It had seen some rough weather.

"Is it going into the garbage?"

"No, mom saw the umbrella man on the corner and said we should get it fixed. In case we need it tomorrow. We would look stupid all dressed up with a broken umbrella."

She handed Tommy a quarter.

"What's this for?"

"That's what he charges."

"Okay."

"Thanks!"

She smiled and headed back into the apartment. He didn't mind. The umbrella guy had some cool stuff, all meticulously arranged on the small wagon he rolled through the neighborhoods. When Tommy walked up to the corner where the man had set up shop, he already had a customer. It was Kevin McCormick with a large knife.

"I found it in Van Cortlandt Park!"

He let Tommy get the feel of it. It was a hunting knife with a wooden handle and a six-inch blade that had a smooth indentation running back from the point. It was rusty for sure but the blade wasn't chipped or bent. The handle was in good shape, too. The umbrella man was all set to go now and took the knife from Kevin. He first put some greasy stuff on the blade and let it set for a couple of minutes. Then he vigorously rubbed it off with a rough cloth. The rust was gone! He had a foot-powered grinding wheel and once it got going, he turned the blade this way and that on the wheel to sharpen the edge. He tested it blade a few times between two moistened fingers until he was satisfied. He held up a piece of note paper and showed how, without any pressure, it sliced right through. That was sharp.

He was going to condition the wooden handle, too, when Tommy noticed Kevin acting funny, kinda all fidgety and nervous. Sure enough he took off, just like that, and ran down Naples Terrace and cut through the alley behind the green gate, the alley that led back to the cellar of Tommy's building. It didn't take Tommy long to figure out what was going on. It was Kevin's father in his best undershirt down on the street looking for him. He had done something again and it couldn't even wait until he got home. Tommy met the father's stare and was ready to respond that he hadn't seen him but was never asked. The father seemed too enraged for words. He soon moved off and went back into their building. Tommy would report the sighting to Kevin when he showed back up.

But he didn't show and the umbrella man was finished refurbishing the wooden handle with some oil. It looked beautiful. He placed the knife in a small drawer and took the umbrella from Tommy. He must have seen a lot of them, and probably much worse, because without any comment he removed the bent spokes one at a time and straightened them on a vice-like device he had connected to the side of his wagon. When he was done they were as straight as a bull rush, the father's old expression from Ireland. He reassembled the spokes back on the umbrella and stitched the connections where needed. He held the umbrella in his hand and told Tommy the fee.

"Ten bits."

Tommy was a bit confused. He held out his quarter in the

palm of his hand. The umbrella man took that and handed him the umbrella. Tommy asked about the knife.

"That's the other eight bits—one dollar."

"I don't have a dollar."

The umbrella man took the knife out of the drawer and felt the blade between his fingers.

"That's a shame. It's a fine knife. Guess that means it's mine."

Another gent had arrived and presented a sorry-looking umbrella with loose fabric hanging from the spokes. The umbrella man got right to work on it and when Tommy asked again about the knife he was told to shove off.

"But it's not your knife. You should give some sort of ticket so Kevin can get it back."

"Beat it, kid."

"What's the problem?"

She got fierce stares from both men but it was the umbrella man who spoke.

"None of your business."

"Maybe it is, maybe it ain't. Tommy, what you got to say?"

"He has my friend's knife and won't give it back unless I pay. But I don't have the money."

The singing lady turned to the umbrella man.

"How much?"

"One dollar."

She turned her back and went hunting through her big pocketbook. After a minute she turned back and handed him a bunch of coins.

"There's your dollar. Count it if you want, my arithmetic is good."

The umbrella man was stuck. She had a witness, the other customer. He threw the coins into the drawer and slapped the knife into her hand, coming very close to cutting her with the sharp blade. The singing lady took the handle and held the blade upwards, between her and the umbrella man.

"Could do a right job of cutting with a knife like this. Always best to be careful."

She handed the knife to Tommy and started off down Naples Terrace. She would make the big building at the foot of the hill her last stop. Her feet were tired.

* * *

Tommy was on his way to the roof across the street, the roof with the pigeon coops. But first, he dropped off his umbrella, said hi to Bob who had stopped by and evaded Mrs. Hyde who always badgered him about associating with juvenile delinquents like Kevin McCormack because that's what the communists would want him to do. Speaking of Kevin, he showed up in the vestibule of the pigeon building, sneaking out from under the stairwell.

"Do you have the knife?"

Tommy took the knife out from his back pocket and unwrapped it. Since there was no leather holder, Tommy had cradled it in three sheets of aluminum foil to allow him to carry it around in his pants. He was careful not to let anyone in the house see him or it would start a chain of unnecessary questions, like: What do you need the tinfoil for? Then: Where did you get that knife? And on and on. Best to keep things like a hunting knife secret.

Tommy showed the knife to Kevin and he was impressed by the transformation.

"It looks brand new! Give it here."

When Kevin went to reach, Tommy snapped it back, making

him grab air. Tommy then slipped it underneath his belt, right over his hip. Something Jim Bowie would do. Kevin wasn't liking this at all.

"Hey, what's the big idea?"

"Aren't you forgetting something?"

"What?"

"The buck fifty it cost to get it sharpened and cleaned up."

Tommy added his own vig to the bill, something he learned from going to the bookmaker with his father. Kevin stared and scratched his head.

"Wow, that was a lot, but I'll pay you."

"When?"

"Now."

"Cash money."

He didn't answer but crept back under the stairs, sat down, and took off his Keds, black canvas Hi-Tops. Tommy looked on and saw that Kevin had made an undetectable slice along the inside of each sneaker, creating a little pocket. He put his pinkie in the pocket and took out a dollar bill neatly folded to the size of an airmail postage stamp. The other sneaker's pocket held the coins and from here he extracted two quarters. He handed the money to Tommy and got to tying up his sneakers again. When he stood up Tommy handed him the knife. Kevin gathered up the discarded tinfoil and rewrapped it to put into his back pocket. When they went out into the building lobby Kevin got nosy.

"How come you had so much money on you?"

"I didn't."

"Then how did you pay for it?"

"I didn't, but I'll pay her back when I see her."

"Who?"

"The singing lady."

"She paid!"

"She took the money out of her tips."

"Tips? You mean those tissues that people throw down at her?"

"I pick them up when she's at our courtyard… what's the matter?"

"I didn't think anyone really gave her money. I wrapped up a peach pit once and threw it out the window."

Kevin started making strange faces and mumbling to himself. Although the impulse was to punch him in stomach, Tommy refrained and gave him time to rearrange the things that went on in his head. But once he returned, he wasn't thinking about peach pits anymore. He had a bigger problem.

"My father is after me."

"Why?"

"It's the knife, it belongs to my uncle."

"You stole it!"

"Kinda. He lives alone on Heath Avenue. We went there yesterday. He has a lot of neat stuff from the army. He shot a lot of people!"

"He should've shot you for stealing."

"Ha! No, when he was in Germany in the war. He showed me these neat pistols that he took off dead soldiers. Lugers. They weren't supposed to keep them but he snuck them back."

Tommy was pondering this kleptomaniacal tendency in the male members of the McCormick clan when suddenly a prohibited but irresistible possibility took command of his mind.

"Did you take a gun?"

"I tried, but my father was watching. Later they went into the kitchen to drink and I was able to sneak out an old knife that was in the box with his souvenirs. I didn't think my uncle would notice."

"What happened?"

"When I was leaving the house today I heard the phone ring. That's never good. When I saw my father down on the street I figured it was my uncle who called."

They both got quickly quiet as an old lady, Rosalind's grandmother, struggled at the front door of the building with an armload of groceries. Kevin immediately ran over, opened the door, and relieved her of the packages. He disappeared for a few minutes, having escorted her to her apartment. When he returned Tommy asked if he got any money for helping.

"I wouldn't take any money from her. She's old. What am I gonna do?"

"Go home and show your father the knife."

"You're crazy! Then he'll know I took it."

"Why did you take it?"

"What do you mean why?"

"You took it to sharpen it and make it look new to surprise your uncle."

"I did?"

"He's always been nice to you and you wanted to do something nice for him."

Kevin's face was working overtime again but this time he came out of it with a smile.

"I'll go down to the card store and get a nice box and have them wrap it all up."

"Your father can't be mad when he sees that. You're covered."

He ran off to get his gift box from Green's card shop. Tommy laughed. He wouldn't be able to steal it and have them wrap it, too!

* * *

"Dondi, look what I brought."

Tommy opened the door to Coop Number One and let the

bird jump up on his arm; he could smell the Social Tea crumbs in his hand. Tommy spread them out on the floor evenly and after rubbing the head of the black pigeon with just a touch of white in her tail he stepped out of the coop and re-latched the door so it wouldn't thrash around in the breeze. Bald Henry hopped over to have a look and Dondi, always being a gentle soul, shared his treat with his friend. The other birds formed a chorus on the top shelf and cooed cheerfully at their old friend looking in. He had forgotten how soft their voices were.

"Hiya, Squirt!"

Tommy half jumped and turned around to see Rosalind grinning at him. She was dressed in her Aquinas High School uniform and had a flush on her cheeks from running up the stairs.

"Whatcha doing?"

"Checking on them."

"Not as many, huh?"

"Not any in Coop Number Two."

"What about that one you found?"

"Orphan Annie? She right there. But no more Dick Tracy."

"Which one was that?"

"The big white one. That was her boyfriend."

"So, he flew the coop. Just like my Elgin."

"No, somebody shot him with a BB gun. We saw him dead on the roof of the barber shop. I went down and got him to bury in Ewen Park. That was right before Elgin left for the Navy. He said Tracy was an easy target."

"Let's hope Elgin isn't as easy."

"You miss him?"

Rosalind took out her pack of Viceroy's, put one in her mouth, and tried lighting a match. The breeze was too strong so she asked Tommy to come over and cup his hand around the match while she got the cigarette lit. She took a drag and looked at Tommy.

"You smoke?"

"Not yet."

"How old are you now?"

"Eleven."

"You're not such a squirt any more. You're taller than me."

"Elgin said you were a shrimp."

"He did?"

"No."

"Wise guy!"

She went over and sat in the old upholstered chair but immediately jumped back up. She should have realized it would be soaked from the morning's rain, and now her seat was wet. She convulsively grabbed her skirt and starting flapping it around trying to get it dry. She was still at it when she noticed they had company.

It was Elgin's brother Nigel who had come up to check on the pigeons. He was three years younger and nothing like him. Small, unathletic, he went to Bronx High School of Science with a bunch of other squares. He really wasn't interested in the pigeons but had promised his brother he would look after them. Elgin was his idol. He was glad to see Tommy because he knew everything would be okay and he could get back to his geometry book. He nodded toward Rosalind and then left as quickly as he appeared. Rosalind went over to Tommy.

"Did he see me?"

"He had his glasses on."

"You know what I mean! You shouldn't have been looking either, but he's such an odd duck. I mean, just his name, Nigel! I asked Elgin how did your mother come up with that. He said she liked anagrams. That's right, I had to look it up! Can you believe it? Anyway, let him tell his mother, she already hates me."

"Why?"

"I'm not the girl for her precious Elgin."

"His father hates you, too?"

She took out another cigarette and Tommy didn't have to be asked. He came over to cup the match for the light. When she blew out her first puff she said:

"I shouldn't tell you this but the father likes me too much. He's been warned to keep his hands above the Mason-Dixon line."

Tommy had heard the term in history class but wasn't sure what it meant. Maybe Elgin's father thought he was Abe Lincoln. He went back to simpler things like sweeping out the pigeon coop and filling up the grain dishes. He was holding Orphan Annie when Rosalind came over to say she was leaving.

"You're a good friend to them… and Elgin, too."

"How's your uniform?"

"It's okay. I'll only need it for another week. Then I graduate."

"Will you go to college?"

"Me? No, I got a full-time sales job at Lerner's on Fordham Road."

"Betty Ann's getting married tomorrow."

"Oh, that's right, your sister Betty. I saw Eileen on the bus last week and she told me."

"I'll be one of the altar boys. You can come and see me."

"I don't think so."

"Why not?"

"I don't feel like it."

"She's marrying Bob."

"Yeah, I know him."

"He was in the Navy and he came back."

"Thanks, Squirt. See ya."

* * *

"Hey, hurry up!"

It was Mark yelling at Tommy as soon as he walked out of the pigeon building. A gang had assembled: Richie, Philip, Paulie, Bobby, Sonny Boy, Gary, Daniel, Dennis, and Patty Morgan. They were hurrying down the Terrace with a decided destination in mind. Tommy didn't run to catch up, but instead he used a fast walk to give him time to evaluate. Nobody was carrying any baseball paraphernalia so they weren't going to Van Cortlandt to do that and they weren't carrying any mop handles, either, so it wasn't a fight with another block. It seemed like a cheerful enough expedition so Tommy sped up to catch Mark, always bringing up the rear.

"Where are we going?"

"The river."

"The Harlem or the Hudson?"

"Both."

Mark laughed and Tommy got it. There was a place where the two rivers came together, Spuyten Duyvil. It was right under the Henry Hudson Bridge, a highly explorable area Tommy first saw many years ago in Billy's car as he drove underneath it. There was an old local train station and a swinging drawbridge connecting the Bronx to the tip of Manhattan. It was the summertime adventure park for the kids of Kingsbridge.

Marching in a rowdy manner, they crossed 230th Street and cut through the freight train yard. This would be the last year of full operation for the yard. The value of real estate in this part of the Bronx was increasing and big projects, including a new high school, were planned for this expansive tract of land. It was too bad because it was a romantic throwback to the days of big steam engines and red cabooses and all sorts of great train stuff. Tommy's father had brought him down here when he was six years old. As was his habit of always running into someone he knew from Sweeney's, this occasion presented one of the engineers of the big freight locomotives. They decided that Tommy would enjoy a ride and, on the face of it, why not? The only drawback was Tommy never met the man before and the father wasn't coming along. Tommy was whisked away into the huge, noisy engine and stood next to this stranger who smelled of beer as they quickly took off down one of the connecting tracks without saying a word. Tommy figured he was being abducted and began pleading to go back; the engineer finally reversed the locomotive and delivered the boy back to his father. So much for riding high iron.

The gang from the Terrace edged along the yard, not drawing too much attention from the yard workers. They were technically trespassing but the workers knew the kids from the neighborhood took a shortcut through the yard on the way down to the river. Unless they started hopping on the equipment, the workers ignored them. Some of the boxcars did present interesting targets to see what they were carrying. At night there were occasional raids when a tip targeted cargo that could be fenced on the street quickly. Top of the line items would be liquor and cigarettes. Ice cream was stolen once with the joke being to eat it fast because it was "hot."

At the end of the train yard were the remnants of the old depression-era shantytown. You had to be careful passing by because there were a couple of shacks still occupied, guarded by dogs you didn't want anything to do with. The old community garden was there, too, but badly neglected. Tommy had a classmate from this area and he was always secretive as to exactly where he lived. His family might have been one of the last. The shacks would soon be vacant and knocked down in a couple of years. That's how things were in the early sixties, on the cusp between the old and the new, with sweeping changes ahead. Tommy got a last glimpse before they disappeared forever.

After shantytown you were at the main line of the New York Central which meant crossing over four busy tracks with third rails. Tommy was instructed early on how to step over and not on the wood-covered electrified rail. If you touched an exposed area you would be knocked flying with the voltage and possibly killed. To further keep you on your toes there was a sharp curve that was chiseled out of solid rock called "the cut" from which the trains emerged without any warning traveling at high speeds. You didn't have much time to react if you were crossing the tracks the same time as the *Lakeshore Limited* was speeding back from Chicago. You'd better move fast!

Finally, at the water's edge, the comrades were quickly noticed by a large group of older teenagers diving and swimming in the river. It would be up to Dennis, being the oldest, how to proceed. Dennis struck up a conversation with one of the boys sunning himself on a rock. He carefully approached the one where no girlfriend was present, knowing too well the complications that can arise if any simple politeness is misinterpreted. The stranger looking over the group saw that this younger migration posed no threat to their hierarchy and told them the water was great. At that moment one of the more advanced swimmers jumped off a particularly high spot from the side of the cut where it faced the river. He made a big splash and when he resurfaced was set upon by his buddies in the water, indicating some sort of initiation horseplay. They were having a great time, no doubt about it. And it was a boys-only moment in the water because the girlfriends were out and dry and clustered around a couple of large rocks smoking cigarettes and talking seriously.

Tommy, standing a on discarded grapefruit crate, had been surveying the scene and admiring the bravery required to jump and swim. There were about twenty teenagers in the water splashing about and returning to shore where they would re-dive back into the swirling waters. The fact that he wasn't wearing a bathing suit was a good thing for him. It took away the option and would be a good excuse if some of the others were going in. He knew that he was not able for the rough waters where the two rivers met. Actually, the location had a terrible reputation for strong whirlpools and several drownings had occurred over the years. His previous swimming experience had been limited to a few treks to the public swimming pool at Tibbetts Brook Park, one of the visits being shortened because of a bleeding foot, requiring some minor medical attention at their Red Cross station. The episode ended up with Tommy and Betty Ann being driven home by one of the county police officers with a stop at the Carvel Ice Cream shop on Broadway for the poor injured boy. The only other swimming opportunity Tommy had was the annual altar boys' outing to Rye Beach Playland where they spent a couple of hours in the saltwater pool. The adventures at Rockaway could not be included in possible swim times. The terrific undertow made it barely possible to get in and out of the surf. He did not go above his waist because of the danger and his limited swimming ability. Of course, true to his nature, Tommy never asked anyone for help in learning to swim. He would figure it out himself. This approach in checkers or horseshoes might mean losing a few rounds before catching on. In swimming it might mean losing your life. Tommy would wait until he could swim better.

"Here she comes!"

It was one of the teenage girls with an exceedingly screechy voice. She was effective, however, because, as if rehearsed, all the boys in the water splashed hurriedly toward the shore and scrambled to different perches on the cut. Just in time too. She was gliding smoothly beneath the Broadway Bridge and loaded with sightseers on this sunny June day: *The Circle Line*. The boys would give her a show.

It was technically considered a yacht but was duly licensed by New York City to carry passengers around the island of Manhattan, roughly a three-hour journey. The captain always enjoyed seeing the divers up on the cut ready to go; it was good for business. He gave them a toot and slowed the boat down to a complete stop and off they went, jumping in a somewhat coordinated fashion. It wasn't Billy Rose's Aquacade but it delighted the mostly out-of-town yokels who were thrilled by the daring of the kids from the Bronx. In gratitude they would throw down coins that the boys could catch, swimming up closely to the boat after their dive. Tommy watching from the shoreline was glad Kevin McCormick wasn't a passenger. He probably would have thrown them an anchor. Once all the boys had jumped from the cliff and collected their money, another toot signaled she was under way and the boys swam back to the shore to count the loot. On a good day, with four or five boats passing by, they would make enough to put together a beer party in Ewen Park. And it didn't feel like work.

The Terrace gang was all set to proceed up and over the cut towards the Hudson River side when Patty Morgan became embroiled in a fierce battle with two teenage girls. It seems a remark was rendered about Patty's purpose for traveling with a bunch of boys. That was all she needed to launch herself at the insulting duo sitting apart on a shared rock. Patty had knocked over the bigger one with such force she took out the smaller one at the same time. It reminded Tommy of the bedpost shot he learned on the shuffleboard game. Patty was swinging away madly when she got flipped over and had her arms pinned above her. Now defenseless, she was getting smacked pretty good when Sonny Boy came over and pushed both girls off Patty. This didn't sit well with the older teenage boys who were enjoying the entertainment. The biggest one stepped up and told Sonny Boy:

"Let 'em fight."

"No, she's had enough."

The tale of the tape showed a height difference of ten inches and a weight advantage of eighty pounds. Tommy had already envisioned the heave-ho towards the river that Sonny Boy was destined to receive at the hands of this giant but fortunately all flight plans were rescheduled due to a request for further clarification.

"What did you say?"

"I said she's had enough."

"And just who do you think you are?"

"I'm her brother!"

Up to this point there had been a general snorting and snickering among the crowd of teenagers watching the unfolding spectacle but all that abruptly stopped. Sonny Boy had just laid claim to a male street privilege that was universally honored: sticking up for one's sister. The giant was stopped in his whacks.

"Your sister?"

The question hung in the air as the gaping teenagers took their assessment. Sonny Boy was as tan as an avocado nut and Patty's pasty Irish skin looked like it never saw a sunbeam. He had dark curly hair; she was a strawberry blonde. Brown eyes versus blue eyes. And the strangest, he was a shrimp and she was tall for her age. The Terrace gang stayed silent and held their breath. It was a classic Sonny Boy deception but a hard con to pass off and Patty wasn't helping. You could see the fire in her eyes. She was being set up as the helpless damsel being rescued by, of all people, Sonny Boy! Hopefully she would keep her mouth shut. The giant actually was going to make it easier for her to swallow.

"Adopted?"

"No."

Leave it to Sonny Boy. He was going to take this the whole way. You were never going to catch him in a small lie. The giant seemed stunned.

"Stepsister?"

"No."

"You don't look anything alike!"

"We take after different sides of the family."

This was where all his experience in dodging consequences kicked in. Sonny Boy had made the preposterous plausible in the mind of his accuser and would now take the initiative. He went over to Patty, put his arm around her and walked her away from her oppressors. When she was safely in the fold of his companions, he told the giant in a voice loud enough for all to hear:

"She said she was sorry."

On cue, the Terrace gang started to move away toward the cut. It all seemed to be going according to plan when one of the teenage girls yelled out, "Hey, you going to let him get away with that?"

Sonny Boy had already turned to catch up with the others when he heard the giant announce, "Yeah. Let 'em go."

* * *

Instead of climbing up and over the cut using the guide line provided, the Terrace gang took the quicker exit and trekked through the opening along the tracks. They needed to stick tight to the carved wall in case a Manhattan bound train came roaring through. Once out, they continued along the tracks for a good half hour until they recognized the area that corresponded to the Riverdale section of the Bronx. Here they would spread out comfortably on the solid granite boulders that were placed along the shore. Excavated from the original Grand Central Terminal building site, their new purpose was to provide protection from the river and a natural border for the new train tracks spreading out from Manhattan. That may have been the official reason but to Tommy and his friends they were front row seats to the unique loveliness stretching out before them: the majestic Hudson River.

New York State history was still an essential subject in the local grammar schools and the Hudson River was always at the center of its development. Tommy enjoyed the stories of Native Americans and their complex interdependence with the river, and later Henry Hudson's amazement at its beauty when first experienced aboard the *Half Moon*. His humble arrival was not yet considered an invasion. Later, Tommy learned that the river was critical to the commerce and protection of the early Dutch settlers and even more so when it became a colony under British rule, brought to life by those pen and ink sketchings of small sailing ships in the mouth of the harbor. The American War of Independence provided numerous examples of the strategic value of the river, but Tommy always favored those colorized drawings of Robert Fulton's *Clermont* on its inaugural voyage to Albany showing the awe-stuck villagers waving from the riverbank. A whole new way of life was coming at them. Next came the connection of the river to the Erie Canal, a technological marvel made possible by strong Irishmen plying their banjos. With the inevitable development of large manufacturers along the river, the waters became dirty and contaminated with new and threatening chemicals, wiping out most commercial fishing and making even swimming hazardous. However, as the Terrace gang looked out on the Hudson on that sunny June day in 1964, things were starting to turn around for the health of the great river of the Haudenosaunee people. Pete Seeger's *Clearwater*, guided by the Great Spirit, would soon become a symbolic repudiation of Fulton's steamboat and the environmental destruction that followed in its wake.

"Wanna sip?"

The gang was on their way back to Naples Terrace, straggling through the fiefdom of Fieldston, where, from the safety of gated estates, they were identified to sheltered daughters as examples of what to avoid whenever possible. Happily unaware of their poor appraisal, they were excited to see the giant trees of the main boulevard full of prickly green pods, showing great promise for a bumper crop of good fighting chestnuts. The gang would return in the fall to collect the fallen and attach them to leather cords ready for the game D.H. Lawrence called Cobblers. Tommy was grateful for Mark's offer to share his can of Krasdale Cream Soda. He was exhausted and the sugary drink gave him the energy to keep up as they rounded Manhattan College Parkway on their way home. He had two pennies in his pocket that had been placed on the tracks and flattened by a passing train. He would put them in the drawer next to the Dolan Nickel. He didn't know why, but that seemed to be the place for them.

Patty Morgan had screamed at Sonny Boy down at the Hudson for claiming she was sorry to the giant. Why did he say that? She was still sore by the time they arrived at the big house at the foot of Naples Terrace but when she saw Sonny Boy's sister tear into him for not letting anyone know where he'd been all day she quickly came to his defense and told her if she was a real sister she wouldn't be yelling at him all the time and she should be glad to have a brother who sticks up for you. The sister protested that he never sticks up for her but quickly acquiesced to the fiery Patty and gave her brother a big hug. Everyone laughed as Sonny Boy became the conquering hero and again escaped any fallout from his appalling behavior. Tommy thought about his own disappearance and if anyone was looking for him. When he entered his apartment, he was relieved to see the spread of cold cuts on the table in the living room with Aunt Betty and Uncle Pat in attendance again for a wedding eve feed. He was home free.

But he was soon out again. The party was fun and he liked seeing his mother enjoying the company, but after he finished his potato salad and custard pudding, he was ready. The long June evenings told him there was action down on the street and he wanted to be a part of it. So, using the excuse of taking out the garbage, he knew once out of the house he would be forgotten and he could find out what was happening. It didn't take him long.

There was a big commotion on the corner with the Bungalow Bar Ice Cream truck. The driver was out of the truck chasing some half pint who kept dodging this way and that. Tommy could see that it was a ruse started by the older kids to occupy the driver while they raided the freezer in the back. There was nothing unusual there but what Tommy didn't see that this was no ordinary raid. It was a full-on hijacking orchestrated by the Murphy kid. Looking like he had a generous helping of leprechaun chromosomes, the Murph always had a scam up his sleeve and Tommy first became acquainted when he heard of a card game after hours in the school yard. It was Murph's game and he showed Tommy how to be the dealer. Tommy always loved his card delivery. He would snap each card down on the board and announce: "Possible straight."

Or… "Possible flush."

Or…"Possible full house."

But Tommy's favorite was when he snapped a card down and cheerfully proclaimed:

"No help!"

Murphy was also the one who popularized Hav-A-Tampa Jewels, the slender small cigar with the wood tip. You couldn't help but to try one. Since they were mild you usually didn't end up being sick and they added a sophisticated dimension to the card game. The Murph was an exciting guy to be around.

But on this evening Murphy asked, why just grab a few ice creams when you can have the whole truck? The simulated bungalow on wheels was a manual drive with a tall clutch stick. When parked on a big hill like Naples Terrace all you had to do was release the break, put the truck in neutral and give it a shove. Down it would go. The half pint was doing a good job of distracting the driver so Murphy got to slip in behind the wheel. But that's where phase two came in. Three teenage girls made a noisy show of opening the side freezer door and each grabbing an ice cream sandwich, right in front of the driver, and prancing off towards the alley. He naturally wasn't going to let them get away with that and started after them. Phase three clicked in with the boyfriends giving the truck a great big push and Murphy was off.

The teenage girls, knowing their mission was accomplished, ran up to the driver and pushed the frozen treats into his hands. Relieved and thinking that he had appealed to their better senses, he turned to go back to his truck and saw it was gone, disappeared. All the other kids had run off and he was left alone holding his ice cream sandwiches. Mercifully, the woman with the ugly baby yelled to him from her first-floor window.

"When you get your truck back, give me an orange popsicle. I'll throw down the money."

"Where did it go?"

"Got me. I only saw it turn the corner at the foot of the hill."

Murphy was no Newton but he knew his gravity pretty well and figured out that he would be able to keep the truck rolling until it leveled out at Broadway. There, waiting in felonious expectation, were his accomplices, equipped with brown shopping bags and ready to unload when Murphy's Express came to a halt. They were almost finished when the poor out-of-shape driver came puffing down the hill in pursuit of his livelihood. He didn't bother to try to chase them once they ran. He was just grateful to get the truck back. He took a look into the freezers and they were cleaned out. He still held the three ice cream sandwiches and decided to give two of them to a young, freckle-faced girl on a red scooter. One was for her and the other was for the woman who always called down from her window. She was happy to deliver. The third one the driver unwrapped for himself as he got behind the wheel. He was done for the day.

Tommy had gone to the corner to see about the truck when he felt a tap on the shoulder. It was Mark handing him a frozen fudge bar. He had two more in his hands.

"Where did you get these?"

"A teenager had them. They were three for a nickel."

"How much for one?"

"Two cents."

Tommy didn't think he had any money but then he remembered. He never got a chance to put them in the drawer.

He handed Mark the two flattened pennies.

"Here."

Mark thought it was hilarious and started coughing convulsively, as he had just taken a big bite of the frozen pop. He was still trying to catch his breath when Gary, Richie, Paulie, Daniel, Philip, and Bobby came through the alley and yelled out to Tommy and Mark, "Come on!"

They marched right past and down the hill. Mark was sufficiently recovered to walk and they followed leisurely behind while eating their ice cream. They had no idea what was up but they half ran, half walked up Broadway and cut through the Safeway parking lot. Tommy knew where they were headed now: the bocce courts. During the early evenings the courts would bring out the old Italian men for their games. They liked that the boys came to watch and would nod to them in appreciation of a younger audience. They were the first generation and still spoke their own language but were happy that their sons and daughters learned English and were doing so well in this country. That's why they came to America, for their children. Yet with their friends on the bocce courts they were home again and they could have their small drink together and curse and argue together and for a short while things were like the way they always were and that was enough. From the bocce courts you could smell the cookies being baked in the Stella D'oro plant a few blocks away. It was appropriate enough; the founder of the company came from Italy in the 1920s but in typical New York whimsy some of the most loyal customers were Orthodox Jews because the pastries were made without dairy. To them, the round fudge cookies were their shtreimels. The boys watched for two complete games and then went down through the high reeds to the freight train tracks that led back to the Art Steel truck lot. Tommy only then found out the reason they were there. Some sort of initiation would be held in the back of one of the empty canvas-covered trucks that were parked overnight. They were just waiting for it to get dark.

There was a rope swing on a high tree that they played on until they were told it was time. The leader was ready. Unknown, he was already positioned in a truck and he had two recognized assistants waiting outside, one who was acting as a guard standing beside the truck and the other performing the job of lining up the boys and keeping order. Each boy was handed an unlit candle and told not to talk. Tommy had no idea what was going on but since everyone was partaking of the ritual and it was something different, he went along. Tommy was near the rear of the line and got a good idea how the thing worked. When a boy got up to the truck, he had his candle lit and in he went. About five minutes passed before he came out again and his candle was extinguished. He was told not to talk to anyone when it was over and to take off back home through the truck lot. Finally, Tommy's turn came; he had his candle lit and got a boost up into the truck. These were the last of the canvas-covered eighteen-wheelers to be on the road and the empty cargo space seemed cavernous and was pitch black, except for the shimmering of a candle up front. He was told to come forth. Using his own flickering flame as a guide he made his way up toward the shadowy figure sitting on the floor where he was ordered to sit down next to him. Tommy's eyes had adjusted by now and he recognized this Bronx shaman as the older teenage brother of one of his street pals. The teenager proceeded to rattle off some incomprehensible mumbo-jumbo that sounded like it came out of the Thuggee Temple scene from *Gunga Din.* Tommy had been watching his candle intensely so the dripping wax wouldn't burn his hand when suddenly the teenager reached over and grabbed between his legs. Tommy rolled off to one side and stood up. Even though Tommy knew this teenager well there was something strange about him now and he moved back. The teenager acted like nothing unusual happened and told him he could go. Tommy jumped off the back of the truck and went home. That was one of the last times that Tommy ever saw him. They said he went off to college.

* * *

It was almost ten o'clock when Tommy got home and the company had left. His mother was a little annoyed that he stayed out so late but didn't make a fuss. She was too busy. There seemed to be a general panic about Betty Ann's bridal headpiece. She was making some last-minute alterations in the kitchen. Good, everyone was distracted. Tommy took an unprompted bath just because he figured that's what he should do and put on his summer pajamas. It was getting warm and the light cotton felt cool against his skin. There was still some commotion going on with preparations, and at Eileen's suggestion, he said good night to everyone. He was exhausted.

Lying in bed he thought about his day. He did a lot of the usual fun stuff but it was a very strange day, too. There was something about Rosalind and the way she looked at him. Then there was the whole Patty Morgan thing and what those teenage girls said about her. The truck ritual was the oddest of all and he didn't understand the reason behind it. Initiation into what? The tiredness from being out in the strong sun was starting to force his eyes closed. Tomorrow he would be on the altar for Betty Ann's wedding. It would be an exciting day but after that she would be gone, just like Kathleen was gone, and he didn't like thinking about that. He was just about to fall asleep when he wondered where Deidre was. He hadn't seen her in a while.

TUESDAY 9PM

After the mentally challenging *Happy Days*, old Tom got a break with the next show on Bridie's strict schedule: *Laverne & Shirley*. No flashbacks, and he could relate to them working at a beer factory; it reminded him of the old Bronx breweries that were closed at the beginning of the war. He also liked Laverne's father and the landlady that looked after the girls. The show's happy conclusion, however, brought them to that perilous nine o'clock viewing juncture. Would Bridie allow Tom to choose a program? Providentially, no decision had to be made because just then the phone rang and Bridie got up to answer. Tom cautiously listened for her distinctive disconnect directed towards any salesman having the temerity to call their number, but after a full minute she was still talking, prompting Tom to get up and change the channel. There it was: *The CBS Tuesday Night Movie.* Tonight, *Barnaby Jones*, an old guy he could understand. He was home safe.

After about fifteen minutes Bridie returned and told Tom to go in and pick up the phone. but predictably, he was now completely absorbed and had replaced his wife of thirty-eight years with Lee Meriwether.

"If she doesn't watch out, she'll be the target next."

"Will you hurry up? It's Eileen, calling long distance."

"She's on the phone?"

No answer, so he scrambled to his feet and went into the kitchen. Since there was already too much yelling on *Barnaby* for Bridie's taste, the TV got switched to *Three's Company*. She got comfortable on the sofa and waited. And waited. Finally, when he returned, she asked, "You have everything said by now?"

He was quiet as he sat next to her on the sofa, staring absentmindedly into the television. California was such a far-off place for Eileen to be. Would he ever get to see her again? It was only at the commercial that he turned to Bridie.

"Everything was said."

Later, after the eleven o'clock news, when old Tom was making his way toward the upland—the place he always called bed—Bridie asked if he was all right.

"Why wouldn't I be?"

"You might be sad. They've all grown up and moved off in every direction."

"We're back to just the two of us. Like the days at the dance hall. They were the best of times."

She gave him a kiss on his cheek and straightened the covers once he was in bed. She was to have her yogurt yet, and then settle in to watch Johnny Carson. She was in luck; Buddy Hackett was a guest and he was one of her favorites.

SEPTEMBER 1967

As soon as the train doors opened, Tommy dove in and grabbed the last two seats in the corner. He put his book bag on the seat next to him to reserve it because Kevin Grogan, his more sedate and chivalrous classmate, stayed back to hold the doors open for a late-rushing lady. He always was the gentleman. It was a half-hour ride on the subway to 86th Street and worse than standing all the way was the pushing and shoving that went on when you had no seat. Kevin was grateful for Tommy's foresight in securing accommodations. By now they were traveling over the Broadway Bridge and Tommy turned to look at the river and the cut and all the familiar places, quiet with the coming of fall. Kevin, not so nostalgic, got busy right away with some paperwork and arranged everything neatly on top of his book bag to fill in on the ride downtown. Tommy was glad for his preoccupation. It was the first day back to school and he didn't feel like talking. The summer took a lot out of him.

There was the first full-time job, a junior counselor at the parish day camp. Assigned the eight-year old boys, they were still cute and manageable enough but not as dopey as the smallest group, the Midgets. His cousin put the word in for him when there was an opening and since he was the senior watchdog for the group, Tommy would work under him. They went on bus trips to different pools and lakes and when it rained, they played basketball and indoor games. At the end of the summer they put on a stage version of *Oliver!* The kids and Tommy got along pretty well considering he had no experience with younger siblings growing up. Maybe because of it. And he got to be out in the fresh air and have fun instead of in some stuffy indoor job packing shelves like some of his friends. The kids were the easy part. What became challenging was Emma Marie Wertheimer.

She was the Midget Girls junior counselor. A few months younger than Tommy, she was almost as tall with short, blonde hair and an athletic build. She came from a large family and lived in an apartment down on Naples Terrace where the father was the super. A tall man, he was suspicious of Tommy from the start and it would be safe to say that the two of them were never going to share a bag of Chee-tos even in the best of circumstances. Emma Marie and Tommy became friendly being in close proximity on the buses and at the pools and putting their hands over their ears at musical rehearsals. So, it was natural enough that Emma Marie invited Tommy to a picnic at the end of the camp season. It was just the two of them and they had to walk for over an hour through Van Cortlandt to arrive at a small park area in Yonkers. She brought the food and Tommy brought his appetite. The sandwiches were very tasty and she had cold sodas and slices of cake for dessert. They were spread out on the grass to have their lunch and when it was done Tommy became fascinated by the small white polka dots on Emma Marie's blue cotton pants. How many were there? He started to point to each one and count and she loudly laughed when suddenly she thought better of it. She wasn't angry but some sort of social conditioning kicked in. She told Tommy to stop counting and he did and they both hiked back to the Bronx in good humor. Afterwards, Tommy looked forward to seeing her but as she was just starting high school, she suddenly got very busy. He wasn't sure if that was it.

The other big change during this summer was drinking beers with the friends down at the bocce courts in the evening. It started simply enough. Tommy was sitting in a long line of guys just listening to the chatter as usual when this can of beer appeared. He saw that everyone was taking a sip and passing it on and he did likewise. It was no big deal but the secret ritual soon became an accepted occasion. By the end of the summer there were regular collections being gathered for the beer parties and Tommy would make sure he got his money's worth. It was something he looked forward to.

On the days that Tommy wasn't at the camp he palled around with the Naples Terrace gang playing the usual ball games and hanging loose up on tar beach, eating watermelons and smoking cheap cigars. The pigeon coops were gone now; the new super said they were a health hazard. Tommy would go over to the spot where they used to be to look around. In the distance, he could see pigeons underneath the platform of the elevated subway station—their new home—and thought he could recognize a couple but wasn't sure. It was okay that the coops were gone since he wouldn't have that much time for them anymore. He did find a feather once, a black one with just a touch of white, and put it in his pocket. He knew it belonged to Orphan Annie. The roof during the summer would have a bunch of sunbathers spread around; some in half-battered deck chairs, some on blankets and some just standing about trying to get a bit of a tan. Transistor radios were all the rage and depending where you were on the roof you might hear the ball game or *Penny Lane* or a dull talk show. On a Saturday, in the far corner of the roof, the old Italian barber from apartment 4E would listen to the broadcast from the new Metropolitan Opera House. He said this was as close to heaven as you can get. With the big crowd, Tommy always kept an eye out hoping that Rosalind might show up but she never did. He had heard from one of the older teenagers that Elgin was in Naples, Italy with his ship. Wasn't that funny! Him from Naples Terrace. That summer was the last time there was high excitement about going into the service. The ramifications of the Vietnam war were seeping into the country's consciousness and serving in the military would soon present a moral dilemma for many, tearing apart friends and families, another unforeseen casualty of an escalating, undeclared war which no one could understand or justify.

But in that pivotal summer of 1967, it was an insignificant, one-off event that changed Tommy's life. His pal Paulie had for years performed a very recognizable imitation of a chimpanzee, complete with bent-over walk and mimicking chatter. He would do it for amusement and for a non sequitur when everyone was getting too serious. It was his thing and everyone was used to it. On this particular muggy day, a gang of guys were hanging out in the alley talking big about all the things they were going to do in life when Paulie segued into his routine. In an instant—without any warning, after being a favorite for so long—his act was old and Tommy knew it. With everyone staring in silence, Tommy jumped in and mimicked Paulie being insignificant. It was a hit! A raucous, cutting laughter encircled Paulie and Tommy was pleased that he had his finger on the pulse. Pleased until he saw Paulie's face. He was hurt and humiliated. Tommy never said anything to Paulie then or later. What was he to say? Tommy survived on his wit and everyone knew it. But to himself, Tommy resolved not to use his humor cruelly to put anyone down or cause anyone pain. In a funny way this new restraint gained him more respect and made him more confident. His circle had expanded again.

The subway made good time running down Broadway this morning. At 125th Street, Tommy again looked out the window. It was one of the highest stations in the system and gave a good view of the neighborhood before the train ducked back into the tunnel. Last year, when Tommy first started traveling down to the all-boys high school in Manhattan, he used to imagine Broadway as the Mississippi and the subway was the steamboat taking people to all different stops along the river. He of course was the captain, just like his uncle Pat. There was even the time when he looked across the seats and saw Deidre all dressed up as a fancy southern belle with a white lace dress and great hat. Scarecrow and Teddy were sitting on each side of her looking like riverboat gamblers with aces peeking out from their shirt sleeves. Not very slick of them. They were sure to get caught.

As the train pitched Tommy into the darkness of the tunnel, he was sad because he knew he wouldn't see Deidre on the train anymore. Or anywhere else. It was only a few weeks ago, just before school started, that his mother asked him to straighten out the old toy box that was in the living room. Bridie's new grandchildren liked to rummage through it and drag out what was still there. He was told to get rid of any toys that were old and broken. Looking through the box there was no question about the metal skates, they were rusted and you couldn't use the key to tighten them anymore, so they were on the way out. But it was underneath them that Tommy found his old red motorcycle policeman. He hadn't seen him in a long time. He rubbed the wheels and they still moved smoothly. He thought it kind of silly but he went ahead and ran the policeman though the wide valley of the living room floor and up the side of the sofa for a good last view. It made him happy. Just then Tommy noticed that Deidre was standing nearby and watching the whole time. She looked exactly as Tommy had seen her that first time in Ireland when she invited him to tea. She was smiling but waving good-bye. Tommy didn't understand.

"Where are you going?"

"I can't be with you anymore."

"Why not?"

"You have all sorts of grown-up things to do now. I am quite late already going back but when I saw you pick up your red policeman..."

"Will I ever see you again?"

"Normally not. Grown-ups don't have time for me and can be quite mean. And you will be awfully impressed by all the things that grown-ups do. For a while anyway. But if you grow tired of the real world, I will let you know that I am near. Good-bye."

Scarecrow and Teddy showed up and gave Tommy a big hug. She then took them by the hand and walked into the bedroom, the room where the boy imagined all the people he wanted to be and all the things he wanted to do. When he looked in, they were gone.

JUNE 1990

When I was young, I had no sense,
I bought a fiddle for eighteen pence.
The only tune that I could play
Was "Over the Hills and Far Away".

He had just rushed back from the smoking section and sat down to look out the window. There was great excitement. You could see Ireland!

It was sixty-one years since old Tom had enjoyed the jug of buttermilk his mother sent along for his journey to America. Sixty-one years and he had never been back. Oh, he was always going but something always came up, whether real or imagined, and like a lot of things the more you put it off the more it will never happen. But Tommy had visited Ireland the year before and all the relations said how wonderful it would be to see Uncle Tom, and if those reassurances weren't enough, the pictures of the old house had great effect on him. He would go the next summer with Tommy. He received a new passport and booked the Aer Lingus flight through Grimes, the good-old Irish travel agency in New York. He was worried about the long flight and maybe feeling trapped but quickly overcame any nervousness when onboard due to the camaraderie of fellow passengers and the friendly flight crew. He never slept a wink but made several trips back and forth to the rear of the plane to have a Chesterfield and to share a memory. The eight-hour flight went by quickly for him. When he re-took his seat the last time before landing he could see the white puffy dots that were the sheep in their fields and the flashes of color that were the horses in their paddocks. They would be glad to see him.

They took the train out to Tullamore where he was received with great enthusiasm by all the nephews and nieces. No time was wasted in organizing teas and notifying old friends that Tom had returned and every day the old house was filled with smiling school friends and nosy neighbors. On one particular afternoon, Tommy had just put down his cup of tea when he looked around the room and saw four mice, three geese, and a polecat sitting around the table talking excitedly. He decided he needed some fresh air and went out and around to the back of the old house. It wasn't long until his cousin Noel found him. He was holding the red wooden top.

Noel gave it a great throw and quickly doubled the string to gently lift the spinning top and place it into Tommy's open palm. This time Tommy spoke the words, sounding like the man in the church:

"It's been said, holding a spinning top makes time stand still. We can stay here forever and never get old."

With a big smile on his face, Noel took his top and rushed off to bring the car around to the house. They were going to take old Tom to the graveyard behind the church. The place where his mother was buried. His last memory of her was waving good-bye at the train station. She would be happy to have him back home.

Tommy was about to return to the party when he noticed a flash of black and white—a kitten! She wanted some attention so Tommy bent down to give her a rub. She looked familiar. When Tommy picked her up, he was convinced.

"You waited for me all these years!"

She got to wiggling and squirming, and as soon as Tommy let her go, she took off. He never hesitated. It was only after running down the lane a short distance that Tommy saw the girl with the splendid head of yellow curls. She was holding the kitten.

"Good afternoon! My name is Deidre."

"Is it still make-believe?"

"It's not make-believe if you believe in me!"

"I'd like to."

"Then share what's in your heart."

Tommy didn't have to wait too long. The idea came quickly.

"I think I'll write a story. A story about a horse, a young horse, a foal—no, twin foals! How they grow up and all the things that happen to them. People would enjoy that and it would be fun."

"Ooh, how delightful! I will show you how."

And so she did. And many other stories, too. Deidre no longer feared the heavy footsteps and had no reason to run away.

The End

ABOUT THE AUTHOR

Thomas Marshall grew up in New York City, the son of Irish immigrants. He is the author of numerous works of fiction, including the novel ***Stride for Stride***. He currently resides in Spain with his wife and an itinerant cat.

OTHER BOOKS BY THOMAS MARSHALL

Stride for Stride

Hopewell Manor

G.V.

Blackbirds for Christmas